MW00532028

Make a Wish for Me

Books by Lenora Mattingly Weber

BEANY MALONE SERIES

Meet the Malones 1943

Beany Malone 1948

Leave it to Beany! 1950

Beany and the Beckoning Road 1952

Beany has a Secret Life 1955

Make a Wish for Me 1956

Happy Birthday, Dear Beany 1957

The More the Merrier 1958

A Bright Star Falls 1959

Welcome Stranger 1960

Pick a New Dream 1961

Tarry Awhile 1962

Something Borrowed, Something Blue 1963

Come Back, Wherever You Are 1969

The Beany Malone Cookbook 1972

KATIE ROSE BELFORD SERIES

Don't Call Me Katie Rose 1964

The Winds of March 1965

A New and Different Summer 1966

I Met a Boy I Used to Know 1967

Angel in Heavy Shoes 1968

STACY BELFORD SERIES

How Long is Always? 1970

Hello, My Love, Good-bye 1971

Sometimes a Stranger 1972

NON-SERIES BOOKS

Wind on the Prairie 1929

The Gypsy Bridle 1930

Podgy and Sally, Co-eds 1930

A Wish in the Dark 1931

Mr. Gold and Her Neighborhood House 1933

Rocking Chair Ranch 1936

Happy Landing 1941

Sing for Your Supper 1941

Riding High 1946

My True Love Waits 1953

For Goodness Sake! (cookbook), with Greta Hilb, 1964

Make a Wish for Me

LENORA MATTINGLY WEBER

IMAGE CASCADE PUBLISHING
CALIFORNIA

A hardcover edition of this book was originally published by Thomas Y. Crowell Company. It is here reprinted by arrangement with HarperCollins Publishers, New York.

First *Image Cascade Publishing* edition published 1999.
Copyright renewed © 1984 by David Weber.

Library of Congress Cataloging in Publication Data
Weber, Lenora Mattingly, 1895–1971.
    Make a wish for me.

(Juvenile Girls)
Reprint. Originally published: New York: Thomas Y. Crowell, 1956.

ISBN 0-9639607-8-4 (Pbk.)

Make a Wish for Me

1

BEANY MALONE sat in front of her dressing table with its yellow plaid skirt, which she had made herself, and extracted bobby pins from tight little snails of hair. On this Saturday morning in mid-January, an early sun slanted through the yellow plaid curtains—also made by Beany.

Strange, she thought, how a certain tingly excitement seemed to go with yanking bobby pins out of one's hair. It seemed the right prelude to dressing up and going places and doing things.

A whisk of the comb through the flat little curls transformed them into a fluff of bangs. She wished momentarily that her hair were either brunette or blond, not "roan." She pinned her two stubby braids across the top of her head.

Every once in a while she thought of cutting her hair—and then she thought of Andy Kern who sat across from her in her French class and ate lunch with her every first-hour lunch period at Harkness High. Whenever she mentioned cutting off her braids, Andy said, "No, child, no! Beany without braids would be like a hot dog without mustard—or a band without a drum."

Carefully she pulled on her best nylons, and stepped into her black ballet slippers. Now for the new print blouse which her friend Kay had given her for Christmas, and which she had saved for this very special Saturday.

In her small room at the head of the stairs, she could hear the family stirring through the house in the usual Saturday morning hubbub. The uneven rat-a-tat of a typewriter meant that her older brother Johnny was getting out a paper on early-day events for his history professor at the university. Johnny earned his tuition by helping him. The occasional mumble of voices told her that Carlton Buell, the boy next door and Johnny's inseparable, was with him.

The smell of oil paints filtering through the house and up to Beany's room announced that Adair was already at her easel. The new and youngish stepmother of the Malones was a portrait painter.

The double clunk in the room next to Beany's meant that her sister Mary Fred was stamping her feet into jodhpur boots as she made ready to go out to Hilltop Stables and teach a children's class how to ride. "How to

2

jounce properly," Mary Fred put it. Sure enough, just as Beany reached for her skirt, Mary Fred came in to have Beany fasten the studs in the stiff French cuffs of her white shirt.

Mary Fred was almost three years older than Beany, and a sophomore at the university. Her short curly hair was a dark, glinting brown. They both had the same blue-gray eyes with a dark fringing of lashes—"Blue eyes put in with a dirty finger," the Irish described it. It seemed to a regretful Beany that the dirty finger had also been shaken over her own nose, leaving a sprinkling of freckles. The time and money Beany had spent on freckle creams and lotions!

Mary Fred's eyes rested on Beany's print blouse above the gray-checked skirt she was zipping.

"Kind of a gruesome combination, chum," she commented, holding out a wrist with its gaping cuff.

"I'm just wearing it as far as the House of Hollywood on the Boul, and then—"

"You *are* in the upper brackets. Buying clothes at the Hollywood."

"Just a skirt." Beany grinned, working the round stud through a stiff buttonhole. She and Mary Fred had often admired a sweater combination or a formal at the smart little shop, only to be jolted back to reality by one glance at the price tag. "It's a moss-green wool—lush is the word for it—and it's already paid for. Simone, who runs the Hollywood, said she'd have one in my size this morning—"

"That Simone with her airs and graces," Mary Fred inserted. "Her right name is Simmons."

"—and so I'll wear the new green skirt on to work, and then to the luncheon at the University Club."

"The University Club yet!"

"I told you about it. This is the annual luncheon our nice old principal, Mr. Dexter, gives for the staff of *Hark Ye*."

"Oh, of course. And Beany Malone, feature writer, should come in for her share of laurels. No one works any harder on that school paper than you do, little Beaver." Mary Fred lifted her other cuff for Beany to fasten.

Beany asked suddenly, "Mary Fred, did you ever want something so bad that you couldn't even think about it without getting goose pimples?"

"Of course I have. What are you goose-pimply about?"

"You know what the Quill and Scroll is?"

"Yessum. It's what all school papers are members of."

Beany said breathlessly, "It's like this. There's to be a Quill and Scroll convention in Cherry Springs next month—"

"And you have your heart set on going? But won't the editor and a senior boy on the staff be the natural delegates? You're just a junior, hon."

4

"Jennifer Reed is the editor," Beany explained, "but her brother is getting married in Los Angeles that week end, so she and her folks are flying out for it. She told Mrs. Brierly, our sponsor, about it—and you know how easy-going Brierly is?—she just told Jennifer to name someone on the staff to go in her place."

"What's Jennifer like?"

"She's a love," Beany said warmly. "Even though the Reeds have lots of money—"

"Is that the Christopher Reed Realty Company? I'll say they have," Mary Fred put in.

"—yet it doesn't make any difference to Jennifer. She wears simple dark things—"

"From Simone's, no doubt," Mary Fred muttered ruefully.

Beany had an instant mental picture of the girl. Slender, brown-eyed, with close-cropped dark hair. Jennifer Reed had poise. Only occasionally was there a hint of arrogance about her. She was a good executive, as though she were used to giving orders and having them carried out.

"Everybody at school looks up to Jennifer," Beany mused. "She has her own column in every issue of the *Hark Ye*—'Between You and Me,' it's called—and it's so witty that all she has to do is make some wisecrack and everyone in school picks it up. Do you know Jag Wilson, a freshman at the U?"

"Who doesn't?"

"He was Morley Wilson last year when Jennifer made some crack about his new Jaguar. From then on he was Jag." Beany laughed. "I guess there are times when she wishes she hadn't been so bright. Because now she and Jag date each other."

"I hope your Jennifer is the long-suffering, forgiving type. Because Jag is definitely on the prowl for any pretty girl who looks his way. . . . Has she intimated that she'll pick you to go to the Press Convention?"

"Just—kind of. She's always telling me she couldn't get out the paper without my filling in whenever someone else on the staff lets her down—"

She paused, and then burst out wistfully, "Gee, Mary Fred, here I am, a junior at Harkness, and I'm the only one of my crowd—and the only one of the Malones—that isn't an OH. [OH meant "Outstanding Harknessite."] Johnny was one because he was such a genius in writing plays for the school to put on. You were one because you were always winning ribbons in horse shows—and chosen Prom Queen. Kay is one because she's good in Art and won the city-wide poster contest. I ran her picture and a swell write-up about her—"

"And your Andy Kern is one because of his charm, I suppose," Mary Fred said.

"Andy always gets things done when he's on a committee," Beany defended. She added thinly, "Do you realize, Mary Fred, my picture has never been in the

Hark Ye that I work so hard on? I draw squares on our dummy where other girls' pix are to go. I'm just the handy man."

Mary Fred said sympathetically, "And you can't even get credit for your Saturday job."

Their father, Martie Malone, was a columnist on the morning paper, the *Call.* He always said the young Malones had cut their teeth on his typewriter eraser.

The *Morning Call* ran a half-page of letters to and answers by a mythical Eve Baxter. These letters about love and family problems, signed "Neglected Wife," "Desperate," "Please Help Me," were read at thousands of breakfast tables, along with Eve Baxter's salty, sympathetic, sometimes scolding answers.

During the week, Eve Baxter dictated her letters to a typist at the *Call* office. But partly because she liked to stay home on Saturdays, partly because she was fond of Beany, she dictated to her on those days. Beany drove to her residence in her brother's jalopy, took down Eve Baxter's answers. Then at the *Call,* she typed both letters and answers and turned them in to the Copy Desk.

The Malones all knew that Eve Baxter was, in reality, a seasoned newspaper woman named Evelyn Bartlett. But because the *Call* wanted her identity kept secret, Beany answered any questions at Harkness about her job with an evasive, "I do typing for the *Call.*"

Mary Fred was saying, "Beany, couldn't you sit yourself next to Jennifer at Dexter's luncheon this noon?

And couldn't you very adroitly lead up to the Quill and Scroll convention?"

A small shiver of hope and fright passed through Beany. "I could try."

She was wriggling into her coat and Mary Fred was reminding her, "Gloves, too, you hillbilly, if you're lunching at the University Club," when the telephone rang.

Beany caught it on its third ring. Her hello was answered by the roguish voice of Andy Kern.

"Hi, Beany. Is the luck of the Irish with you today?"

"Uh-huh."

"Don't say uh-huh to me, say sir."

"Uh—yes, *sir*. What do you need Irish luck for?"

"That, knucklehead, is a secret until our date tonight. I want to bowl you over."

"Andy, is it something you're going to *tell* me—some news?"

"No, it's a something I'm going to *give* you. That is, if your luck and mine holds out."

"A something for me!" she squealed. "Just tell me this much—is it big or little?"

"Never mind the dimensions. It's not my heart, but it has one thing in common with it."

"You mean it's shaped like a heart?"

She heard his low chuckle. She could picture him lounging at the phone, even as he lounged carelessly across from her in their French class. She could picture his eyes crinkling.

"Never mind the shape," he said. "And it has something in common with your dog, Mike—"

"Oh, is it alive? Does it move?"

"We-ell, it moves if you work on it."

"Is it animal, mineral, or vegetable?"

"Hey, this is no Twenty Questions program. Get on with you. I got to polish my shoes for my ushering job at the Pantages."

"Andy, give me another clue—just one more."

"O.K. It has something in common with a fat lady's girdle."

"A fat lady's girdle! I can't wait till tonight."

"Good. I like gals that can't wait for a date with Andy. If you've got a shamrock, pin it on for luck—"

"I've got dozens of 'em on. I'm wearing my new blouse with shamrocks in it."

"Bye now, doll."

"Andy, does it make a noise?"

He hung up on another chuckle.

She replaced the receiver, laughing excitedly herself. Madame, who taught them French, always spoke of Andy's *joie de vivre*. He not only got joy out of living, but passed it on to his girl, Beany. Not that they were steadies as many of the couples were at Harkness. It was more an easy and delightful camaraderie.

Beany's thoughts flashed back to a year ago when she had been Norbett Rhodes's girl. There was nothing easy—though it was often delightful—about their relationship. Last fall when Norbett had written that he was staying back in Ohio to attend college there, Beany's world had shaken under her.

But then her world had been shaky when Norbett was close at hand. Mary Fred always said, "When bigger and better fights are had, Beany and Norbett will have them." I was so crazy about him, Beany mused. He took up all the room in my heart. Nothing else mattered. He could be so dear—and so mean. . . . No, Andy Kern was less demanding, less distracting. You could be Andy's girl and still have room in your heart for other dreams.

Mary Fred came down the stairs and reached for her bright red jacket in the hall closet. "Dating Andy tonight, I suppose, from the purring look on your face?" she asked. "The usual foursome?"

Beany nodded. The usual gay, free-and-easy foursome of her friend Kay with her brother Johnny, herself and Andy. Andy ushered every evening, except Saturday, at the Pantages movie house. Andy could and did get his three friends in free several times a week.

"Andy's got a present for me," Beany said. "Can you think of anything that's like Andy's heart, and our dog Mike, *and* a fat lady's girdle?"

Mary Fred smiled knowingly, as though she might be in on the surprise. "Maybe," she said.

10

The front door pealed and Mary Fred said, "That's one of my mothers." She meant that it was the mother of one of her riding pupils who would drive her out to Hilltop Stables. She was buttoning her red jacket as she hurried out.

Beany glanced at the hall clock. Ten minutes to nine, and she was due at Eve Baxter's at nine. She called up the stairs to Johnny to throw down his car keys. He couldn't hear her over the rumble of his typewriter, and she raced up the stairs.

"Johnny, give. Your car keys."

The rat-a-tat of typewriter ceased. Johnny leaned back in his swivel chair which was the kind that tipped back scaringly if you relaxed wholly in it. Johnny alone knew just how far to tempt providence.

Strange, Beany thought, how certain pictures of certain people seem to etch themselves on your mind. She always pictured Mary Fred in riding togs, her cheeks wind-reddened, hurrying up or down stairs. When she thought of her father, Martie Malone, she always saw a tall, thoughtful man, fiddling with his pipe, and smiling at her over or through the nice smelly veil of smoke. She always pictured Johnny as looking up at her from that swivel chair, his dark absorbed eyes taking a minute to focus on her and the present. Miss Hewlitt, the Lit teacher at Harkness, said Johnny was a writing genius because he had such powers of concentration, of forgetting the world about him.

Johnny was six feet tall, with dark hair that looked like wet feathers and always seemed to need cutting. His smile was warm and beguiling.

"My car keys?" he repeated. "Oh forevermore, Beany—I was going to clean out the fuel line, but I started pounding out a paper on Indiana Sopris who started the first school here in a blacksmith shop and—"

"Johnny, you ghoul. I've got to go."

Carlton Buell, who was sitting on Johnny's bed, said promptly, "Take my car, Beany. I won't be needing it till late this aft."

"You're a lifesaver, Carl," Beany said gratefully. "I'd a lot rather drive your three-year-old than Johnny's relic. Yours runs."

Johnny gave her a down-twisted grin.

"Come on," Carlton said.

Carlton wasn't the kind to toss her his car keys and let it go at that. He was the kind who would walk out to his car with her. Nice old Carlton, Beany thought. She couldn't remember when he hadn't been Johnny's shadow. The two had worn a path between the widespread Malone home and the more severe red brick house of Judge Buell's to the north.

Carlton was not so tall as Johnny. He was broader of shoulder, and hadn't Johnny's light-footed grace. Carlton's crew-cut blond hair was never in need of cutting. "This way I can comb it with a towel," he admitted.

12

The Buell family was wealthy and moved in a sophisticated and successful circle, and Carlton was their only son. Yet he went through his days with shy modesty. Last summer when his parents toured Europe they had been irked because Carlton preferred to stay home and teach swimming and athletics at a community center out in the stockyard district.

As Beany and Carlton went out the side door, there was the small but vociferous Mike ready to hurl himself upon Beany. She cried out in alarm, "Grab him, Carl—I've got on nylons."

Carlton obligingly scooped the tornado into his arms and thrust him back into the house. They were always either shutting Mike in the house or shutting him out.

"Hold it," Carlton said, "while I clean all the basketball debris off my front seat."

Beany stood a moment, blinking in the bright January sun. Her stepmother was standing in the yard at the foot of the stairs which led up to the room over the garage. And beside her stood a heavy-set man in a sheep-lined coat. Oh yes, Beany remembered, Adair had said she was going to have a carpenter replace those worn steps.

Adair was saying reproachfully to the workman, "But you promised me that you would build the new steps for us right after the first of the year."

"Yes, missus, but some urgent business came up down in the south of the state. I figure I better look into it. I'll be back—now don't you worry. I'll take care of those steps for you."

Beany sensed in the man a fidgety eagerness to be off. There was something boyish about the amiable smile he turned to Beany and to her stepmother, and with another, "I'll be back," he went hurrying to his car.

Adair gave an exasperated *tch-tch-tch*. "That man. Judge Buell recommended him. He said he was the best carpenter he ever had work for him. He remodeled their upstairs back porch into a room. But, just as the Judge said, 'Now you see him, and now you don't.'"

Beany listened with only half her mind, for she was thinking of Andy Kern and his surprise for her. Something in common with his heart, and their dog Mike, and a fat lady's girdle? What in the world could it be?

She climbed into Carlton's car and started toward the Boulevard and the House of Hollywood. What a full and exciting day loomed ahead. First, the acquiring of a new green skirt. Then on to Eve Baxter's, and from there to the *Call* editorial rooms. She would have to hurry with her typing of the Eve Baxter column so as not to be late at the staff luncheon at the University Club.

She was glad she had Carlton's smooth-running car. If Jennifer wasn't driving the car she shared with her mother, Beany would offer her a ride home, and surely—oh, surely, Jennifer would say, "Beany, how would you like to go to the Press Convention in my place?"

2

THE door of the House of Hollywood was locked.
Beany stared at it in startled dismay. But there in front of
her eyes was the printed explanation:

OPEN
MONDAY THROUGH FRIDAY
9 A.M. TO 6 P.M.
SATURDAY
9:30 A.M. TO 6:30 P.M.

Of all the times she had passed the shop, and even
gone through the door, she had never noticed the large
black lettering on it until now.

But she couldn't wait around for it to open. Eve
Baxter expected her about nine. She peered around the
drawn blind in the door and saw someone moving
inside. She rapped on the door. If that someone would

just let her in, let her take her new and already paid for skirt, let her step out of this clashing checked one and into it— With relief she heard the bolt slide. The door was opened by a woman in a sewing apron with scissors jutting out of the pocket, and with a tape measure around her neck, who smiled at Beany and said, "The store isn't open yet. I'm just the alterations woman, and I came early because we promised to have a suit ready for a customer."

"Couldn't I get my skirt? You see, I planned on wearing it to a luncheon at the University Club, and I won't have time to come back—and you can see how weird this checked one is with a print blouse—"

The woman's kind eyes rested on the blouse with its pale green, bright green, and blackish green shamrocks against a gray background. "No, you couldn't go to a luncheon like that," she said. "Come on in. Our new skirts aren't unpacked yet. They're still in the stock room in the basement. I'll go down and look."

The shop was divided into two sections. On one side of it were the sport clothes and their accessories; on the other the formals with theirs. While Beany waited, her eyes rested on a manikin wearing a breath-taking formal. Beany gave a sigh of pure longing. The strapless basque was of black lace. The ankle-length skirt was a billowing cloud of white tulle with a facing of black tulle and black lace medallions edging it.

She reached over and edged the price tag out from where it was carefully tucked out of sight under the bodice. Eeks!—$89.50—no wonder it was so mouthwatering. It was not for Beany Malone, who dressed herself on the five dollars a week Eve Baxter paid her.

The woman entered with a large carton and set it down. She was panting from the exertion as she pried it open. She extracted a softly pleated, green wool skirt. "These are your size. Slip into that first dressing room and we'll try it on."

A second disappointment. The waistband of the skirt was too large. The woman's face reflected the disappointment in Beany's. She said, "We haven't it in a smaller size. But look, here's a seam in the band I can take up. Let me rip it out and pin it, and then you try it on. It won't take me but a minute to stitch it for you."

In the small dressing room with Beany, she took out her scissors and ripped the belt seam deftly.

"I surely appreciate all this trouble for me," Beany said.

"That's all right, honey. What did you say your name was?"

"Beany Malone."

"How old are you?"

"I'll be seventeen next month. On St. Patrick's day."

"I have a daughter who is already seventeen. So I know what it means to a girl to plan on having something new to wear."

"Does she go to Harkness?"

"No—no, she doesn't go to school." The woman's gentle face clouded. "You see, we moved here last November, and she didn't want to start in a strange school right in the middle of a term. Your new term starts soon, doesn't it?"

"Monday after next."

"Now try this with my pins in it." Beany tried it and found it a perfect fit. "You wait while I stitch it. I'll be right back with it—and no one will ever know it's been taken up."

Beany heard the whirr of a sewing machine in the back room while she folded the offensive checked skirt in a small suit box. The woman reappeared shortly with the new one.

Beany pursued their conversation. "I hope your daughter will like Harkness."

The woman leaned almost wearily against the wall. "She doesn't want to go. She says she won't know anyone—and she hates to be a stranger and left out."

Johnny Malone always said Beany was a born helper at heart. It was true. She felt a certain warm glow at the thought of doing something for someone. She said impulsively, "I'll help her get acquainted. All of us Malones have gone to Harkness. I can introduce her to the teachers and make out her program with her. She can eat lunch with our crowd until she makes friends of her own."

"Oh, would you, dear?" the alterations woman asked hopefully. "Would you stop in and tell her that? You'd better telephone first because she works too. Our name is the kind you have to spell, L-u-n-"

Beany didn't catch the rest of it, for just then the door to the shop opened and Simone, the manager, called out, "Mrs. L—Mrs. L, is that Adele suit ready? I see Mrs. Reed driving up."

Mrs. L. hurried out, explaining, "The skirt is ready, but not the jacket. The Malone girl came for her skirt— you remember you told her to come this morning?—and I had to alter it."

Beany, peering through a crack in the dressing-room curtain, saw a different Simone from the suave and sugary one who dealt with the customers. This Simone snapped out, "We promised Mrs. Reed we'd have it ready when the store opened. A customer who buys an Adele suit shouldn't be kept waiting. You had no business wasting time with a skirt. The Malone girl could have come back later. The Reeds are *good* customers."

Mrs. Reed. That must be Jennifer's mother.

As the front door opened again, Simone went through another metamorphosis. She greeted the woman with dripping graciousness. "Your skirt is ready. Just step into our large dressing room. Perhaps I could show you

20

some blouses, while you wait a minute or two for the jacket."

Once Simone and her *good* customer were in the large dressing room, Beany slipped out the front door. She felt jolted, somehow, to have heard the arrogant Simone—whose right name was Simmons—sharply scold the woman she called Mrs. L. for taking care of the Malone girl. Beany felt doubly grateful to Mrs. L. It would have been so easy for her not to have unbolted the door, or to have answered through it, "You'll have to come back later."

Beany resolved, I'll stop in and get her address and her daughter's name. She's probably some bashful small-town girl. Again Beany's heart swelled with the thought of helping a stranger over her first bewildering days at Harkness.

Beany's way led past the big Park Gate apartment-hotel. Here Kay Maffley, Beany's inseparable, lived with her mother. Kay, who knew Beany's schedule as well as she knew her own, was waiting on the wide marble steps, her rosy-red coat and blond shoulder-length hair making a bright blob of color.

Beany slowed to a stop and Kay ran out to the car to say, "Let's see your new skirt with the shamrock blouse. Oh, Beany, that's fabulous—I was afraid it'd be one of those grassy greens."

And then Kay, who knew Beany's dreams as well as she knew her own, asked, "Has Jennifer given you the word to go to the Quill and Scroll convention yet?"

Beany shook her head.

"She will," her best friend assured her. "Today, I bet. . . . Is Johnny or Andy calling for me tonight for our double date, and what time, and what are we going to do?"

"Andy will chauffeur us all tonight. I don't know what we'll cook up. 'Bye for now—I'm a little late."

Her next stop was at Eve Baxter's. Beany had been coming to this narrow, prim two-story residence for over a year, yet it still gave her a thrill to have the elderly housekeeper, named Araminta, in ruffled cap and apron, open the door for her. It was always like something out of an English novel to have Araminta say, "Come in, Miss Beany. Let me take your coat, dear. Miss Eve is expecting you."

She supposed Araminta was what you called a faithful family retainer. After Beany's coat was carefully hung on the hall tree, Araminta said, "Come, dear, I'll show you upstairs."

But the minute Araminta announced, "Here's Miss Beany, Miss Eve. Now I'll go about my marketing," and started down the stairs, all illusion of the faithful ministering servant was gone. For Eve Baxter, a slender woman with gray sprinkled through her reddish hair, blurted out, "Soon as the door closes behind that woman, go down and make me a pot of coffee."

It was a feud of long standing between employer and employee. Araminta insisted that coffee was ruinous to a woman's disposition and complexion. She served Miss Eve tea instead. "When I do browbeat her into making coffee," Eve Baxter often grumbled to Beany, "I swear she puts a geranium leaf or a dash of nutmeg in it."

This morning, as usual, when Araminta departed, Beany hurried down to the old-fashioned kitchen and put on a percolator of coffee. She carried it up to Eve Baxter in the large sunny upstairs room.

It was a room with a dual personality. The part of the room where Eve Baxter and Beany worked was businesslike, with large cluttered desk and files and comfortable, mannish, leather chairs. But the alcove off the room was sheer femininity. Ruffled curtains and bedspread of pale green taffeta. Wallpaper with a lacy flower pattern in it. An array of cut-glass perfume bottles on the dressing table.

As Eve Baxter sipped her black coffee appreciatively, she said, "Beany, I'm always getting letters from girls who want to know should they or shouldn't they be loving in order to be popular."

"You do?" Beany said with interest. "What are you going to tell them?"

"I've given quite a bit of thought to it," Eve Baxter said thoughtfully. "In my day we called it 'petting.' And it did a girl no good to be labeled a 'petter.' You'll notice, Beany, it's always the girl who is labeled, never the boy. As I say, it's a man's world. What's the word for petting now? I can't keep up with it. Smooching?"

"No, that's baroque—meaning old-fashioned. Now it's loving-it-up. Only at Harkness we have a new word—more-thanning—and the girls"—come to think of it, Beany realized, it *was* always the girls who got tagged— "who are extra ardent are called 'more-thanners.' "

Eve Baxter repeated it, mystified, "More-thanners?"

Beany explained, "Melinda Page—she's the drama teacher—put on a play in December called, *Our Darling Daughter*. It was a riot. It was laid in the Gay Nineties—only what was so gay about those boned collars and squeezed-in waists? It seems that a heavy date in those days was boy plays girl croquet with a chaperone on the sidelines—"

"Even in my day, when boy took girl to the opera, he bought three tickets—one for the chaperone," Eve Baxter commented. "But where does your more-thanning come in?"

"The grand finale of the play was when the girl was caught holding hands under the porte-cochere with the young tenor in the choir. So the whole family gathered for a kind of inquisition, and the father chewed the poor girl out—her name was Adeline—and he gave this ringing speech about how a girl was allowed a brief

24

handclasp in greeting her escort, and he could take her arm in crossing a street, and her dancing partner could put his arm around her waist—with a handkerchief under his hand when they waltzed. But more than that no well brought-up young lady ever permitted."

"It must have been a riot," Eve Baxter commented dryly, "for you free-and-easy kids of today."

Beany continued, "Of course, all the kids at Harkness had to kick that around—the part about 'more than that no nice young lady may permit.' So now it's more-thanning at school."

Eve Baxter turned her keen eyes on Beany. "What about you, kidlet? Do you have problems with that beau of yours, that Andy?"

Beany's blush drowned out the sprinkling of freckles across her nose. "Not with Andy." (But who knows what problems she might have faced with Norbett if he hadn't stayed back in Ohio?) "Andy keeps it light."

"In my day," Eve Baxter went on, "a boy never used endearments until the girl wore his engagement ring."

Beany laughed. "You couldn't call what Andy calls me endearments. Once in a while it's hon or sweetie, but usually knucklehead or stupe or monkey-face."

Eve Baxter said gravely, "Customs change, Beany, but human beings don't change as much as we think. I imagine that the young men of today in their T-shirts and jeans aren't too different from the men in their Norfolk jackets and straw sailors of a generation or so ago. Men have always felt the need to look up to a woman. It has always been up to the girl to set the pace."

She sighed, and her eyes and her attention shifted to the letters her slim nervous hands were shuffling.

"No, human nature doesn't change. Do you realize, Beany, that today we have the equivalent of the old gold-rush days? Only today it's uranium. The same old gambling, get-rich fever. And it's the same as in the old days—the men have the fun and excitement of it, and the wife and children have the hardships—"

Oh dear, Beany thought, I hope she doesn't take up too long talking about uranium seekers. Not this morning, when I have to be at the University Club at one o'clock. Uranium fever, uranium seekers seemed far removed from Beany's life. It was the luncheon of the *Hark Ye* staff which was all-important.

"Letters have been pouring in to me from the womenfolks of these new prospectors with their jeeps and Geiger counters. Their menfolks are giving up jobs, mortgaging homes, to go seeking a fortune down at Four Corners. You know where that is—that plateau region where Colorado, New Mexico, Utah, and Nevada touch? Some of the men want to leave the family behind; some of them want to borrow money and buy a trailer and load up the family and set out."

Beany held her pencil poised over her notebook. Oh, hurry, hurry, she thought. She didn't have a wrist watch,

26

but time was moving on. "Are you going to answer some of those letters this morning?" she asked.

"Indeed, I am," Eve Baxter answered hotly. "I'm going to say what my father always said in the old goldrush days: 'A man has a right to gamble if his losses are his own, but not when it works a hardship on a wife and children who depend upon him—' "

Oh, hurry and dictate, Beany thought. If I'm late at the luncheon, I won't be able to sit next to Jennifer Reed.

3

MR. DEXTER'S luncheon was over.

Beany and Jennifer Reed left the University Club together. Jennifer had gratefully accepted Beany's offer of a ride home.

A half-block from the club building they came upon a girl who had stopped on the street to put on her coat, and who was having somewhat of a struggle to squirm into a coat because she carried a purse, and a knobby and evidently hastily wrapped package.

Beany called to her, "Wait, Peggy—let me help you." This was Peggy Wood, the senior reporter on the *Hark Ye,* who had also attended Mr. Dexter's luncheon.

Peggy explained lamely, "I didn't think I'd need a coat—I mean, the sun seemed so bright—"

As though anyone would think a blue slipover sweater, faded to a near gray and shrunk till the sleeves didn't reach her wrists, would be warm enough on a

January day with a chill bite in the air! With a flash of understanding, Beany realized that Peggy had been ashamed to put on her shabby, long-worn coat in the University Club. Not only was the coat shapeless from years of wear and too small in the shoulders for Peggy, but it was also an odd shade of green that didn't go too happily with either the wan blue of her sweater or the reddish cast to her plaid skirt.

Peggy was a hard-working, likable, round-faced and plump girl whose clothes always seemed to be straining at the seams, and whose dark hair of indeterminate length always looked as though she hadn't had time to do much about it. And she probably hadn't, Beany thought concernedly this afternoon, even as her fingers longed to tuck a stringy lock of it back from Peggy's face. For these were troublous days in the Wood household. Peggy was the oldest of a large family, and her father had been out of work for months.

Beany was holding the newspaper-wrapped package. She tucked a corner of the wrapping over what was obviously the scuffed toes of a pair of boy's heavy shoes. Peggy took the package from her and asked in a low voice, as though she didn't want Jennifer Reed, only daughter of the successful Christopher Reed, to hear, "Beany, isn't there a shoe shop downtown where they half-sole shoes for you right away?"

Beany nodded, and matched Peggy's low voice, "Repairs While-U-Wait, it's called. On Broadway near the bus station."

"I hope it won't take them too long," Peggy murmured, "because my brother— Well, good-by, Beany and Jennifer—" And with a harried smile, she went hurrying off.

Beany watched after her with a pang of pity. Because, Peggy had stopped short of saying, my brother can't go out of the house until I get home with his shoes.

Beany started to say, Poor old Peg is sure having it tough these days. If she had been with Kay she would have; she and Kay often discussed Peggy, wishing there were some way they could make it easier for her.

But Jennifer—somehow Jennifer Reed seemed on a more remote plane. One hesitated to discuss an out-of-work father with her, and a brother with only one pair of shoes. So Beany said, "My car is in the Press parking space in front of the *Call*."

They walked on, chatting about the luncheon.

It seemed a happy coincidence to Beany that, as they neared the *Call* building, they should meet her father, Martie Malone.

Beany felt a warm surge of pride as she introduced her friend to her father. She was proud of Jennifer, the poised and lovely, who always looked so casually right. She did, this mid-afternoon, with her dark wool dress barely showing under her fur coat. The coat was the same rich brown as Jennifer's eyes; Beany wasn't familiar enough with furs to know what kind it was.

And she was fondly proud of her father, too. "Quite a personage," Eve Baxter always said of him. He was tall like Johnny. He never wore a hat; he never "bundled up" with scarfs or overshoes, yet he never seemed conscious of cold winds. With his dark hair graying slightly at the temples and his alert dark eyes surrounded by laugh wrinkles, he looked like an older and more weathered edition of Beany's brother Johnny. They both had the same warm, beguiling smile.

Jennifer Reed said, "I've always wanted to meet you, Mr. Malone. I've been reading your column ever since our Junior High teacher made us read it for Current Events."

"And even that didn't turn you against me?" he chuckled. "I'm always happy to meet editors, too. Did your luncheon go off nicely?"

"No, it didn't," Jennifer said with rueful honesty. "Oh, the luncheon itself was super—"

"We led off with Vichyssoise," Beany put in, "and ended with cherries jubilee."

"—but Mr. Dexter really jolted us in his nice way," Jennifer finished.

"Meaning he came up with criticism," Martie said with his understanding smile. "Editors have to take that from the boss, you know. What was he unhappy about?"

"Tell him, Beany," Jennifer prompted.

"He thinks the whole tone of the paper is too slaphappy," Beany explained. "And wisecracking. He thinks some of it is all right, but that we should also have a sort of uplift or inspirational note."

"And what do you think?" Martie Malone asked Jennifer, the editor.

"I think he's right," she admitted with that same rueful honesty. "We have all been outdoing ourselves in being witty and bright. Mr. Dexter wanted more in the vein of a short piece Beany wrote in our 'Thought for the Week' sometime back. About how there would be less hard feeling if folks would be generous enough to admit their faults—"

"I remember it," Martie Malone said.

Jennifer sighed. "Something thought-provoking, the boss said. Something to do with life's problems. I was just telling Beany that I'm tossing it right into her lap. She's our feature writer—she has a knack for something like that. I haven't."

"But I haven't an idea in my head for anything inspiring or for strengthening Harkness souls. We've just got out our January issue, so we won't need to uplift until our Valentine one."

They parted from Martie Malone at the entrance to the *Call,* and the two girls walked on to the car Carlton Buell had lent to Beany. It was plain that Jennifer was disturbed by their principal's criticism. She roused from her frowning abstraction to say to Beany as they settled

32

themselves in the car, "That's a good-looking outfit you're wearing, Beany. I like you in green."

"Brand new," Beany said, edging out of the parking space. "Kay gave me the blouse for Christmas. I stopped at the House of Hollywood and got the skirt this morning."

The alterations woman's daughter. She must remember and get her address and call on her with friendly encouragement.

"Nice things at the Hollywood," Jennifer said. "I've got my eye on a formal there with a view to our Heart Hop on Valentine's night. This one is different from the usual fluff of pale blue, or pink, or yellow. It's black lace with white tulle."

"Oh, that one!" Beany said with awe. "Yes, I noticed it this morning. Looks like something a movie star would receive her Oscar in. Sort of deliciously wicked." She added ruefully, "The price is wicked, too."

Jennifer made no comment. But then price tags weren't stop signals for the only daughter of the Christopher Reed Realty Company.

They were driving out the long stretch of College Boulevard. Maybe now Beany could bring the talk around to the Quill and Scroll convention— But Jennifer's thoughts had veered back to Mr. Dexter's criticism of *her* paper. She mused, "He's right, too—a school paper can influence students more than we realize." She gave a short laugh. "I ought to know. Just that one wisecrack of mine about Morley Wilson, and now nobody even knows he's got a first name. Oh, that reminds me—Jag is coming over for dinner. And, what with Mr. Dexter and his note of uplift, I forgot to stop downtown and buy some barbecue sauce."

"We can get it at the Ragged Robin," Beany offered. "It's right on our way."

The Ragged Robin was a drive-in which catered to the university crowd. It had recently been enlarged and remodeled. Beany turned off the Boulevard and onto its wide asphalt apron. A sign said, "Blink Lights for Service." She sat for a moment, hesitating as to whether or not one blinked lights for a pint of Ragged Robin barbecue sauce.

Jennifer said, "Well, well! The old Robin *has* come up a notch to have a carhop in uniform."

The carhop was some twenty feet away, clamping an aluminum tray onto a car door. She was wearing a red jacket, fitted revealingly snug, a short pleated skirt, and white drum majorette boots. The girl turned from the car she was serving and, with a wide, delighted smile on her face, started toward theirs.

She was pretty and pert—and startling. Her hair wasn't quite blond, but a light brown, like burnt sugar, and the afternoon sun showed up its glinting gold lights. She wore it in a pony tail which cascaded out, profusely long and wavy and shaped like a plume. In contrast to her golden hair and fair skin, her eyebrows and lashes

34

stood out, heavy and blackish. Beany wondered swiftly if nature had given them to her—or if she gave them to herself.

The girl reached their car just as Beany rolled down her window. She stopped short, and so did her welcoming smile at sight of two girls in the front seat. I suppose, Beany thought, she prefers male customers from the university.

Jennifer Reed said curtly, "We don't want to be served. I'd like a pint of barbecue sauce to take home."

The carhop with the pony tail tossed her head like a mettlesome pony. "So what? You can go in and get it at the counter."

Jennifer's chin lifted. Her tone was quite definitely the tone one used in speaking to a menial. "You're supposed to wait on the customers, aren't you? Why can't you get it?"

"Because I'm too busy taking tray orders, that's why."

There was insolence in the way she said it, in the way she turned her back on them and strutted in her majorette boots back to the car she had served.

Jennifer said angrily as she got out of the car, "A lot of airs for a carhop." But she went to the counter and soon reappeared with her carton of sauce.

Beany was just reaching up to adjust the sunshade against the lowering sun when another car drove in to the Ragged Robin with a premeditated noisy roar. Jag Wilson in his low, bright yellow Jaguar. With the sun slanting on Beany's windshield, he would have had to look close to see the two girls inside.

But Jag Wilson didn't look close. He didn't even glance their way. His eyes were on the girl with the burnt-sugar hair, and he sang out, "Hi-ya, Dulcie. What do we do if we can't blink our lights?"

She smiled boldly at him and made quick answer. "Just blink your eyes and I'll come running."

She walked with her hippy swing over to the open low car. Jag Wilson was lighting a cigarette. She reached out with easy familiarity and took it from between his lips and with a swift glance around—probably to see if the manager of the drive-in was in sight—took an appreciative puff or two before she handed it back. She leaned on the low door of his car, and the two laughed together.

Jennifer watched with narrowed eyes, her lips crimped thinly. She said with a derisive laugh, "Too busy to wait on a couple of girls. Crummy little more-thanner."

Beany asked hesitantly, "Should I honk—so Jag will see us?"

"Heavens no!" Jennifer said shortly.

Beany backed up and drove out. Jag Wilson didn't even glance their way. All his laughing attention was focused on the girl named Dulcie in her red jacket, and her cheeks almost as red from the cold wind, and her lips even redder—because of lipstick wielded generously.

Beany wished, somehow, it hadn't happened. Her sympathies were divided. Maybe if Jennifer had been more friendly and her tone less arrogant, the girl wouldn't have answered so insolently. And, after all, Jag Wilson was as much to blame as the carhop. Jennifer shouldn't wholly condemn her by calling her a crummy little more-thanner.

Beany glanced at Jennifer's set face as they drove on. Beany had noticed Jag's jeweled fraternity pin on Jennifer's soft wool dress at the luncheon . . . No, this was certainly no time to bring up mention of the Quill and Scroll convention. . . .

"That's our house on the corner—the white one," Jennifer said briefly.

The house, on its landscaped corner lot, was the one-story rancho type which needed words like "spacious," "de luxe," to describe it. A breezeway, patio, and many picture windows catching the sun. Even as Beany drew up to the low curb, a maid in uniform came out the front door to pick up the afternoon paper.

This was a new and restricted district called Harmony Heights. Every house had an individual and picturesque elegance of its own. In summer, these Harmony Heights lawns were kept green by automatic sprinkler systems. In winter, the sidewalks were kept clear of snow by automatic warming systems under them.

Oddly enough, the district on the other side of the university was not at all restricted or exclusive. Some of the houses there were old and rundown; some were newly-built, flimsy affairs. There were lawns of sorts, but no sidewalks. Some wit had termed it Hodgepodge Hollow. The campus divided the two districts like the railroad tracks. An address on the east of the campus was so right; on the west, so wrong.

Jennifer roused from her tight-lipped abstraction to say as she got out of the car, "Don't forget your inspirational something for our Valentine issue, Beany."

"I'll start thinking," Beany promised.

She drove toward home dispiritedly. She was no closer to going to the Quill and Scroll convention at Cherry Springs than she had been this morning. If only Jennifer's mind hadn't been so diverted by Mr. Dexter's criticism, and even more diverted by a pert and prancy carhop named Dulcie and the carhop's familiarity with Jag Wilson, for whom Jennifer was buying barbecue sauce.

4

BEANY was driving down the Boulevard and past the bustling shopping center when, on the corner outside Downey's Drug, she glimpsed a familiar bright red jacket and fawn-colored jodhpur breeches. Mary Fred, carrying a large sack of groceries. She was evidently marketing on her way home from Hilltop Stables.

Beany slowed to a near stop and called to her. "How about a taxi to Barberry Street, Miss?"

Mary Fred called back, "Oh my, yes, and much obliged. But park a sec and come on in the drug with me. I want to pick up some saddle soap Downey said he'd order for me."

Beany joined her. She reached into the top-heavy sack and took out the heavy package of dog meat and a tall can of fruit juice to lighten Mary Fred's load a little. They pushed into the drugstore.

Mr. Downey wasn't in the store and neither was Mary Fred's saddle soap. His friendly wife explained, "He went down to the wholesale house to pick up some items—your saddle soap among them, Mary Fred. But he should be back any minute. You girls sit down, and have a coke on the house while you're waiting."

They slid into the corner booth opposite each other. Mary Fred said as she braced the lumpy sack on the bench beside her, "I thought I'd try my hand at meat loaf tonight. I considered Swiss steak, but decided to leave it to my betters—meaning Beany. It's times like this," she sighed, "I wish our Miss Opal hadn't left us with all these culinary problems."

Miss Opal was the elderly, motherly spinster who had lived with the Malones from last October until the first of the year. With Miss Opal in the house you could always open the door on enticing food smells. But two weeks ago, when she had a chance to ride to California with friends, the Malones had all urged her to go. "We can get along while you have a nice visit," they said.

They got along, but not so well. Breakfast had always been a catch-as-catch-can affair anyhow, with the toaster on the table, and the first one up putting on the coffee. School lunches could be handled too, though they were apt to be monotonous without Miss Opal's chicken-salad spread and fancy tarts.

It was the evening meal that was the real chore. Their new stepmother, Adair, tried hard but, as she herself admitted, she was more deft with a paint brush than a mixing spoon. Beany and Mary Fred took week-long turns at marketing and cooking dinner for the family.

"It'll be my turn next week," Beany murmured as Mrs. Downey set their cokes before them. She smiled at their thanks and went on to wait on a customer.

"Tell me about Jennifer," Mary Fred said suddenly. "Did she give you the nod on the Quill and Scroll affair?"

Beany shook her head. "She had too much on her mind." She told about Mr. Dexter's criticisms, about the unhappy stop at the Robin.

Mary Fred snorted, "Playboy Jag!" She added, "He belongs to the same fraternity as my friend Wally."

The very edge to her voice made Beany look up from her cold drink. "Why, Mary Fred! You're dating Wally tonight, aren't you?"

"Yes." Mary Fred peeled the paper covering off her straws. "But maybe for the last time."

"The last time? Oh, no," Beany breathed.

Wally was Sergeant Wallace Thomas who, though stationed at the air base, took classes in Radar at the university. He drove a yellow convertible. He was whole-souled and generous and likable, and he had been Mary Fred's most devoted escort since last October.

Mary Fred laughed raggedly. "I have problems. Wally is the amorous type. I'm getting so tired of having to 'rassle' with him, or to outwit him so we're never alone together."

"Goodness," Beany said. "This is the second time today the amorous problem has come up. Eve Baxter was talking about it. But Wally's pretty crazy about you, Mary Fred. And you like him, don't you?"

Mary Fred leaned back against the gray imitation leather of the booth, the collar of her white blouse half in, half out of the red jacket. Old bubble-and-bounce, Johnny always called her. Her friends always said, "Oh, Mary Fred, it won't be a party without you." Because she was so vital and sparkling, her soberness always seemed extra sober.

"Yes, Wally's pretty crazy about me—in his way," she said slowly. "He has fun coming to our house because he feels at home with all of us. Yes, I like him—he's fun to go out with, fun to dance with—but, by darn, it isn't love on his part or mine and that's why—well, it's a problem."

From the moment Beany had slid into this corner booth, Norbett Rhodes's presence had seemed to be hovering near. How many times she and Norbett had sipped cokes here at Downey's Drug! She felt again the excited ecstasy of her first date with him. It had been a foursome and they had crowded into this very booth. Beany had eaten blueberry pie, and Norbett had looked across at her and had sung out lustily,

"I dream of Beany with the light blue teeth . . ."

42

She murmured, "I was nuts about Norbett. Maybe I'd be having problems too if he hadn't stayed back in Ohio."

It was always nice, these brief interludes when Beany and her older sister took out their hearts and examined them. Beany said around the chunk of ice she was crunching, "Does Wally want to go steady with you, Mary Fred?"

"Yes, he does. For the same reason that a lot of the couples on the campus—yes, and at Harkness—do. Because going steady or being 'pinned' seems to make it O.K. for being *quite* affectionate, to put it mildly."

Both girls peered out of the booth as the drugstore door opened. It was not Mr. Downey, but two little boys to buy comics. Beany resumed, "I thought going steady on the campus meant being engaged."

"Engaged to be engaged," Mary Fred said wryly. "Maybe it's me, but unless it's the real thing and you can start plans for getting married, all this *amour-amour* seems a little on the cheap side. Gosh, Beany, I'm no touch-me-not. I like holding hands in a show, and watching the moon with my head on a guy's shoulder, and kissing him good-night—"

"Girls write to Eve Baxter," Beany put in, "asking if they have to be loving on dates to be popular."

Mary Fred was flattening, pleating one of her coke straws into small lengths. "I guess every girl worries about it and is haunted by the specter of being left out. I certainly was confused when I started at the university last year, and I kept wondering if my conscience was too prim and Victorian . . ."

"Why?"

"I suppose every campus has girls that are called Hot Lips. That's what mixed me up—because, lordee, what a wild rush the fellows made for those girls. They had dates stacked up—the Hot Lips—early dates, late dates, later dates. And then I noticed that these gals didn't get asked to the campus affairs—the games and formals and firesides . . ."

"That's funny—funny-peculiar, I mean," Beany said. "Because Eve Baxter said that in her day it did a girl no good to be labeled a 'petter.' I thought maybe it was just an older woman deciding it ought to be like that. She said a man always felt the need to look up to a girl."

The straw between Mary Fred's fingers was like a miniature accordion now. She said, feeling out her words, "And maybe a girl feels the need of a man looking up to her. I know I'd hate to have remarks tossed around about me like those I heard the fellows make about the Hot Lips." A thoughtful pause and then Mary Fred added in an even lower voice, "Besides, let's face it, hon, it's the heavy loving scenes that lead up to—well, last year one of the Hot Lips had to get married in a hurry. And this year one of them dropped out of school, and a lot of ugly whispers buzzed around—"

44

Mr. Downey called, "Here's your saddle soap, Mary Fred."

They had been so engrossed in their airing of hearts they hadn't even heard him come in. Both girls put their hearts back under their coats and stood up. Mary Fred paid for the saddle soap and dropped the round, flat can into her sack; they thanked Mrs. Downey again for their cokes and left.

Carlton Buell was waiting when the two girls reached home. He was in gym shoes and was dribbling two basketballs on the sidewalk. This was the evening he coached basketball at his community center, he explained.

Mary Fred said, "Pardon me, while I scurry in and make with a meat loaf."

Beany lingered to voice her appreciation for the use of the car, and Carlton grinned and said, "That's all right. You'll have to pay through the nose for it by teaching me how to shag."

Imagine Carlton wanting to improve his dancing!

"Any time. You got yourself a girl, Carl?"

His only answer was a flush that ran up into his short crew cut.

"What is this—a secret love?" Beany wanted to know. He didn't answer that either, but said, "Johnny got his fuel line fixed," and climbed into the car.

Beany entered the Malone house. In the big living room Adair had visitors. She was doing the portrait of an elderly woman, and her family had come to view it. This was the third time they had all come, Beany realized.

A letter lay on the newel post. For Beany Malone. Why, it was from Norbett Rhodes, and it had a small bulge inside the envelope that she could feel through the folded sheets of writing paper.

She carried it up to her room. She sat on the bed, slid her coat off her shoulders, and looked at the envelope curiously. It was well-covered with penciled, "Not at this address. Try————" and another number on another street written in. Norbett had addressed it wrong. He hadn't put South in front of Barberry Street. The letter had been long delayed in its travels.

She tore it open, and a small tissue-wrapped lump dropped in her lap. She unwrapped it and gazed at a tiny silver leprechaun, holding what was supposed to be an even tinier pot of gold. The leprechaun wore a pointed silver cap and pointed shoes, and had eyes that were emeralds no bigger than pinheads.

Wonderingly, Beany read the hurriedly-written note:

Beany, I need your Irish luck. Since I wrote you last, my world has cracked up. Please fasten this charm to our bracelet—remember we always said it was a charmed bracelet?—and wear it to bring me luck.

What was Beany Malone anyway—a four-leaf clover who was supposed to bring Andy luck and Norbett luck?

46

The letter ended;

I'll write more later. In a rush now, so you'll get this right away.

He had been in such a rush that he had misaddressed the letter and she hadn't gotten it right away. And if this silver leprechaun was to bring Norbett luck by dangling on the charm bracelet on Beany's wrist, then Norbett's luck would be delayed.

Unpredictable Norbett. He had written her last October to take off the charm bracelet. As though Beany didn't know the words by heart. As though she hadn't cried herself to sleep the night after reading them:

There are a lot of years ahead before we could think of going steady, with me in college back here and you in Denver. So you take off our charm bracelet.

Beany got up slowly. She fumbled under her handkerchiefs in a drawer of her chest and lifted out the silver link bracelet.

The dangling charms tinkled tunefully as she did— those charms with their special sentimental significance for Norbett Rhodes and Beany Malone. The miniature car which represented Norbett's red car and which Beany used to keep touched up with bright red nail polish. The little bottle that Norbett said stood for her unsuccessful freckle remover. (Norbett liked her freckles.) Even a miniature typewriter, because they had met first in typing when Norbett asked her, "What is it two of in *occasion?*" And because in typing class they used to pass typed messages, sometimes friendly, sometimes stormy, back and forth.

Beany hunted for her nail file in the squeaky drawer of her dressing table. She dropped back on her bed and with the file pried open the small ring attached to the good-luck leprechaun. She had to turn on her bed light to attach the new charm to the link bracelet. She laughed as the light caught the green eyes of the little man, turning them into twin twinkles.

There now. He was firmly attached. She fastened the bracelet in its old place on her right wrist. She gave it a twist or two to hear the old jingle she knew so well. That was strange. The very putting on of the bracelet seemed to bring Norbett close. It seemed to change Beany back to the Beany of a year ago when the very weather of her days depended on Norbett Rhodes.

And what changeable weather it had been. Because Norbett himself was so changeable.

There was the show-off, wise-guy Norbett who bragged about his newspaper job and mentioned big politicians and celebrities by their first names. And the moody, trigger-edge Norbett who could needle Beany until her temper flared— "When bigger and better fights are had—" There was also an appealing, heart-warming

48

Norbett who could say, "Ain't you the one!" which was his way of saying, "Beany, you're wonderful," and hearing it, Beany would be lifted to the clouds.

But perhaps it was the unwanted, lonely, orphaned Norbett who pulled the hardest at her heartstrings. He had lived with his aunt and uncle at the Park Gate, that luxury apartment-hotel where Kay lived. "I'm just the poor relation," he would say bitterly.

It was that Norbett who had given Beany the bracelet. The bracelet had started life as a heavy silver-link necklace. Beany could still remember the day he had pulled it out of his pocket along with his car keys. She could still remember the self-derision in his voice as he told her of buying the necklace for his Park Gate aunt with the first money he earned, distributing advertisements from door to door.

He had hoped to please his Aunt Mae, the social climber, by buying her what a twelve-year-old boy thought was a beautiful piece of jewelry. She had never worn it. And then, years later and a few days before Beany had seen it in his pocket, his aunt had asked him to carry down a box of discards for Good Will and Norbett saw his necklace among them.

"Don't know why I thought it was worth picking out of the other junk," he had said with an offhand laugh that didn't hide his hurt.

That was when Beany said, "It would make a bracelet—the kind you put charms on."

A year ago Christmas Beany had unwrapped the heavy silver chain, cut down to fit her wrist and already complete with the charms that meant so much to them. She had worn it, its jingle music to her ears, until last October when Norbett wrote her to take it off.

What had happened that Norbett's world had cracked up? His Ohio aunt had wanted him to stay with her after her husband died. What was troubling Norbett? Beany felt the old ache of wanting to help him.

Was it indeed a *charmed* bracelet, so that she had only to feel its weight and jingle on her wrist to become again the Beany who cared so deeply about the red-headed, unpredictable Norbett?

Mary Fred burst open the door. She was still in her jodhpurs and white shirt, but a cellophane apron with pink roses was tied around her waist and loose sandals flapped on her feet. She said, "I put the meat loaf and the potatoes in the oven, and then I thought I'd better ask you—will one get any done-er than the other, come dinner time?"

Meat loaf? Potatoes? . . . Beany's mind had difficulty coming back to such mundane things. "Not if the meat loaf isn't too thick," she said absently.

"What're you sitting here mooning about, toots?" Then Mary Fred's eyes fell on the bracelet on Beany's wrist. "Shades of the past! Don't tell me that jangly bracelet and your jangly squabbles with Norbett are with us again."

Beany said stiffly, "He sent me a good-luck charm for the bracelet—this little leprechaun—"

Mary Fred leaned over and examined it. "Cute. The little codger winked at me."

"—and he asked me to wear it on the bracelet, because he needs all the luck he can get."

"What for?"

"He didn't say."

Mary Fred snorted. "Old cloak and dagger Norbett. The man of mystery. I thought your torch for Norbett had burned itself out."

"I thought so too," Beany mused. "I thought I was all over caring. Of course, whenever I make peppermint-stick ice cream—remember how crazy he was about it?—or when I'm with Kay and see his little red car sitting in the basement garage under the Park Gate hotel, I feel a sort of pang of missing him. . . ."

"First love," Mary Fred said sadly. "I admit there's something sweet under Norbett's burry, cantankerous hide. But you two had a rough go of it—and you bruise too easily. You know, little Beaver, I have a hunch that if he came back into your life again, it wouldn't be the same. Like that old saying, 'You can't go back.' "

She perched herself uncomfortably on the footboard of Beany's bed, her sandals hanging precariously from her toes. "It's funny how we go along with the same names and the same faces, but we're really different people at different times in our lives. What I mean is, you're a year and a half older than when you first met Norbett and handed him your heart, as they say in stories. You've had other boy friends, other interests—you're a different you now."

Her philosophizing broke off at the sound of feet on the stairs. Johnny? Only Johnny usually took the stairs two at a time, and these feet were progressing slowly, stumblingly. Yes, it was Johnny, for he yelled out, "Man in the dorm!" and, in another instant, kicked open Beany's door.

They stared at him in amazement, as well they might. On Johnny's dark wet-feather hair rode a wide, stiff, flower-trimmed hat. A multitude of long rustly skirts were wadded under one arm. Thrown over his shoulder, as though they were shoe skates, hung a slim pair of high laced shoes with pointed toes.

They still watched in speechless amazement as he deposited his armful of skirts and shook the hat off his head onto Beany's bed. He extracted from under his other arm a rolled white something from which long strings dangled; evidently the strings were what he had stumbled over coming up the stairs.

"What in the world is that?" Beany asked.

Mary Fred reached over and shook it out. "It's a corset, the grandma of our form-flo girdles of today."

"Stays was the word, my pets," Johnny said. "I have more." From the pocket of his Levis he pulled out something that looked like a brown hair pincushion.

52

"The rat," he murmured, and fished deeper for a handful of bone hairpins.

"There, I guess that's it," he said. "Stand up, Beany, and let's try you for size."

"Try *me* for size?" Beany repeated, as she got to her feet. "*Me?*"

Johnny picked up a weighty skirt of cherry red silk from the bed; it was gored and lined, and had a geometric braid design around the bottom. He halved its narrow waistline and held it up to Beany's middle. "Looks like a tight squeeze, even if Melinda did say she thought you were the same size as this Darlene person who has the mumps."

Melinda? That would be Melinda Page, drama teacher at Harkness. This Darlene person? That must be a Darlene McDaniels who belonged to the drama club and who had a walk-on part in *Our Darling Daughter*.

Johnny was saying, "Didn't Melinda get hold of you, Beany, before you left Eve Baxter's? She said she would try to. You knew, didn't you, that the Harkness cast is putting on *Our Darling Daughter* for the soldiers out at the air base tonight?"

Yes, Beany knew.

"And just this noon, Melinda got word that Darlene McSomebody was down with the mumps. Melinda called some other girls in the drama club to fill in, but they were either skiing or halfway down with the mumps. She was simply out on a limb, and so I—"

Beany's eyes were aghast. "Johnny Malone, you didn't tell her I'd be in it?"

"Why, sure. Why not? I'd take a part myself if I were still in high school. I've already done all the legwork for you. I gathered up all these ruffles and rats because Melinda says the dressing rooms at the Service Club are practically nil, and the cast will please get into costumes at home."

"But I can't act," Beany said.

"You don't have to *act*," Johnny said. "You just have to help fill up the stage. You remember the play, and how they had a lot of swishy skirts around? All you have to do is fiddle with a croquet mallet and—"

Mary Fred's bubbling laugh rang out. "And look frail and flowerlike. Sure you can do it, Beany. It'll be fun." She was holding up the very narrow shoes. "Oh, groan!— I'll bet you'll wish these were open toes before the evening is over. No wonder ladies minced along in those days."

"I don't think I can take a step in those," Beany said. Johnny put in encouragingly, "You can kind of lean on the croquet mallet in the first act, and in the second you get to sit down and sip tea."

Mary Fred was now holding up the shirtwaist with its high boned collar. "*Sip* is right, with this cinched around your throat."

"And no lipstick," Johnny said. "You have to look like you could faint easily."

54

"I doggone well could in those clothes," Beany grumbled. She picked up the skirt and again tested it by comparing half of its waistband to half of her. "I'll never get it around me."

"That's where the stays come in, lambie," Mary Fred said. "Those strings were meant to be pulled."

"What do you do with the rest of all those white strings?" Beany asked.

"Loop them around your waist," Johnny informed her. "I asked about them when I picked up part of your gear at the House of Mumps. Darlene's great-aunt told me she had worn these clothes. She said that in her day every woman lived in terror for fear a piece of corset string might poke through the placket of her skirt. Think of what zippers could have done for the peace of mind of those poor women."

Beany took a closer look at the stiff, betrimmed hat. The beady black eyes of a red bird, perched beside a cluster of roses, met hers. "The bird on Nellie's hat," she murmured. She set the hat on her head where it rocked loosely. "It's way too big. How'll I keep it from falling off?"

"Hatpins," Johnny said. "Look—two hatpins."

"What do you put the hatpins through?"

"The rat under the pompadour which we'll have to fashion somehow with the hair in your braids," Mary Fred said.

"What do you fasten the rat to?" Beany pursued.

"Your head, stupid," Mary Fred said.

"Oh, my sainted aunt!" Beany sighed. She made one more helpless demurring. "Johnny, I've got a date with Andy tonight. And you've got one with Kay. Remember?"

"Sure. Andy and Kay and I will go out to the Base and see you in that soul-shaking performance of *Our Darling Daughter.*"

"Yipes," Mary Fred said, leaping to her feet and spilling the white corset and strings onto the floor. "I smell something that could be meat loaf going dry. Better not eat too hearty of my well-balanced menu, Beany. Looks like the Battle of the Bulge ahead for all of us to get hooks fastened into eyes with Beany underneath."

5

YOU could always depend on the Malone family to enter wholeheartedly into any plans that involved the Malones. Mary Fred called Sergeant Thomas at the Base and told him she would meet him at the Service Club because the Harkness cast was putting on their play and Beany was to be in it.

"Beany in the play!" Wally had said. "I'll round up my whole gang and bring them along. Tell her she can count on a lot of clappers."

"But she isn't going to say anything or do anything," Mary Fred explained, "except toy with a croquet mallet."

"Well, tell her we'll clap everytime she gives it a twist."

In all the hubbub backstage at the Service Club before the curtain went up, an uncomfortably dressed Beany peered through a crack in the curtain to locate her family.

She picked out her father in his dark suit in the sea of Air Force blues. There was Adair beside him, her oval, alert face lifted expectantly.

In the same row, Beany saw Kay's taffy-colored head bent to hear something Johnny was saying. Next to Kay sat Andy. That smugly mysterious Andy Kern who had only whetted her curiosity by saying that the surprise was like his heart, like Mike—and like a fat lady's girdle.

Backstage, Melinda Page was taking final inspection of the cast. "It's the guillotine for anyone chewing gum," she warned grimly. She saw the charm bracelet on Beany's wrist, and exclaimed, "Beany, either take off those jingle bells or get them out of sight. Who ever heard of a charm bracelet in the Gay Nineties?"

It meant taking off the red shirtwaist with its lace yoke and putting it on again, pulling the tight-fitting sleeve over Norbett's bracelet. This way the bracelet was silent and unseen, but *felt*. It must be that new charm—the good-luck leprechaun with pointed cap and shoes—which pressed sharply into her wrist.

Curtain going up!

In Act I a nervous and perspiring and hard-breathing Beany stayed well in the background and went through ladylike motions with a croquet mallet. They couldn't be anything but ladylike with sleeves that restricted and the high, boned collar which nipped at every turn of her head. She walked mincingly from one wicket to another.

58

The mincing walk wasn't acting; she couldn't have walked any other way in those tight, high-laced shoes.

Once, another nervous player batted the ball harder than he intended, and it landed at Beany's feet. Without thinking, she gave it a quick whack. Loud clapping came from one side of the audience, and a hearty yell of, "Knock it home, Beany."

Beany blushed. She knew now where Mary Fred sat with Wally and his rooters.

Our Darling Daughter couldn't have played to a more appreciative audience than these service men. They were almost too vocally appreciative at times. They whooped loudly when the chaperone reproved the heroine, "Never so much as glance at a young man to whom you have not been introduced."

Then the final climactic scene where the downcast heroine, Adeline, must face her disapproving aunt-chaperone, the minister, and her parents, and answer for her crime of hand-holding under the porte-cochere with the young choir tenor.

When the tearful mother reproached her daughter, "Have you no maidenly reserve?" loud exaggerated chortles from the audience almost drowned out Adeline's reply.

These same exuberant noises continued throughout the speech of the irate father which was responsible for the terms, "more-thanning," and "more-thanners," in Harkness Halls: "Until the engagement has been announced, no well-brought-up young lady may do more than clasp a man's hand in greeting, or accept his guidance when crossing a street. During a waltz his hand may rest about her waist—with a handkerchief under it—but more than that—"

"Adeline, how could you?" and "What is the world coming to?" the supposedly scandalized audience shouted on.

The curtain went down amidst hilarious cheering and whistling.

Before the curtain touched the floor, Beany was loosening her belt and bending over to untie shoelaces. Nor was she the only one. Other hands, too, were reaching for hatpins, hairpins, buttons, and hooks and eyes.

Johnny came backstage to call out to Beany, "Hey, Kay and Andy and I are going on. Got to stop at a delicatess' and get some rye bread. You come on with Dad and Adair."

Beany was both disappointed and relieved at this arrangement. Disappointed, because she had hoped to find out more about Andy's surprise on the way home. Relieved, because in the car with her parents, she could reach through skirts and untie that suffocating corset. She took off the hat. Adair helped her extract the rat. Beany murmured as their car stopped in the driveway, "If the ground wasn't wet and frozen, I'd take off these shoes and walk into the house in my stocking feet. If I didn't have my best stockings on," she hastily amended.

In Beany's room, Adair helped her out of her hampering garb. They folded and laid upon a chair the clothes that belonged to a young lady of the Gay Nineties era.

Drawing a long, relieved breath, Beany buttoned her own unhampering blouse, and zipped up the short and *unlined* green skirt. She wriggled her numb toes to start circulation, and eased her feet into flat-heeled ballets.

She was rebraiding her hair when Kay came hurrying up the stairs and burst out, "Adair, were you as worried as I was, for fear Beany's hat and rat would both drop if she moved?" She broke off at sight and sound of the tinkly bracelet. "Beany Malone, not Norbett's bracelet again. Not after you cried your eyes out last fall and put it away—"

"It doesn't mean a thing," Beany said swiftly. "He just sent this little leprechaun and asked me to wear it."

Like Mary Fred, Kay bent to look at the new charm. "The little fellow has a sort of—devilish wink."

Beany's stepmother examined it, too. "Yes, but very wise," she added.

"Come on," a flustered Beany said. "Let's go down." They entered the bustle of the living room. Mary Fred's problem, Sergeant Wally Thomas, was lighting the fire in the fireplace. He didn't seem like a problem, but a genial addition to the crowd. Johnny was bringing in a tray on which were piled slices of rye bread and meat loaf.

"Our darling daughter," he greeted Beany, "couldn't you have managed to look paler and frailer?" And Martie Malone smiled and asked, "How does it feel to move back to the present?"

"Wonderful. Every Thanksgiving from now on, I'll be extra thankful for being able to dress and think and act the way we do now."

"Imagine," Mary Fred said feelingly, "having a chaperone at your elbow every move you made. Imagine parents who wouldn't trust a girl to go downtown alone to buy a spool of thread."

Beany sidled close to Andy to ask, "Well, how much longer do I have to wait?"

"Wait for what?" he asked innocently.

Kay said scoldingly, "Andy, stop teasing her. It's in his pocket, Beany."

"These gold-diggers," Andy sighed, but he drew something from his pocket and said, "Hold out your cotton-pickin' hands, sugar." He slipped over her left hand a wrist watch of white gold on an expansion bracelet.

Beany gasped out in amazed joy, "Oh, a watch—and the prettiest one I ever saw. For me?"

"No, for Queen Elizabeth. I'm just letting you wear it."

"A watch!" Beany murmured on. "I *am* bowled over. But you said it was like your heart—"

"It ticks."

"—and like Mike—"

"It has a face."

"—and like a fat lady's girdle."

"The bracelet is stretchable and expansible," he said triumphantly.

Mary Fred said primly, "No well-brought-up young lady may accept an expensive gift from an admirer unless they are affianced."

"It didn't cost me anything but a new bracelet and six months of wondering would it or wouldn't it be mine."

Andy went on to explain that six months ago he had found the watch with a broken bracelet at the Pantages Theater where he ushered. He had followed the rule of entering it on the list of lost articles which was posted in the theater lobby. But no one ever appeared to identify and claim the watch. Tonight had been the last night, when, according to the theater's rules, it became the property of the finder.

"I was scared my luck, plus Beany's luck, wouldn't hold. So there you are, m'love. And, as the brush salesman says when he gives you a sample, 'No obligation whatever on your part, Madam.' "

Martie Malone and the new Mrs. Malone laughed happily with the others.

Beany reached over with her right hand to hold up her left closer to the lamp, the better to admire her new wrist watch. As she did, the charm bracelet clinked remindingly. But that was all it was—just a reminder that she was wearing a charm bracelet. It was as though this bit of white gold, silent and snug on her left wrist, balanced everything—more than that, as though it somehow neutralized her unstable emotions for Norbett Rhodes.

Goodness, what kind of a girl was she? To sit on her bed only a few hours ago and moon over Norbett, and now to stand beside Andy Kern, full of tingly delight over his gift?

Johnny nudged her. "Go taste the cocoa and see if we put it together right. And bring it in while Kay and I get the mustard and trimmings."

Andy went with her to the kitchen to help.

He reached for the mugs on a high cupboard shelf and put them on a tray. Beany added a dash of salt to the cocoa. She glanced at the watch with its small hand at eleven and the large one at three. "I've been wishing and wishing I had a watch, Andy. But I never hoped for one so lovely."

"You like it, hon? I like it on you."

He reached over and in front of Johnny and Kay, in full view of Wally and Mary Fred, who were getting spoons and napkins in the dining room, kissed her on the cheek. "I don't know what bozo gave you that jingle-jangle on your right hand," he said, "but just remember your left hand belongs to Andy."

They sat in the big Malone living room, munching sandwiches and drinking chocolate, and talking—or lapsing into contented silences, watching the fire. Red, the Malones' Irish setter, lay with his head on Martie's shoe.

Andy spoke suddenly, "Kay, is Norbett Rhodes's red car still stored at the Park Gate garage?"

Kay's blue eyes involuntarily sought Beany's. Kay knew so well the part Norbett's red car had figured in the stormy romance between Beany and Norbett. Kay reached back and gave her long taffy-colored hair an upward flip as she always did when she was uneasy.

"Yes," she said hesitantly, "it's still there."

Yes, it's still there, Beany thought, and whenever I see it sitting over in the corner, I can't help turning back into the old Beany and longing for Norbett to come back.

Andy said, "Wonder if he wants to sell it, now that he's staying back in Ohio and going to school. I'm in the car market. I got enough Christmas bonus on my ushering job to dicker for something in the lower-price bracket. I hanker to be a man about town and not have to argue with Dad every time I need the car."

Johnny said, "Beany, why don't you ask Norbett the next time you write him? Ask him if he wants to sell it, and how much he wants for it."

"Do that, Beany," Andy said.

Beany squirmed. Oh dear, that really would be mixing the old love and the new. It wouldn't seem *right* for her to be riding beside Andy in that red car.

She said faintly, "Well, I'll ask him when I write—"

Martie Malone stood up and pocketed his pipe and said on a stifled yawn, "The chaperones are retiring. Come on, Adair."

They were no sooner gone than Mary Fred stood up and said on a wide yawn she could barely cover with her hand, "Mary Fred Malone is retiring, too."

"Oh, no," Sergeant Wally Thomas said with an injured air. "I was figuring on outsitting these young sprouts."

"I had quite a dose of wrasslin' horses today, and I'm tired," Mary Fred said.

Wally got to his feet and appealed ruefully to the others, "With a crowd adored, alone ignored." Yet he laughed too when they laughed in understanding.

Beany watched with half an eye as Mary Fred kissed him good-night at the door; she listened with one ear to Wally's insisting, "Look, Mary Fred, let's go for a drive in the mountains tomorrow and have dinner at some little inn—"

"No. You can't tell about the weather in January."

"But you said you wanted to go up to that dude ranch where you work in the summer and see about your job. How about us making it tomorrow?"

"No, Wally, I have to wait till the owner is there."

66

Mary Fred caught Beany's eyes before she started up the stairs. So far, so good, her look said.

Andy and Kay were putting on coats. As usual, Andy Kern, who went past the Park Gate on his way home, would drop Kay off. There was all the small hubbub of leave-taking in the hall, of Kay's saying, "I'll look for you to come by, Beany, after the nine-thirty Mass so you can copy the notes I took in Home Ec that day you worked on the paper—"

The telephone rang. Even the constantly ringing Malone phone seldom rang at this late hour. Beany, the closest to it, picked up the receiver.

Her hello was answered by a young male voice, speaking low and tensely, "This you, Beany?"

"Yes." And then on a breathless squeak of amazement, " Why, Nor—"

His voice cut in swiftly, "Don't say my name if there's anyone around. Is there?"

"Yes—there is. Kay and Johnny and—" She stopped short on the Andy, remembering Norbett's gusts of jealousy. Her heart was pounding excitedly under the blouse with its multitude of green shamrocks. "Where are you, Nor—?"

"I told you to be careful about saying my name," he fairly snapped at her. "I don't want anyone to know—"

"Know what?"

"Beany, will you keep still and listen? I'm out at the airport. I just flew in on one of these nonscheduled flights. Can you come and get me?"

"Well—I don't know. I mean—"

"You mean on account of the company? When are they going to leave?"

Beany glanced helplessly at Johnny; at Kay and Andy waiting to say their final good-nights. What could she say while they were within hearing distance? Oh, why didn't they go? She turned her back to them and mumbled low into the mouthpiece, "Pretty soon."

"I wouldn't ask you," Norbett said, "but I haven't got the price of a taxi. I didn't figure they'd charge me so much excess baggage, and I'm dead broke. Get out here as soon as you can—I'll be waiting." He laughed the nervous laugh Beany knew so well, though she hadn't heard it for over three months. "Nothing else I can do. You'll see a bum, sitting on a bedroll outside in the dark—that'll be me. Get here as soon as you can."

"I will," she promised.

"I knew I could count on you, Beany. And don't breathe it to a soul that I'm here."

She heard the click of the receiver at his end. She replaced hers.

She turned from the telephone and though Kay and Andy looked at her questioningly, though Johnny asked, "Who was that?" she didn't explain. How could she? She began talking fast to cover her utter ignoring of the telephone call. She said, "Kay, how'd it be if I walked over after church tomorrow? I'll go to the nine-thirty, and it lets out about ten-fifteen, and so I'll be at your place about ten-thirty—"

The odd look on Kay's face checked her rush of unnecessary details. For it was the usual thing for Beany to go to the nine-thirty Mass, and practically the usual thing for her to walk on over to Kay's at the Park Gate. Kay knew well when church was out, and how long it took Beany to walk from St. Mary's to the Park Gate.

Beany turned to Andy to say even more flusteredly, "Thanks again for the watch, Andy."

He laughed as he opened the door. "Look at the watch when you say 'thank you, Andy'—not at the bracelet on the other wrist."

The door closed behind them.

Beany's father called from the head of the stairs, "That wasn't long distance, was it?"

"No—no, it wasn't," she answered. Her father waited a moment for the explanation that didn't come. Beany hurried through the hall and into the kitchen. Johnny followed. He asked again, "Who called up so durn late?"

"Oh—just a friend. You go on to bed, Johnny. I'll just stack these dishes; we can do them in the morning."

"I'm not about to coax you into doing them tonight."

Why couldn't he walk faster up the stairs? Why did he have to be so long in the bathroom?

She picked up and stacked the chocolate mugs with shaky fingers. She heard Johnny's bedroom door close at last. If everyone was asleep, she could go out to the airport with no one in the family the wiser.

She fidgeted in the kitchen, listening. Norbett was waiting, and he was an impatient waiter. She felt her own impatience to be in Johnny's car, driving toward the airport for Norbett.

The big setter, Red, sensing something unusual, watched her uneasily, his tail wagging like a question mark.

She daren't risk going up to her room to get her warm coat. She tiptoed in to the hall closet, and her fingers closed over Johnny's leather jacket. Back in the kitchen, she pulled it on. There was no sound or stir in the house.

She left the light on over the sink. As she reached for the doorknob, Red was beside her. "You can't go," she whispered tensely. She went out, closing the door softly behind her.

Johnny's car was parked on the cement apron of the garage. The motor had never seemed so loud as when she started it, and drove out the driveway onto Barberry Street. Her heart was pounding even harder. She felt guilty, setting forth in the windy, moonlit night without explaining to her family. But a feeling of urgency, of Norbett's waiting, was even greater.

"I knew I could count on you, Beany," he had said.

6

BEANY felt an eerie excitement as she drove up to the airport at this late hour. It seemed strange, after driving through lonely deserted streets, to find this mecca of bright lights and scurry of activity. As she drove slowly past the baggage department, which faced onto the driveway, a tall and hatless figure with red hair, roughened in the wind, came toward her.

Norbett. She stopped the car with a jerk and tumbled out. The wind seemed to blow them together. He clutched at both her arms and laughed raggedly. "Oh, Beany—Beany, I knew I could count on you."

His lean cold cheek pressed hers, and she was suddenly a fifteen-year-old sophomore at Harkness with no thought of anything but Norbett Rhodes. How could she ever have thought she had forgotten him, or that she could change? It wasn't until she felt him shiver in the raw wind that she said catchily, "Norbett, you're frozen. Get in the car."

He had first to load in his grip and the long brown cocoon of bedroll. He carried something in a canvas case that was bigger and of a different shape than a camera; it was about the size of a shoe box. He was very careful to hold it on his lap.

"What's that?" she asked.

He didn't answer, but said, "I never thought about having to pay so much excess baggage. That's why I'm dead broke."

They settled happily in the car; and, as Beany started off, he reached out and gripped her arm again with nervous fervor. "It's wonderful to have someone like you, Beany. One person like you is worth all the rest of the world. With you helping me out—by darn, I'll show them all."

Ah, that old familiar thrill of Norbett's needing her, that old ecstasy of "We two against the world."

She stopped where the airport driveway ended and streets converged, hesitating as to which turn to take. "You want to go to your uncle's at the Park Gate." It was more of a statement than a question.

"Holy Moses, no! He's the last one I want to know about my coming back."

"Oh! Why?"

"I'll tell you later on when—I'd rather not go into it all now."

She turned that over in her mind. "But doesn't your aunt in Ohio know you flew out? Won't she tell your uncle at the Park Gate?"

"My Ohio aunt left on a Mediterranean cruise," he said shortly. "She won't know where I am, so she can't be spilling anything to Uncle Nate."

"Where do you want me to take you?" Beany asked.

He fumbled a letter out of his pocket and held it under the poor light in Johnny's dashboard. "Do you know where South Wyman is? I want to go there—2943 South Wyman."

"It would be west of the university and beyond that big sanitarium," Beany mused aloud. "It'd be in that neighborhood they call Hodgepodge Hollow." Again her curiosity made her ask, "Who lives there? Are you going to stay with them?"

"Fellow's name is Ivor," he said, looking at the letter again but not letting Beany see it. "He writes such a poor hand, I can't figure out the last name. He sounded as though I could bunk there with him until we—" Again he left his sentence dangling.

"Does he know you're coming?"

Norbett laughed. "Beany, don't be such a walking— or sitting-down—questionnaire. I decided all of a sudden to come. I don't know the answers myself—yet. I read once where the proof of a real friend is that he—or she—will stand by and not ask questions. I figured I could count on you to be that kind."

"You can, Norbett. I'm just the curious type, that's all."

"You're just the blessed type," he said warmly. "How's everything going with you?"

"I was in a play tonight," she said, driving toward University Boulevard. "I had to pinch-hit," she giggled, "and I got pinched in numerous spots. The whole family went and then we all came home—"

It was her turn to break off in the middle of a sentence. She couldn't very well go on and say, and Andy Kern gave me a wrist watch that was lost at the Pant. Even the memory of it was uncomfortable. Now that Norbett was back, maybe she shouldn't be wearing Andy's present.

Norbett hadn't noticed her unfinished sentence. He wasn't even listening.

They had reached the Boulevard now. Beany tried a different line of conversation. About their stepmother, whom Norbett had never seen. "At first we were so disappointed because she couldn't cook or sew—it's funny the way she always hums when she paints, and always scowls when she tries to follow a recipe. But she's mothery without being bossy. Johnny teases her a lot. He says right in front of her, 'Listen to our heartless, cruel stepmom—' "

Norbett wasn't listening to that either. "Keep watching for South Wyman," he said.

74

They found Wyman and turned south on it. But finding the 2900 block and number 2943 was quite another matter.

They wouldn't have had so much trouble if it had been daylight and they could have read street signs, or if the sanitarium with its widespread grounds hadn't kept throwing them off their route. Or if the streets beyond it hadn't turned into winding country roads.

But Beany turned corners, found dead ends, backtracked, warmed all the while by a sense of conspiracy, of helping Norbett. They laughed in rueful but intimate glee over the disappearing Wyman.

There was no uniformity about the homes in Hodgepodge Hollow. Some were staid old houses of brick; some were new little frame shacks. Some sat far back, sheltered by tall skeletons of trees; some were shoved close to the street—or road—with bare dirt yards and no shrubbery.

At last their car lights caught a glimpse of a mailbox nailed onto a post and jutting out into the road. On it was crudely lettered, "2943 So. Wyman." Beany stopped. "This must be it. And there's a light on," she said with relief.

She and Norbett sat for a minute, staring through the windy, moonlit night at the outline of the house. It was a small frame building with a flat roof. An addition, made of cinder block and fully as large as the house itself, was in the process of building.

"I'll go see if this Ivor fellow is home," Norbett muttered.

"Norbett, even if you stay here tonight, you can come over tomorrow for dinner, can't you?"

He mumbled an evasive something.

She sat in the car and watched him pick his way through the clutter of building materials, and climb the makeshift steps of cinder block to the door. He rapped.

Almost instantly a light in an unshaded globe over the door went on. And, simultaneously, the door was opened by a girl about Beany's age.

Such a pretty, wide-awake girl, and dressed as though she had just come home from a dance. The light inside silhouetted her full bosom and slim waist. The hard light overhead revealed the brilliants sparkling on the bodice of her pale green dress. Beany wondered if she had used one of those gadgets from the ten-cent store to press the beads on.

Norbett too had seemed temporarily taken aback by such a bright-hued girl opening the door of this shabby little house so late at night. But only momentarily, for the girl answered his questions with a carefree shrug and gave him a wide, friendly smile. She leaned against the door jamb as casually as though there were nothing at all unusual in her answering the door to a stranger this time of night—or early morning.

She must have just come in from a late date, Beany thought.

76

Norbett drew out a cigarette and lit it. The girl reached out and with a roguish, cocksure smile took it from between his lips and drew a deep enjoyable breath—

The carhop at the Ragged Robin! Sure enough, she gave her head a sidewise toss and Beany saw the plume of pony tail the color of burnt sugar. The girl Jag Wilson had greeted, "Hi-ya, Dulcie."

She looked even prettier in that round-necked dress with its sparkling crystals catching the light. She wore silver slippers. Beany wondered again if she darkened her eyebrows and lashes.

Dulcie and Norbett talked on and on while Beany sat behind the wheel with the motor running. She turned it off. She was not more than twelve or fifteen feet from them. You'd think, as long as there seemed so much to talk about, that Norbett would beckon her to join in. Or else bring the girl out to the car and introduce them.

Well! Norbett was finally backing down the makeshift steps of cinder block and coming toward the car. The girl stood in the doorway watching with a friendly half-smile on her face, not seeming to mind the chill of the January night.

Norbett got in beside Beany. She couldn't keep the edge off her voice. "Wasn't your friend Ivor at home? The one you said you were going to stay with?"

"No. He left this morning. That's his daughter. I can't very well stay there—hardly any room in the shack—the girl's mother was asleep inside. Looked to me like Dulcie sleeps on the couch."

H'mm, it certainly hadn't taken Norbett all that time to find out that Dulcie's father was gone and that he would not be able to spend the night there.

Beany pressed the starter. It whirred, but there was no catch to the engine. She pressed the starter harder and longer—

"Holy smoke, Beany—sounds like you're out of gas," Norbett said.

They both leaned over to scan the gas gauge. Beany gasped, "Empty. I never though about it being low on gas—that crazy Johnny never has much in it—and we did drive all over Hodgepodge Hollow to find this place."

The girl called from the doorway, "Out of gas?" and Norbett called back, "Yeh, empty as a gourd."

"Wait a sec," she offered, motioning toward a truck, drawn up in the back of the yard, "and I'll rob the gas tank for you."

She left the front door open. It seemed but a brief moment or two before she reappeared in a plaid shirt, jeans, and loafers. She leaped lightly down the uneven steps, her cascade of pony tail bouncing saucily.

"I'd better help her," Norbett murmured, and climbed out. He added, "You stay here, Beany—it's sort of a mess in the yard."

Dulcie bounced over the piles of cinder blocks and mounds of sand. She picked up a bucket and clunked it hard on the frozen ground to dislodge the sand in it. She found a handkerchief in her pocket and wiped it still cleaner. She found a piece of rubber hose. And all the time she was laughing and joking with Norbett. They walked together toward the truck to siphon gas out of its tank.

Beany couldn't help admiring the girl. She'd like to know this pert and undaunted Dulcie if she weren't so puzzled—yes, and irritated at Norbett's chumminess with her and at his being so careful that Beany shouldn't meet her.

They were laughing even more hilariously when they returned with the bucket of gas. They had evidently spilled some on themselves. "I'm inflammable," Beany heard Dulcie shriek, and Norbett answer, "You're inflammable! I won't dare light a cigarette."

Beany climbed out of the car. Surely now she could strike up a casual conversation with her and Norbett. But Norbett looked up from pouring the gasoline and said, "Get back in, Beany. Now try starting it."

The motor caught readily. Norbett gave the bucket back to Dulcie. Was there a brief conspiratorial exchange of words before he climbed in again beside Beany, bringing with him a reeking smell of gasoline?

"Let's go," he said.

Beany couldn't even wait until she had backed up and turned the car around before she blurted out, "What was the idea of not introducing me to that girl?"

He hesitated. "I didn't know her last name."

"Pardon me," Beany said sarcastically. "In such a hurried conversation, you could hardly ask her last name." She longed to ask, what *were* you talking so long about? She asked instead, "Where are you going now?"

Norbett gave a bitter laugh. "I don't know. What is that about the foxes having their lairs, and the birds their nests? I haven't got the price of a hotel room. If you see a nice vacant lot, or a city dump, just put me and my sleeping bag out—"

"You can come home with me. There's an extra bed in Johnny's room."

He said with strained patience, "Beany, can't you get it through your thick head that I'm incognito and incommunicado and insolvent? I can't think of a better way to broadcast my being back than to stay at the Malones. Sure, with Kay Maffley bobbing in and out. You ought to know how gabby her mother is—everyone at the Park Gate, including Uncle Nate and Aunt Mae, would know I was back."

Beany said with equal impatience, "If you insist on being so secretive, you can stay in that room over our garage—"

"Could I, Beany?" he broke in eagerly. "That's a swell idea. None of your folks need know I'm there."

Her irritation mounted. Why did he have to be so untrustful with her, with all the Malones? She bet Dulcie knew what it was all about.

80

They drove in silence until they reached the Malone house on South Barberry and turned into the driveway. She stopped outside the garage.

"Don't slam the car door," Norbett warned in a whisper. She found herself whispering back, "I'll go up the stairs and open the door for you and your bedroll. I'll carry your grip. Watch out for the second step from the bottom. You have to keep close to the rail because it's worn through in the middle."

He was tugging out the lumpy brown cocoon. "Don't turn on the light up there," he cautioned.

She climbed the steps and stood holding the door open for him. The thin moonlight pushed through the dusty windows and revealed the clutter in the room. For years the Malones had stored castoff furniture, skis, cartons of books here because it was less damp than the basement.

Norbett made another trip to the car for that mysterious canvas-covered case. In the murky light he groped his way to an outmoded radio cabinet and set it down carefully. Again Beany asked him what it was.

Without answering, he flicked on his cigarette lighter to look about. He gave a start as its flickering light revealed a tilted figure in a coy and droopy hat and a faded blanket robe.

"Good grief! Who's—what's that?"

Beany laughed, almost equally startled. "That's Headless Hetty. Didn't you ever see a dress form before?

Miss Opal always used it to fit clothes on. Johnny stuck that old cracked vase in her neck and the hat on top of it."

"Headless Hetty. Is she hollow inside?"

"Down to her hips. Miss Opal kept dress patterns in her."

"Hold the lighter for me, Beany. If Hetty hasn't got a head—and no mouth to talk with—I guess she's one female I can trust to keep a secret for me."

He pulled a sheaf of long envelopes out of his pocket and, lifting both white vase and limp hat, shoved them down the hollow neck. "Yep. *There's* a woman for you. No whys or what-fors from Hetty," he said meaningfully. That remark did nothing to soothe Beany's irritation.

She said, "I think you're crazy to sleep up here in this cold messy place when Johnny has an extra bed. I think it's crazy for you to think you have to hide from everyone."

"Sure it's crazy," he broke in. "Crazy to someone like you who has a nice comfortable little niche in life. You couldn't possibly understand how anyone could get a bellyful of being a poor relation." His words came in a bitter torrent. "That's what I was when I lived with Uncle Nate and Aunt Mae at the Park Gate. Their orphan nephew they'd have chucked in an orphans' home, only they knew people would talk if they did. Then my Ohio aunt gave me a great line about how lonely she was, how she wished I would stay with her to keep her company. And I fell for it—"

"Oh, Norbett, didn't she want you after all? You said she wanted you to stay back there with her and go to school?"

"Oh, sure. To run errands for her. Until some friends talked her into taking a Mediterranean cruise. I heard her tell these friends that she'd feel better about leaving if she could close her house. So I told her to close it—that I had other plans. I'll tell you right now, Beany, I'm through being the poor relation. Yes, and I'm through being soft-soaped by anyone. My Uncle Nate here thought I was so green and gullible that he—" he stopped short.

"What did he think?"

He said shortly, "It must be pretty late. What time is it?"

"I haven't any idea."

"You've got a wrist watch. Doesn't it run?"

"Oh, I forgot I had it." She had. She had completely forgotten the watch and the boy who gave it to her. Again Norbett flicked his lighter and bent to look at it. Beany added foolishly, "I'm not used to having one. I just got this one tonight."

"From one of your admirers, I suppose."

His mocking tone stiffened her. "A boy I know named Andy Kern—he ushers at the Pant and he—"

Norbett laughed savagely. "A very nice boy named Andy Kern gives you a fancy watch and Norbett Rhodes gives you only trouble. Norbett, the nuisance. Go ahead and rub it in."

"I'm not rubbing it in," she flared back. "You asked me."

He went on mincingly, "Why didn't you tell me when I phoned that I was interrupting one of those sweetly tender moments when he was fastening the watch on your wrist and telling you that his heart beat in time to it. I could have sat on my bedroll all night."

Not a fight with Norbett the first night he comes back, she thought in alarm. I won't fight with him. . . .

She clenched her lips tightly.

Norbett had first deposited his sleeping bag on top of a lawn glider on which folded deck chairs were piled. Now he picked up the roll and threw it on the floor with a thud.

"Your lovely little keepsake—which, of course, keeps perfect time—says two o'clock. I'm tired and sleepy. And I've got a heavy day ahead. I haven't got time to stand around yak-yakking all night."

Alas for Beany's resolution. The words left her lips before she knew it. "I notice you had plenty of time to stand around yak-yakking with Dulcie."

He gave the bedroll a vicious kick into place. "There you go," he said. "Honest to Pete, you've got a disposition like a wounded cougar."

84

A wounded cougar! Anger sizzled through her. "Opinions differ," she flung out with a false smile. "Andy Kern always says I'm—I'm—" If only she could think of something especially flattering—

"Never mind, never mind," Norbett broke in coldly. "Go on back to your nice adoring family. My apologies for messing up your routine—and romance."

She turned and stumbled out the door into the cold, windy night. She was half sobbing in hurt fury as she went down the stairs. She forgot to watch for the broken second step from the bottom, and her foot slid through it. She caught herself on the rail to keep from falling, but her shin was scratched and bruised and—worse yet—her best pair of stockings was torn. Her sheerest party nylons which she had been protecting from the vociferous Mike ever since Christmas.

Somehow it increased her rage at Norbett.

She paused a second on the back porch to pull herself together. It startled her to see the kitchen light through the transom, before she remembered that she had left it on. She must open the door softly, then take off her ballets and tiptoe up the stairs. She would undress in her dark room and go to bed with her churned-up hurt and anger at Norbett.

Stealthily she opened the door and eased in, thinking only of quieting Red who whimpered in greeting. Her hand was still on the knob when she looked up—

Her father was sitting at the kitchen table, a glass half full of milk and a plate of crackers before him. She could only stare at him in consternation while a guilty flush reddened her face.

"Did you—wait up—for me?" she stammered.

He nodded. "I got up when I couldn't go to sleep. I was worried about you. It's after two."

Then he had heard her drive off with such thoughtless haste, because Norbett had telephoned and said, "Come." A moment of silence while he waited for her explanation.

"You—you needn't have worried about me," she said lamely.

"That's part of being a parent," he said with a tired sigh. "Where did you go, Beany?"

She said unhappily, "I promised I wouldn't tell. I know it sounds crazy, but I can't—not now. It was—all right."

His kind eyes rested on her flushed face. "Yes, I'm sure it was all right."

She faltered on, "I'd like to tell you but . . . I guess we'd better go to bed. I'm sorry you worried."

"Wait a minute, Beany. I've been thinking while I waited about an idea for your inspirational article for *Hark Ye*. It came to me when we were all talking about the play tonight. I imagine Melinda must have selected that very play to point out the contrast between the young people of sixty years ago and you youngsters today."

"I don't see how the girls stood all that being watched over by parents and chaperones," Beany said, glad of a chance to talk about something other than her unaccounted-for hours tonight.

"Now about your article. You practically said it when you said you were thankful you could dress and think and act the way you do today. But you didn't go far enough. It's the old story of everything in life having its price. The price of greater freedom is greater responsibility."

"How do you mean?"

"Think of this, child. Adeline in the play had chaperones to make decisions for her. She was spared getting into messes—maybe having regrets. You girls today have to make your own decisions. Your conscience has to be your chaperone."

Beany thought back to Mary Fred's saying over their cokes this afternoon, "At first I was so confused—it seemed to me my conscience was too prim and Victorian."

"You'll be seventeen next St. Patrick's day," her father mused. "It's hard for me to think of you as anything but little Beany—maybe fifteen, but not seventeen yet."

If only she could get over feeling fifteen and acting fifteen when it came to one Norbett Rhodes.

Martie Malone was saying, "When my job took me away from home so much, I had to bring you children up on trust. I couldn't have been the policeman type even if I had wanted to. So now I realize it's a little late for me to turn into the heavy-handed father and start tongue-lashing you about why you went out without a word to anyone—"

Why? Because Norbett Rhodes had said, "Don't mention my being here to a soul."

"I would have told you," she murmured, "only—this person—asked me not to."

"Doesn't this *person* realize that the Malones can be trusted?"

She couldn't tell him that this *person* had been in a no-one-can-be-trusted mood almost from the start; no one, she remembered with a stab of jealousy, except a girl named Dulcie.

Her father stood up. "Think over your uplift piece about the greater freedom of today calling for greater responsibility. It's something all of Harkness could stand being reminded of. Don't be afraid of using good old-fashioned words like *conscience* and *duty.* . . . And when you see this *person* again, tell this *person* that being underhanded seldom pays off. Scoot on to bed now, child."

Beany thought suddenly of the stage father of Adeline and his storming and catechizing and humiliating his daughter. He hadn't said to her as Beany's father had, "I trust you."

Beany did not drop off to sleep immediately. She thought of Norbett. Why could he always shake her and infuriate her? Wounded cougar! And why had *she* been so edgy? But she knew why. Because Norbett had lingered so unduly long with that pert and pretty Dulcie. The nice rapport between Beany and Norbett had been lost when they stopped at the house on South Wyman.

Beany never talked to her father that she didn't feel her own inadequacies and long, somehow, to be more generous, more kindly. Now, as she tossed in bed, she felt belated sympathy for Norbett and his bitterness over being treated as a poor relation. She longed to say, Norbett, I do understand.

The very first thing in the morning, she would hurry out to the room over the garage and say it. She ought to know by now that a soft answer turneth away Norbett's wrath.

Everyone always laughed when the Malones told how Red, the big setter, came to Beany's bed on Sunday at seven, as on every other day, to waken her, but that when she said, "This is Sunday, Red," he subsided on the rug by her bed.

But tomorrow morning, Sunday or no, she would get up and, while the rest of the house slept, make peace with Norbett.

Please trust me—and all the Malones. Even if you're in trouble, we'll help you, she would say.

7

BEANY stood in the doorway of the room over the garage, her eyes glued to the approximate spot on the floor where Norbett had so angrily thrown his bedroll not too many hours previously.

No bedroll. No Norbett.

The early morning sky was drear and sunless, the air raw. At Red's first nudging, Beany had hurriedly dressed and slipped stealthily out of the house to bring to Norbett the olive branch of peace. She might as well have slept that extra hour. She shivered and pulled her cardigan closer, conscious the while of small twinges in her grazed shin.

Norbett's bag was gone, too, and the canvas-covered something he had been so mysterious about. There was not even a sign that he had ever been here. Her eyes roamed over the castoffs in the loft room—the lawn glider, the baby bassinet now full of shoe skates, the floor lamp that didn't light, Headless Hetty—

A paper was pinned on Hetty's blanket robe. It read, "I'm counting on you to keep mum."

Only that. No thanks for meeting him at the airport, no apology for calling her a wounded cougar. She wadded up the note and flung it in a dusty corner.

As she reached out to straighten the tipsy hat on Hetty, she remembered Norbett's thrusting some papers in her hollow neck. Beany lifted the white vase and limp hat and looked inside.

They were still there—letters and business papers held together by a rubber band. Had he forgotten them in his haste to be off? Or did he intend to come back? Of course, one never read another's letters, but business papers? If she looked at them, surely they'd shed some light on the mystery of Norbett.

She stood for a full moment with her fingers resting on them in their niche, while curiosity and conscience warred . . . and then she took her empty hand out of Hetty's neck. She replaced the vase and hat. She left the loft, watchful of the broken second step.

Again when Beany entered the kitchen, expecting to find it empty, someone was there. This time it was Adair. She was making coffee.

"I came down to get the paper for Martie, and I decided to take him up a cup of coffee, too," she explained.

The Malones always fortified themselves with coffee before going to Mass. They enjoyed a leisurely and filling breakfast on their return.

When Beany's father had first described their stepmother-to-be to her stepchildren-to-be, he had said, "Adair's easy to look at and easy to laugh with." They found her easy to be serious with as well. Her dark eyes were warm and responsive. This morning they looked large and heavy in her oval face, and Beany realized that Adair, too, had lain awake last night until her stepdaughter returned. Yet, like Beany's father, she was neither prying nor condemning.

Beany said impulsively, "You're sure swell, Stepmom."

Adair's smile was a little tremulous. "You're pretty swell yourself, Beany. I guess that's why Martie and I worried about you last night."

"I thought I'd be able to explain about it this morning," Beany said slowly. "But I can't. I gave my word."

Again she felt a gust of resentment at Norbett. He had no right to slip away after putting her in this questionable situation with her father and Adair. No right to order her, by a message on Hetty, to go on keeping everything secret.

She tried not to think of him through all the hubbub of the five Malones getting ready for nine-thirty Mass. First, Mary Fred, the sleepyhead of the Malones, had to be called repeatedly. Of course, once Mary Fred was on her feet no one could make herself ready with such swift, synchronized movements as she. She could button her blouse with one hand, zip up her skirt with the other while she slid feet into loafers. She could run a washcloth over her face with one hand and a comb through her hair with the other. She could trip down the stairs and call out blithely, "Well, what are we waiting for?"

Secondly, Mike, the obstreperous young dog, must be caught and locked in the basement to forestall his following them. The more mannerly Red always went with them as far as the steps of St. Mary's. He then stretched himself out on the side of the top step and waited for them to come out.

Mike, on the contrary, had been known to come darting into the church, much to the giggling delight of all young worshipers and the consternation of the Malones. It always meant that Johnny had to corner him, carry him out, trot the five blocks back to the Malone house, fasten him inside, and then return, red-faced and breathless.

This gray Sunday morning, when Mass was over, Beany parted from the family outside the church and turned toward the Park Gate. She wished she could tell Kay about Norbett's return. She longed for the relief of talking it all over with her Kay, the wonderful sounding-board.

Beany took her usual short cut through the park, feeling now and then a hurting reminder as her ankle twisted on the rough frozen ground. She came out on Park Street, the ten-story apartment-hotel looming ahead of her.

Her heart suddenly leaped high in her throat. A familiar red car was coming down the street. Norbett's red car, which had been lodged in the garage under the Park Gate hotel since last September. Even its jerky gait, the roar of its motor as the driver gunned it, was familiar.

Automatically Beany stepped closer to the curb; her every nerve, every muscle quickened with joyful excitement. Now she could make peace with Norbett. Oh, perfect, perfect—to climb into that red car with Norbett again—

Norbett was not at the wheel. Dulcie was. You couldn't mistake the tilt of that cocky head and the dark-gold swirl of pony tail. She didn't see Beany. She was too busy racing the cold engine and gauging the oncoming traffic into which she must turn. There, she found a break and spurted bumpily around the corner.

Beany, lips apart, watched the red car out of sight. Norbett had sent Dulcie to get his car. Maybe he had said to her, "You're the only one I can depend on."

The familiar old ache of jealousy was sharp under her ribs. Mary Fred was wrong. Maybe some people could change with the years, but not Beany. She was fifteen again, and so hurt that she longed to hurt Norbett—yes, and that cocksure, flaunting Dulcie. She found herself muttering through set teeth, even as Jennifer Reed had yesterday, "Crummy little more-thanner."

She chuckled bleakly, remembering how she had thought Jennifer far too harsh in condemning Dulcie. Oh, it had been easy enough to be lofty and charitable when it was Jennifer's vanity that was wounded. What was that quotation about its depending on whose ox was being gored?

She walked on leadenly toward the Park Gate.

Kay Maffley was waiting for her on the wide stone steps. Kay often sighed out, "Things are always happening at the Malones." Kay, an only child, lived with her mother in their seventh-floor apartment; her engineer father was home only on occasional visits. For a brief moment as Beany climbed the steps, she envied Kay the serene monotony of her sheltered existence.

"Hungry, Beany?" Kay greeted her. "Mother made some cinnamon rolls for us to eat while we work on our Home Ec notebooks."

Kay's mother was of the dainty school of cooks. Her cinnamon rolls, Beany knew, would be what Johnny called "one-biters."

Kay added, "I came downstairs to meet you because I want to tell you something. Here, sit down in the lobby a minute."

Beany dropped into a green leather chair, and Kay sat on the edge of a carved bench close beside her. Kay asked, "Beany, is it still top-drawer secret about your telephone call, just when we were leaving last night? And the who, why, where of your dashing off the minute we left?"

Beany was untying her scarf. Her fingers froze on the knot while she stared at her best friend. Did everyone know about her supposedly secret mission last evening?

Kay went on, "I thought I'd better tell you that Andy and I saw you driving out the Boulevard. You know how Andy always likes to take candy or ice cream home to Rosellen?"

Yes, Beany knew. Andy was devoted to his younger sister who had been a polio victim and was now on crutches.

"So we stopped outside of Downey's Drug, and Andy went in and got ice cream. He came back to the car, and we were just getting ready to drive on when you passed us in Johnny's car. Andy even started to honk at you—and then I guess he changed his mind."

Still Beany could only stare into Kay's concerned blue eyes without answering. Kay added, "Funny about timing. If Andy hadn't stood inside the Drug and visited with Downey—but you know how friendly Andy is—we'd have been gone before you came out the Boul."

Beany found her breath. "What did Andy say? Was he mad?"

Kay laughed softly. "Andy mad? I live for the day to see Andy Kern mad. No, he just said, 'So that's why Beany was in such a hurry for us to leave.' "

"Is that all he said?"

"That's all. Then he started telling me to watch out that the ice-cream carton didn't leak on my coat. Gosh, Beany, why did you go sky-hootin' off by yourself that late at night?"

Kay waited. Beany was suddenly sick of people waiting for her to explain. Suddenly sick of not being able to. She tugged unhappily at the knot under her chin. "It's all so cockeyed, Kay. I promised . . . . Golly, it worries me, but I can't tell you—not yet, anyway. I wish I could."

"It must be awfully undercover if you can't even tell me," Kay murmured. She waited invitingly again, while Beany twisted her flowered scarf. . . . Norbett had said, "I don't want Kay to know—you ought to know how gabby her mother is. Everyone at the Park Gate, including Uncle Nate and Aunt Mae, would know!"

Kay stood up. "Well, come on. Mother wants us to eat her cinnamon rolls while they're warm."

As they were walking across the lobby toward the elevator, a middle-aged couple passed them. The stout woman, a little too bedecked with brilliants, smiled and spoke to Kay. The man nodded. His eyes rested on Beany in half recognition; he hesitated, as though debating whether to stop and speak to her. But the woman took his arm, and they walked on toward the dining room off the lobby.

Kay said as they stepped into the elevator, "You remember the Rhodeses, Beany—Norbett's Uncle Nate and Aunt Mae?"

"Oh!" Beany breathed. Norbett's aunt and uncle who must not know that he had flown here from Ohio. "Norbett's uncle looks so much thinner than he used to," she added.

"Yes, he gets thinner and his wife gets fatter all the time. I don't know why, but I feel kind of sorry for him. She works so hard, trying to get into society—"

The elevator stopped.

Beany had never felt entirely at ease in the Maffley apartment. The thick-piled carpet, the color of peach fuzz, didn't seem meant to be walked on. Beany hated to think of what that carpet would look like after a day's hard wear in the Malone home. It was quite evident that the fireplace with its shiny brass fixtures had never been touched by flame or smoke. As further proof that it was purely decorative, a vase of silver leaves sat in front of it. Beany always compared it with their own big utilitarian fireplace in which bushels of popcorn had been popped, hundreds of wieners and marshmallows had been roasted.

And Kay's mother was so fluttery and gushy. Her name was Fay, and she preferred to have Kay call her that, rather than Mother. She often said to Beany, "You don't have to call me Mrs. Maffley—it sounds so old. Call me Fay." She was fond of saying proudly, "Folks always take Kay and me for sisters." It was true. Mrs. Maffley's blond hair was only a shade darker than Kay's, her waistline only a fraction larger.

But Kay had not her mother's talky, fluttery ways. Kay was quiet, gentle, thoughtful. "Praise be, she takes after her father," Johnny always said.

And Kay's mother always said proudly, "I do all my own housekeeping." But it was a playhouse brand of housekeeping, what with plugging in electric appliances and pressing buttons for janitor or maid service.

Sure enough, the cinnamon rolls Mrs. Maffley set before them were about the size of pin curls.

Absently, shakily, Beany copied on the loose-leaf notepaper Kay supplied her, and which would fit in her Home Ec notebook, the time and temperature charts for roasting meat.

It had been a jolting day. Norbett's disappearance when she had expected to make everything right with him—and with her father. Then seeing that brazen blond Dulcie, driving away from the Park Gate in Norbett's car. And now this further uneasiness of knowing that Andy Kern had seen her, Beany, leaving on a "late date" a scant hour after he had given her the watch on her left wrist. The charm bracelet jingled—no, jangled—on her right.

100

She wrote, "Allow twenty-two to twenty-five minutes per pound for well-done roast—"

A lot Norbett cared that he had jangled up everything for her. A lot he cared that she'd had to face her father. Or that she had skinned her shin and ruined her best nylons. . . .

She murmured to Kay while Mrs. Maffley listened to a TV program, "I wonder how Andy will act tomorrow at school. I mean, I wonder if he'll keep on eating lunch with me—"

It wouldn't seem right at Harkness without Andy asking her and Kay if they had an extra sandwich or cooky or banana. Or without Andy waiting in the hall to walk with her to French, and putting on an act of usher with a flashlight showing her to her seat—"Watch out for the step, Madam."

"I don't know," Kay answered. "All I know is, he didn't *act* mad."

Beany was glad that Kay didn't offer to ride down to the lobby with her. Because Beany did not get off the elevator at the lobby. Instead she rode on down to the basement garage. She often drove in and out with Kay in the Maffley car; she had even driven in and out with Norbett, and she knew the old attendant, named Nick.

He was sitting in front of the large rack, on which a great array of keys hung, reading the Sunday comics. Beany commented as casually as she could, "I see Norbett Rhodes's red car is gone."

"Yeah, just went out about an hour ago."

"Did he sell it? The reason I'm asking is because a friend of mine was thinking of buying it."

"I don't know, Miss, whether he sold it or not. All I know is, he sent me a paper, saying to deliver said car to bearer. And the bearer drove off with it."

He was very carefully referring to the girl with the pony hairdo as "bearer." Tactful of him, she thought wryly, because he remembered the many times he had seen a girl with braids in the front seat of that red car with Norbett.

"So—there we are," he ended, quoting a current comedian on TV.

So there we are. Beany sauntered ever so lightheartedly out the entrance, up the cement ramp, and into the dour day. She didn't want Nick to think she cared. It wasn't until she reached home that she realized the sheaf of notebook pages had been clutched so tightly in her hand that they were sadly crumpled.

She went to school Monday with anger and hurt at Norbett still lumped under her ribs.

She saw Jennifer Reed when all the student body were milling into the Harkness auditorium for an Assembly. Beany was sure Jennifer would hail her and ask, "Have you thought up your new uplift piece yet?"

A distrait Jennifer didn't even see her.

Instead it was Beany who had to push up to her and say, "Father gave me a swell idea for an inspirational article."

Jennifer didn't even ask what it was about, but nodded absently. "I knew I could count on you. Write it up as soon as you can."

The speaker in Assembly was a native of Korea. He told of the hardships of Korean children. A pencil, which boys and girls in America took for granted, was a rare and valued thing there. He told of his childhood and his learning to write by using a stick to scrape out the letters on the ground. A sympathetic Beany felt her old stirring of wanting to do something about it.

So when the meeting was over and Miss Hewlitt, Lit teacher and sponsor of the Scribblers' Club, stopped Beany and said, "You know, child, I was wondering if our Scribblers couldn't put on a pencil drive for Korean children," Beany answered readily, "Sure we could."

"We could put receptacles in the halls and ask each student to drop in a pencil or two," Miss Hewlitt. planned. "You get behind it and talk it up. Maybe your staff artist on *Hark Ye* could letter some signs—"

Beany had only time to say, "I'll ask him sixth hour," before she hurried to her next class.

The heavy lump under Beany's ribs was miraculously dissolving. Perhaps it was Jennifer's saying, "I knew I could count on you"; perhaps it was Miss Hewlitt's saying, "You get behind it and talk it up."

Were there two Beany Malones? One who had only to be with Norbett Rhodes to fall under the old spell—that nothing-else-matters spell? And one who, after a few hours at Harkness, was Beany Malone, almost seventeen, a junior in the thick of school activities?

Andy Kern belonged in the milieu of this Beany Malone. So that the real uneasiness under her yellow slipover was now not her quarrel with Norbett, but the facing of Andy. Supposing he said to her, "Sorry if I held you up for your late date"? How could she justify herself? Or, even worse, suppose he completely avoided her at lunchtime—and from here on out? Then what did a girl do about her wrist watch which had already occasioned many a "Lucky you!" from admiring classmates?

First-hour lunch period.

Beany stood outside the lunchroom, clutching her paper sack tightly and letting the hurrying clusters of boys and girls sweep by. Kay had been detained in clay modeling, and Beany was glad. If there was to be a blowup with Andy, she preferred it to be private.

Here came Andy. He was sauntering happily along, his broad shoulders swinging easily under his white shirt. He caught sight of her, and his gray eyes lighted.

"Hi, knucks," he said in his old way and took her arm. "Is it because you boast a timepiece that you're so prompt?"

104

Andy wasn't mad. . . . "I live for the day to see Andy Kern mad," Kay had said.

Beany stood, looking into his teasing eyes. "Andy, that telephone call Saturday night—it was someone at the airport who needed a ride in—and I—I mean, I don't want you to think—"

"Thanks, hon, for not wanting me to think. All morning long, every teacher has been urging me to the contrary."

He was keeping it light. Beany stammered on, "I mean I don't want you to feel that—"

"I don't want to *feel* either, if I can help myself," Andy said with his twisted grin. "I make a point of that. Some day I'll tell you more about Andy Kern. . . . What kind of sandwiches you got?"

"Chicken," Beany said promptly. Relief, like a tidal wave, swept over her. After Norbett's moodiness, his lashing out at her—wounded cougar!—it was soothing as ointment to have Andy keeping life bland and easy.

They made their way to their corner table. Andy, the observant, asked, "What're you humoring your left foot for?"

"I skinned my shin," she said evasively.

"How?"

"Oh—on those rickety steps to the room over the garage." She changed the subject quickly, "We're going to start a pencil drive for Korean children."

"Good idea. There must be a dozen or so lost ones at the Pant I'll gather together and donate."

The mention of lost articles at the Pant reminded her of the lost article Andy had watched over anxiously, until such time as he could present it to her. She ventured in a hesitant voice. "I thought maybe you'd—you'd be sorry you gave me the watch."

"I told you once, turnip—no obligations on your part. . . . I brought a couple hard-boiled eggs left from breakfast."

As they unwrapped sandwiches in the noisy, food-smelling din of the lunchroom, Beany asked, "Andy, you stop at the Ragged Robin sometimes, don't you?"

"Not too often—not since they've gone so ritzy. They charge fifty-five cents for a hamburger with about three potato chips and a slice of dill pickle cut with a razor blade."

She couldn't leave it at that. Curiosity was nagging at her. "Have you seen that blond girl with her hair in a pony tail named Dulcie?"

"The carhop in her drum majorette outfit? You can't help seeing her. She hits you right smack in the eye, even when you're brooding over the price of a hamburger de luxe."

"Do you know her very well?"

He shook his head. "She's got her sights raised higher than high-school studes. She turns on her charm mostly for the Varsity boys."

106

Kay joined them then. Andy said, *à la* a prim parent, "I hope, little girl, you washed your hands after playing in your mud pies." He added, *à la* Andy, "Don't have an extra cupcake in that fancy lunch kit of yours, do you?"

8

BEANY rode home from school Tuesday afternoon with Kay in the Maffley car. Kay was full of talk about the poster she was making in Art for the Heart Hop to be held Valentine's night. Beany sat silent and inattentive.

By now curiosity overrode even her anger and jealous hurt at Norbett. Was he staying out at that house in Hodgepodge Hollow with its unfinished addition? Did he think it safer there than on the Malone premises? Had he confided "all" in Dulcie?

"Our Heart Hop is really a reunion dance," Kay was saying. "You know they used to call it 'Auld Lang Syne.' The committee is sending invitations to old Harknessites."

"Are they?" Beany murmured, preoccupied with her own thoughts.

Well, she had a perfectly good excuse for going out to the South Wyman house again, didn't she? It was only courtesy for her to ride out and pay Dulcie for the gasoline which had been siphoned out of the truck for Johnny's car. Or, at least, offer to pay. She felt a cold shakiness under her ribs. Suppose Norbett's red car were sitting in the driveway?

"I'm on the decorating committee," Kay went on. "Of course, we'll have the usual festoons of red and white hearts, but I've been thinking it'd be fun to rig up a wishing well in the middle of the gym. And all the girls could throw in a flower out of their corsages and make a wish."

"Yes, that'd be nice."

"Do you realize, Beany, the Heart Hop is just a little over three weeks off? It doesn't seem possible that the new term starts next Monday, does it?"

The new term. Beany thought fleetingly of the alterations woman at the House of Hollywood and her own promise to help her shy and friendless daughter in starting the new term at Harkness. But Beany had her gnawing curiosity about Norbett to satisfy first.

"This is your week to cook dinner at home, isn't it, Beany? Want me to stop at the store for anything?"

Beany shook her head. "There's enough roast beef to serve cold. Such is the power of suggestion that after copying all those time charts, I had a medium rare one last night."

"It's cooking charts on fowl tomorrow. If I'm working on my poster, you take down the notes and I'll get them from you. Funny thing about teachers," Kay mused as she stopped in front of the Malone house. "The better you are in anything, and the more willing you are to work, the more a teacher piles on you. The Bitter One expects me to make posters and still have a clay modeling figure to put in the exhibit."

They hoped that the art teacher, who was a nervous, unhappy, sarcastic young man, would never know that his students called him The Bitter One.

"And it's the same with you and your writing for *Hark Ye*," Kay went on. "You work harder than anyone else on the staff. Yet if someone falls down on his copy, Jennifer always turns to you. Has she said any more about your going in her place to the big Press doings in the Springs?"

"Not a word," Beany admitted. "But then Jennifer's got something else on her mind."

"What?"

Beany said with relief, for this was something she *could* tell Kay about, "Last Saturday when she came home with me from Mr. Dexter's luncheon, we stopped at the Ragged Robin for barbecue sauce because Jag Wilson was coming to her house for dinner. And Jag came roaring in in his Jaguar and there, right in front of Jennifer's eyes, was enacted a chummy little scene between him and the blond carhop at the Robin. Her name is Dulcie."

"Yes, I know. Didn't Jag see you and Jennifer there?"

"No. And I could tell Jennifer was seething about the whole thing."

"Wonder if she gave Jag back his pin. But this Dulcie carhop is friendly as a pup," Kay defended. "I kind of like her."

So did I, Beany thought, until I saw her driving Norbett's red car down Park Street Sunday.

"And I feel kind of sorry for her," Kay added. "One evening Johnny and Carlton Buell and I stopped at the Robin, and we heard the manager lacing her down for being too visity with the customers. Carlton felt terrible about it, because he blamed himself for talking to her. You know how chivalrous Carlton is underneath his crew cut and snub nose."

"And idealistic," Beany added, thinking of the boy next door.

"So is Johnny," Kay said with that fond flicker of smile that crossed her lips whenever she so much as mentioned Johnny Malone.

"Yes, but Johnny's more lenient with human frailties—"

"Listen to the dictionary words," Kay put in.

"Carlton's shy with girls—not with Mary Fred or me, because he grew up with us and we've taught him to

111

dance. Not that he's much credit to our teaching, but then neither is Johnny."

Kay laughed. "Johnny'd be all right if he wasn't always thinking about something else when he dances."

Beany pursued, "That crazy Carlton always has to put a girl on a pedestal. I remember once, years ago when I was in Junior High, Carlton was far gone on a cute little brunette who worked behind the fountain at Downey's Drug. His heart always goes out to someone who has it hard. One day this little black-eyed girl was behind the fountain and Johnny and Carlton and I were in a booth, and Carlton was sitting there, mooning over her, when a little boy tipped over his glass of coke at the counter and it spilled on her white uniform. Whew, I'll never forget how she called the little kid a nasty name and reached over and slapped him. And I'll never forget the look on Carlton's face. Disillusionment."

"What'd he say?" Kay asked.

"Not a word—neither to her, nor to us. But from then on the little brunette was just a soda-fountain fixture to him. Carlton's like that."

Beany glanced at Andy's present on her wrist. After four already. She couldn't waste time talking about the boy next door when curiosity about a boy named Norbett roiled inside her. She said, "There's something I have to do, Kay. See you tomorrow."

Beany hurried through the house and found Adair in the kitchen, leafing through a cookbook. Beany asked her

112

if Johnny was home, and she answered that he was over at the Buell's with Carlton.

Beany said, "There's someplace I have to go. Will you tell him I'm taking his car?"

She was glad her stepmother wasn't the kind to ask, "Where?" For Beany couldn't explain that she had to call on a girl named Dulcie to ferret out more about Norbett's appearance—and disappearance.

Adair nodded. "I'm going to try my hand at cornbread. I thought it'd be nice with the cold meat."

"You don't have to help, Adair. You've got your portrait to work on."

"I wanted to get away from it. Honestly, I've fiddle-faddled over the lips all day." She laughed ruefully. "Whistler once defined a portrait as a picture of someone with the mouth not right. . . . Should I double this cornbread recipe?"

"Yes, double it," Beany advised, her hand on the door, "and then we can toast what's left for breakfast. I'll be back soon."

She had no trouble finding the house on South Wyman which had been so bafflingly elusive that windy moonlight night when she and Norbett hunted for it. There was the workman's truck sitting well toward the back of the lot. There was the unfinished addition. There was Dulcie herself, snatching a pair of stockings off the clothesline.

But there was no familiar red car anywhere in evidence.

The two girls met at the cinder-block steps. Beany said self-consciously, "I'm Beany Malone. I'm the one who ran out of gas Saturday night. I came out to pay you for it."

"Oh, never mind that little dribble of gas," Dulcie said largely. "The truck will never miss it." She was opening the door. "Come on in."

Inside, Beany's eyes flitted over the large room which was living room, dining room, and kitchen. One end was curtained off, evidently for a temporary bedroom. There were all the evidences of remodeling that had come to a standstill. The window on the west had been cut down into a door, and had been hastily boarded up. Some plumbing on one wall had been roughed in, so that the laths under the plaster showed.

Dulcie said with a belittling laugh, "Isn't this a weird dump? An uncle of Mom's left it to her, and nothing would do but that we move up here. We supposed, of course, it would be a real house—not a shack like this. Dad and I wanted to take an apartment, but oh no! Mom insisted on living here while the addition was being built. She wants to settle down here. She's always said that her ambition is to be in one place long enough to have ivy growing clear over the front of the house. Can you imagine anyone wanting to stay put that long?"

Beany didn't know what to answer. "Have you moved a lot—you and your family?" she ventured.

"We're always on the move. Dad and I are rolling stones that don't want to be mossbacks. How many places have you lived in?"

"I was born in the house we're living in now."

"You were!" Dulcie exclaimed with scorn. "I've lived in as many different places as I am old. I'm seventeen, and we've moved seventeen different times."

"Does your father's work keep you traveling?"

Dulcie hesitated. "No, not necessarily. He's a contractor, and he can make good money any place. But he's a gambler and a dreamer," she defended, "and he says that when there's big money to be made, he's going to be in on it. And I don't blame him."

Dulcie had dropped down on a low stool. She kicked off her loafers and pulled on her stockings, explaining, "I wasn't supposed to work at the Robin this evening, but the other girl wanted off, so I told her I'd work for her." She pulled on the white flared boots and stood up.

"What hours do you work?" Beany asked politely. She was still self-conscious.

"Four to ten on Thursday, Friday and Saturday. The boss gives me the busiest days because I'm a lot faster than the other girl. I make a lot more in tips, too."

An awkward silence fell. And lasted. Dulcie turned mischievous eyes upon Beany. "Why don't you ask what you really came out to find out? Where is Norbett and what is he up to?"

Beany's telltale flush betrayed her. Dulcie gave her head a pert toss. "You can search the premises in case you think I'm hiding him."

Beany flared out, "I don't think you're hiding him. I think he left for someplace—I don't know where—in his red car that you got out of the Park Gate garage Sunday."

"You think right," Dulcie said cryptically.

Another silence. So Dulcie was giving out no information. She was even taking great relish in keeping Beany in the dark. And to think that once Beany had thought she would like to know this bouncy girl with the wide smile.

At least one of the minor questions in Beany's mind was satisfied. Dulcie *did* darken her brows and lashes. She stood before a small oval mirror on the wall and blandly used a blackish pencil on her brows; silently, carefully, she applied a moist black brush to her eyelashes. She left off to open the door and glance down South Wyman Street, which was more of a country road.

"I'm looking for a ride in to the Robin," she said.

Beany stood up. "You can ride in with me," she offered stiffly.

"Oh, I mean I'm waiting for my ride to show up." She glanced through the open door at Johnny Malone's little, scuffed car. "You wouldn't expect me to ride in

116

with you in that puddle-jumper when I can go roaring in in a Jaguar, would you?"

"Frankly, no," Beany answered out of her seething fury.

"Is that your brother who drives that car to the Robin? Dark-haired, and a nice smile?"

"That's Johnny," Beany said coldly. And to still any predatory ideas Dulcie might have, she added, "Johnny goes with my best friend Kay."

"So?" Dulcie said with a toss of her head. "Jag Wilson goes with that snooty Jennifer Reed, but I can still date him any time I please. Jag is the hot-blooded type," she added meaningfully.

Defeated and nettled, Beany stepped to the door. She longed to puncture the airy triumph of the unperturbed Dulcie. But how?

Even as Beany reached for the door, it was opened by a woman with a scarf over her head, who carried a large bag of groceries.

Dulcie promptly took the bulging sack from her arms with a murmured, "I didn't expect you home so soon. Mom, this is Beany Malone." She added, her eyes bright with malicious glee, "She was so nice to come clear out here to call on me."

Beany took a backward step in surprise. It was the alterations woman at the House of Hollywood who had gone to great pains that Beany might have her new green skirt to wear to the staff luncheon—the woman whose daughter Beany had promised to befriend.

There was little chance for greeting, much less for conversation, for there came the unmistakable roar of a car outside. Her mother said as Dulcie grabbed her coat, "Oh, honey, I didn't know you were working. I hurried home so we could have dinner together."

"Had a chance to make a few extra bucks," Dulcie explained, "and I need it for all those yards of black lace for my new formal."

The car outside honked loudly. Her mother expostulated again, "You oughtn't to have that boy in the Jaguar calling for you—"

Dulcie kissed her mother and said, "Don't worry about me and Jag Wilson. There's someone else my heart goes pitty-pat over."

Beany's heart started an uneven pitty-pat. Did Dulcie mean Norbett?

Dulcie, from the doorway, was adding with that same mocking smile, "Thank you for coming, Beany. I'm sorry we didn't have longer to talk."

The door slammed behind her.

Beany's first surprise was that the woman with the tired, troubled eyes was Dulcie's mother. Her second surprise was that Dulcie's mother should so completely misinterpret her coming to the house on South Wyman.

She beamed at Beany gratefully as she took off her wraps. "You certainly were nice to come out to see

Dulcie. I hoped you would. I was afraid you didn't get the name straight at the Hollywood Shop, even though there's only one Lungaarde in the phone book."

Beany squirmed guiltily, remembering her well-meaning offer and her procrastination in carrying it out.

"Did you talk to Dulcie about starting at Harkness next Monday? And tell her that you'd introduce her around so she wouldn't feel such a stranger? What did she say?"

The woman was so anxious, so concerned. Beany couldn't say, I don't like your daughter. I can't think of anyone I'd rather *not* introduce at Harkness. Instead she muttered, "I just got here—and we—we didn't get much chance to—"

Mrs. Lungaarde nodded in understanding. "I'm sorry she had to leave. I hate to have her working such late hours—and having to get rides back and forth with those college boys. Dulcie hasn't any girl friends—"

For a very good reason, Beany thought grimly.

"—but we've never been in one place long enough for her to make any."

"She said you'd lived in seventeen different places."

The woman sighed. "That's right. But I'm praying this will be our last move. Once the addition is finished, we can have a nice, homey place here." Her face glowed as she gave details of the addition, which was to be two bedrooms and a living room with a picture window facing the mountains. There would be a patio under the apple tree. She even showed Beany samples of drapery material, and told her that Dulcie was as handy as she was herself at making slipcovers and curtains.

Beany couldn't follow all the details, but it was easy to gather that this was Mrs. Lungaarde's dream—this having a home where Dulcie could bring her friends.

Beany saw by her watch that it was five-thirty. She said uneasily, "I have to hurry home and see about dinner. Dad gets home about six."

Mrs. Lungaarde detained her at the door to say, "I'm so afraid that if Dulcie stays out another term, she'll never go back. You know how it is when a girl gets a taste of making money and buying her own clothes. She's already behind for her age. She says she hates to start and be in a class with others younger than she is."

"What year is she in?"

"She'll have to start as a junior. We left New Mexico to come here early in November, so she'll have to repeat her first half. Oh, I hope she can make friends and live like other girls—like you do. You see, honey," again that deep shadow touched her eyes, "I'm one against two. I'm the one who wants to put down roots. Dulcie and her father like the excitement of always being on the move."

Beany went out the door and down the shaky cinder-block steps. Mrs. Lungaarde's final words were, "I think you can do a lot with her, Beany. A girl her own age will

120

have so much more influence on her than anything I can say. You're so good to do this."

Beany's final words were a murmured, "Well—I'll talk to her about it."

A befuddled, regretful, and resentful Beany drove home. Now what was she going to do? Why had she ever glibly promised the woman in alterations at the Hollywood that she would take her daughter under her wing? But Beany had pictured a shy, small-town girl. She had never supposed she was the kind who would play up to Jennifer Reed's boy friend—

Oh dear, Jennifer wouldn't take kindly to Beany's sponsoring of the girl she had called a crummy little more-thanner.

No, and Beany had never supposed the daughter of the alterations woman would come between her and Norbett, or gloat over Beany's curiosity. Who else could she mean but Norbett, when she tossed off, "There's somebody else my heart goes pitty-pat over?"

9

HOW Beany dreaded the thought of her heart-to-heart talk with Dulcie on enrolling at Harkness next Monday!

And how thankful she was the following day, Wednesday, to have a good excuse for putting it off. A staff meeting of the *Hark Ye* was held after school. It was to plan their next issue which would come out the Friday before the Heart Hop on Saturday, February fourteenth.

Jennifer Reed, usually so crisp and capable in giving out assignments, in visualizing the whole layout, seemed vague as to which ones should write up, or how much space to allow, the Forensic Contest or the Heart Hop.

"Have you done your uplift something?" she asked Beany.

"Not yet. I've got the idea but I don't know how to slant it. I can't think of what Dad would call a vehicle for it. Maybe if we talked it over—"

"I haven't any more bright ideas than you," Jennifer said shortly.

Claude Metz, who always proofread the dummy and took it to the printer, nudged Beany. "Jenny's not herself," he said in a low voice. "She's got heart trouble. The scuttlebutt is that Jag is late-dating a plushy blond number."

I've got heart trouble, too, Beany thought wryly, because of the same plushy blond number. And on top of that I'm supposed to urge and inspire her to start in at Harkness.

It was after five when Beany reached home. She had dinner to prepare for the family. A girl's first duty was to her family, wasn't it, not to a cocky little carhop who probably didn't want to go to school anyway?

But a promise is a promise, her conscience prodded her; Dulcie's mother is counting on you.

Thursday afternoon she tramped home from school in a sleety snow. She called through the quiet house, "Anybody home?"

Mary Fred came to the head of the stairs, a towel lumped about her soapy, dripping hair.

"Johnny drove Adair downtown in her convertible, for a tube of umber. They're to pick up Dad and bring him home. I'm washing my hair," she imparted unnecessarily. "Going to ride in the horse show tonight. Oops, soap in my eyes." She ducked back into the bathroom.

In the kitchen Beany started dinner. Pork chops and potatoes, covered with milk and baked in the oven. She was sliding the big casserole into the oven when Mary Fred, her wet hair tousled about her flushed face, sought her out.

"Here, Beaver, part my hair straight for me." She handed Beany a comb and bent her head. Her muffled voice went on, "And then will you be a lamb and drive up to the Varsity Shoe Shop and get my jodhpur boots? I left them there to have the heels straightened, and I forgot all about them. I have to wear them tonight, and I can't go after them with my hair sopping wet."

Beany was a lamb and went, driving Johnny's car through the wind-driven snow. She got Mary Fred's boots and started back.

Her way led past the Ragged Robin. She could see that there was little drive-in trade because of the snowstorm. Why not stop and talk to Dulcie about starting to school and get it over with? At least, she would be living up to the letter of her promise, if not the spirit. She hated the very thought of talking to Dulcie, much less offering to befriend her at Harkness. But she had promised.

And if Dulcie didn't want to quit her carhop job and the big tips she bragged about—fine! "Doggoned if I'll coax her," Beany muttered to herself. "I'll just speak my piece and call it a day."

124

With her square jaw clamped determinedly, Beany took the turn into the driveway and onto the wide cement apron that spread out on all sides of the Ragged Robin. There was Dulcie standing on the lee side of the building, waiting for the customers in the one parked car to blink their lights as signal for her to remove their tray.

Dulcie looked like a ragged and half-frozen robin herself. She had pulled a warmthless spring coat on over the fitted red jacket with its gold frogs. Like a shivery robin, she stood on one foot with the other drawn up under the short pleated skirt. There was nothing pert or prancy about her as she huddled there in the snowy dusk. Even the pony tail hung limp and bedraggled. She was holding a paper plate over her head to keep off the snow. Her face under it looked blue and drawn—and somehow defenseless.

Sudden pity was like a hand clutching Beany's heart. She swerved Johnny's car up close to where Dulcie stood.

Lifelessly, Dulcie left her shelter at the side of the building and came toward the car. She stopped short, said, "Oh, hello, Beany."

Beany said, "I came to talk to you about starting in to Harkness next Monday when the new term starts—"

Dulcie's eyes under the darkened and wetly-smeared lashes stared at Beany. For one brief, unveiled moment Beany saw the loneliness, and the dread of loneliness, in their depths. Dulcie lowered them swiftly and gave a scoffing laugh that was like a snort.

"Not me. I'd rather take a beating. I know what it'd be like. Everybody has her own nice little clique. I'd have to scuttle around by myself. Everybody else would have someone to eat lunch with. I'd be sitting off in a corner alone—"

"No, you wouldn't," Beany said impulsively. "You could eat with Kay and Andy Kern and me. We'd introduce you to all the kids we know. The teachers, too. Kay and I will help you make out your schedule and—"

She saw the sudden push of tears in Dulcie's eyes, the crimping of her lips, before she jerked her head toward the customer in the car. She muttered thickly over her shoulder, "I got to get their tray."

She came back after she had slid the tray of empty dishes across the counter into the drive-in kitchen. Beany said, "Hey, don't stand out in the snow and get wetter. Climb in. It's all right, if there aren't any cars for you to wait on, isn't it?"

A shivery Dulcie climbed in beside Beany. She said in that same thick voice with her head turned toward the window, "You're the first girl that ever—ever offered to give me a hand. Gosh, I don't know why *you* would." She added forlornly, "If you've never gone into a strange school, you can't imagine how awful it is."

"Yes, I can. But you needn't worry. You'll like Kay—you know, the girl who comes in here with Johnny? She's so kind—she's a wonderful friend—"

"So are you, Beany," Dulcie said with childlike frankness.

Her cold, clammy hands were trembling in the abbreviated lap of pleated skirt. Beany reached over and covered them with her own warm ones. "We'll help you over the humps," she promised.

The snow was swirling down in a white cloud. The manager of the Ragged Robin, his coat collar turned up against it, came to the car. He said, "No use your sticking around, Dulcie. We won't have any drive-in customers until after the first show. You can go on home for dinner. But be back again around eight."

He hurried back to the haven of the lunchroom.

"Big-hearted of him," Dulcie said with a caustic laugh. "He doesn't want to pay me for a few extra hours. He *would* let me off the evening Mom has to work late. I'll have to tramp all the way out to Hodgepodge Hollow and rustle up something to eat—"

"Come on home with me," Beany offered. "I just chucked our dinner in the oven before I left."

"You mean it?" Dulcie asked with that same childlike candor. "Will it be O.K. with your family?"

"Oh, sure," Beany said heartily, as she started the car. "We always cook enough for one or two extra."

Beany herself had to talk around a catchy lump in her throat. Why, this Dulcie was all right; she just didn't know the rules too well. She was lonely . . . and she surely hadn't meant Norbett when she said her heart went pitty-pat over someone other than Jag Wilson.

Beany left the car in the driveway, and the two girls came in the side door into the back hall. Her stepmother was in the kitchen, unwrapping a pumpkin pie she had brought home. Mary Fred was in the one-time butler's pantry, pressing the long-sleeved white shirt she would wear under her riding coat that night.

Beany started the introductions, "This is Dulcie Lungaarde—"

"Lungaarde?" Adair said. "Why, you must be—"

"It's L-u-n-g-a-a-r-d-e," Dulcie broke in. "I go through life spelling it and pronouncing it."

Whatever Adair was going to say, she seemed to think better of it. She smiled warmly instead. "We're glad you came home with Beany. Goodness, child, your jacket is soaking wet."

"And my feet," Dulcie said.

"Come upstairs with me," Adair offered, "and I'll find you a blouse and some loafers. You can dry your jacket and boots by the radiators."

That was strange. Dulcie's very swagger and strut seemed to come off with the flared boots and fitted jacket. She had wiped off the smeared mascara, and the wise audacity of her eyes seemed wiped away, too. She was all eagerness to please, to help.

And she was a competent helper to Beany in setting the table, in cutting up fruit for salad. Perhaps because she had made do in those seventeen different kitchens, she felt at home even in a strange one.

The Malones made her one with them. At the dinner table, Johnny teased her about giving an extra handful of potato chips to the college boys she liked best when they came to the Robin.

"You'll have Carlton Buell eating out of your hand— the one that dishes out the potato chips," he said.

It surprised Beany that Dulcie could blush like a twelve-year-old.

Martie Malone with his beguiling smile talked to her about herself. "So you're starting at Harkness this coming Monday. What are you interested in as a career?"

She looked at him blankly, and he explained, "Mary Fred is majoring in psychology, but she can't decide whether to follow that up or run a dude ranch so she can work with horses."

"Maybe both," Mary Fred said. "I could psychoanalyze folks and advise them to spend a month or two on my dude ranch." She reached over and lifted Beany's left wrist to consult the new watch; Beany's was more dependable than her own. "Pardon me, all, if I grab my pie and eat it while I dress. I have to be all spit and polish to impress the judges."

Martie Malone continued, "What do you like to do best, Dulcie,—or what do you think you do best?"

Dulcie's face lighted. "I'm awfully good at designing clothes and making them. Once I thought I'd like to be a model, but now I'd rather be a designer."

"I imagine you'd be good at it," Adair said.

"In the school I went to in New Mexico I was the best in our sewing class. Of course, it was a small-town school. I made a two-piece purple faille suit, and it would have been in the school fashion show—I'd have modeled it, of course—except that we moved before they held it. Criminy, I look at those formals that old phony of a Simone sells for eighty-nine fifty—and I could buy the material and make them for a fourth of that." She turned to Beany, "Does the sewing teacher at Harkness let you go ahead, or does she hold you down to making silly cotton dresses any sixth-grader could make?"

Beany winced inwardly. She had just finished a cotton sunback and was now starting denim pedal pushers.

"No, Mrs. Hilb gives us our head. Just so we've learned enough to tackle something hard."

"I want to make a formal," Dulcie announced confidently.

With that, Mary Fred came into the room. She was garbed as an equestrienne in shiny black boots, snug jodhpur pants, and fitted jacket over her white shirt. Even the stiff hat was placed just right over her short brown hair. But she was holding her arms out strickenly.

"My coat sleeves are too short. Lila gave me this coat of hers because my own is so tacky, and the buttonholes worn through. But I never thought about my arms being longer than hers. Why, I'll look like a hayseed—the judges'll never let me place."

She looked helplessly at them all.

Dulcie was the first one to her feet. "Take it off, Mary Fred—and somebody get me a needle and black thread. See, there's enough of the cuff turned under so I can let it out for you. Beany, get out the ironing board and a pressing cloth."

Dulcie worked with flying, deft fingers. She pressed the let-down cuffs. "There," she said happily, "no one would ever guess but what it was tailored that way." Just as the automobile horn honked outside for Mary Fred, Dulcie was holding the remodeled coat for her.

"Whew!" Mary Fred breathed, "that was a close shave. If I win a ribbon, Dulcie, I should cut it in two and give you half." And the whirlwind that was Mary Fred, complete with white gloves and white carnation in her lapel, was out the door.

Dulcie insisted on helping with the dishes. She told both Beany and her stepmother that if they ever saw anything they wanted at the House of Hollywood to let her know, and her mother could get it for them at her employee's discount. "Or any time you want me to help with any sewing, you just holler," she offered.

She dressed again in her red jacket and white flared boots. Johnny drove her up to the Ragged Robin to catch any after-the-show customers.

Beany and Adair stood in the back door and watched the car drive off in the snowy night. Adair burst out feelingly, "That man! He makes me so mad. Just wait till I see him—I'm going to tell him what I think of a man who would—"

"What man, Adair?"

"Oh, that carpenter who promised me he'd have those new garage steps in for me right away. He's such a good workman. I know any number of jobs he could get, if you could only depend on him."

Beany barely listened. . . . It wouldn't be the painful chore she had anticipated to sponsor this new Dulcie— this new warm-hearted and whole-souled Dulcie—at Harkness.

Of course, there was Jennifer Reed—

Oh, but surely Jennifer would understand when Beany explained that Dulcie had always gone to small-town schools and needed help over the hard gap of getting acquainted. Jennifer was fair. She wasn't the kind to carry personal animosity too far. Maybe Beany and Kay could hint to Dulcie not to turn on her charm for one Jag Wilson.

Beany wished Dulcie hadn't had to go hurrying off. Maybe if they could have had a visity time alone, their friendly Dulcie wouldn't be so maliciously secretive about Norbett.

10

ON Monday morning, Beany and Kay pushed through the heavy front door of Harkness. They stood for a moment until their eyes grew accustomed to the hall's dimmer light after the bright glare of sun on snow.

Beany's eyes were still blinking as they sorted through the new pupils standing in line to register at the desks set up in the hall. She didn't see Dulcie but she heard her— "Hi, Beany! What do I do first?"

Dulcie was standing alone near the football trophy case. Beany breathed out, "Oh, no!" For the girl with her vivid coloring and jaunty pony tail was wearing the dressy purple faille suit she had made for the fashion show in her school in New Mexico. And certainly that suit with its full gored skirt and fitted jacket with buttons of brilliants would have brought a round of applause at any fashion show.

"I wish," Beany breathed on, "I had told her everyone at Harkness wears sweaters or blouses and skirts."

"I wish," Kay murmured back, "we could have told her not to make up her eyes."

Beany and Kay walked toward the girl who was clutching a notebook tightly in one hand, the mimeographed schedule of Harkness' classes in the other. If Beany's vision hadn't been still a little blurred from the brightness outside, she might have glimpsed the shaky fright of the newcomer.

Instead she heard Dulcie laugh loudly, and say just as loudly, "You can tell me which teachers are pills—"

Not only the pupils in line, but the teachers at the desks, as well as those passing in the hall, turned to look at her. Beany said hurriedly, "Here's a program for you; we can go someplace and fill it out."

Dulcie's eyes rested on Kay's pale blue sweater and black skirt, on Beany's much-washed yellow one topping her gray-checked skirt. Dulcie said defensively, "I wore this suit so the sewing teacher can see what I can do. So she'll let me start on a formal."

If only you'd brought it in a suit box, Beany thought regretfully.

"It's very becoming," Kay commented. "We want to fix up your class schedule so you'll have first-hour lunch with us."

"Yes, and I want that Mrs. Hilb for sewing that you told me about, Beany. And a class in dress design."

"You'll have The Bitter One for design," Kay said. "We call him that, but if he likes you he isn't bitter."

"With me he's bitter, because I never get any farther than ashtrays in clay modeling," Beany contributed.

Dulcie was studying the list of subjects. "Do I have to take gym? I get all the exercise I need, dancing. I have late dates for dancing every night in the week."

Again heads were turned in Dulcie's direction. Beany said instantly, "Let's go upstairs, and see if Miss Hewlitt can take you for Lit."

She turned toward the stairs, Kay and Dulcie following. If only Dulcie hadn't doused herself so heavily with perfume. Heavensent, Beany's nose diagnosed it.

If only they hadn't met Jennifer Reed as they reached the first stair landing!

Jennifer was coming slowly down the stairs so that the three who had reached the landing had a moment of seeing her in her dark and simple perfection. Navy blue tailored skirt, navy blue soft sweater with small and immaculate wings of white collar. Her short dark hair had a well-brushed glint. No make-up except lipstick. No jeweled buttons. Not even Jag Wilson's fraternity pin on her sweater, Beany swiftly noted.

Jennifer's preoccupied eyes rested first on Beany who was in the lead, and Jennifer stopped. "Beany, I've been wanting to talk to you. About the Quill and Scroll doings in the Springs. I have to fly out to my brother's wedding, so I thought—"

136

She broke off at the sound of swishing silk skirts, at the sight of the girl who was responsible for the pin's absence from her sweater. She stiffened, and her dark eyes turned cold. The figure in purple faille stood stiff and glaring, too.

Beany said flusteredly, "Jennifer, this is Dulcie Lun—"

Jennifer interrupted, her chin lifting a noticeable degree, "We've already met at the Ragged Robin."

"I'll say we have!" Dulcie snorted.

The two girls, one from Harmony Heights and the other from Hodgepodge Hollow, stood like enemy dogs with hackles rising. Beany tried to fill in the dangerous silence by rushing on, "Kay and I are going to help Dulcie fill in her program. You see, she's never gone to a city school before and—"

Jennifer's eyes raked over the purple suit, the sparkling buttons, the mascaraed eyes; her nostrils quivered as they caught the strong aura of Heavensent. She didn't say a word but the belittling twist of her lips said, That's quite evident.

And Dulcie, as though answering that unspoken slur, said fliply, "I'd like to ask you if you ever found a lipstick—"

Beany didn't let her finish. Fearsome instinct told her that the rest of the sentence would be, —in Jag Wilson's car? She grabbed Dulcie's arm and said, "Come on, we have to hurry."

Kay took the other arm, and they almost propelled her up the stairs. Why, it was like grabbing hold of Mike, the young Malone dog, to keep him out of a canine fray.

At the head of the stairs Beany paused limply and let her hand drop from Dulcie's arm. She wished bitterly she had never laid eyes on her. Heavensent, indeed! But for Dulcie Lungaarde, Jennifer would have finished her sentence, "—so I thought you could go in my place."

But for this feisty small-town girl, Beany could announce gladly to Andy Kern at lunchtime, "I'm to be acting editor for *Hark Ye* at the Convention." She could go home and look over suitcases, piled in the garage loft, and start planning her trip. Darn her eyes, she thought viciously.

Kay's troubled glance rested on Beany and then on Dulcie. She said, "Jennifer Reed is an OH—outstanding Harknessite. She's editor of *Hark Ye*."

"And my boss, incidentally," Beany said flatly.

"Everybody looks up to and thinks a lot of Jennifer," Kay added meaningfully.

"I can name one who doesn't," Dulcie said between set teeth. "An OH, huh? Well, just let her start something with me, and OH, she'll be sorry."

So will I, Beany thought bleakly. Because I'll be right in the middle.

Kay had to leave them and go to her art class and the Heart Hop poster she was working on. Beany pulled herself together with an effort. After all, Dulcie was a

138

first-half junior and Jennifer a second-half senior. Surely their paths wouldn't cross. Beany said, "Here's Miss Hewlitt's room, Dulcie."

Miss Hewlitt was one of the older teachers at Harkness. She knew the Malones well, having taught Martie Malone as well as each Malone as he or she left Junior High and entered Harkness. She was especially devoted to Johnny, and predicted a literary future for him.

This morning she looked questioningly at Beany, dubiously at the gay bird of paradise Beany introduced. And when she had signed Dulcie's program and the girls started off, she called Beany back.

"Is this girl some special friend of yours, Beany?"

"Well—she's new, and I wanted to help her off to a good start here at Harkness."

The gray-eyed, gray-haired, gray-dressed Miss Hewlitt said bluntly, "Tell her she'll get off to a better start if she washes that axle grease off her eyelashes."

The room for math classes was across the hall. Beany introduced Dulcie to the math teacher. He studied Dulcie's program, studied Dulcie. "My fourth-hour class is practically all boys," he said.

"That's all right with me," Dulcie said blithely.

His eyes raked over her again. "I'll sign you up for fifth," he said dryly.

It went off better in the sewing room.

This was the third-hour sewing class in which Beany sewed on the days she didn't go to Home Ec. Mrs. Hilb was young, energetic, and enthusiastic. Nothing delighted her more than a pupil with initiative who made garments with style and verve. Mrs. Hilb was always looking ahead to her Easter Parade fashion show during spring vacation.

Her eyes quickened with interest when Dulcie asked, "Can I start right in on a formal?"

The girls in the class looked up with almost startled unbelief. They, like Beany, had been content to make full cotton skirts, simple blouses. Some of the more daring had made colorful fiesta dresses, the tiered skirts gay with metallic braid or rows of rickrack.

Mrs. Hilb asked, "Can you sew well enough to tackle a formal?"

"Oh, sure," Dulcie said largely. "I've made scads of cotton things. I've made all my own clothes since I was twelve. I made this suit."

She turned around like a fashion model on mincing steps, preening herself in it. She even unbuttoned the sparkling buttons to show the finished seams underneath. Mrs. Hilb's critical eyes noted the flare of skirt, the smooth lapels, the bound buttonholes.

Dulcie opened her notebook and drew out a folded piece of white wrapping paper. Over the crackle of unfolding paper, she said, "See. Here's a drawing of the dress I'm going to make."

140

Several of the students were standing about Mrs. Hilb's desk to question her about their work. Others pushed up, frankly interested in this cocksure new pupil. Wherever Dulcie is, Beany thought, she somehow gets the center of the stage.

Beany peered over the shoulders of two girls to see. Dulcie sketched well. Black lace bodice which held itself up without benefit of shoulder straps. A white cloud of ankle-length tulle skirt. And around the bottom of the skirt an uneven hem of black tulle, edged with black lace medallions.

Beany caught her breath. Why, it was a copy of that "deliciously wicked" dress Beany had seen on the manikin at the House of Hollywood with the startling price tag carefully tucked out of sight. The dress Jennifer Reed had said she had her eye on for the Heart Hop. And a price tag would neither startle nor deter Jennifer, the only daughter of Christopher Reed, Realtor. Beany felt an uneasy stirring.

"I'm copying an Original," Dulcie was saying. "I turned it inside out and saw just how it was put together. I even took all the measurements."

Beany waited hopefully. Surely Mrs. Hilb wouldn't let Dulcie start on something so breath-taking, so difficult—

But Mrs. Hilb was saying thoughtfully, "Of course, this new nylon lace isn't as slippery to work with as silk lace—"

"That's what I'm using. Here's a sample of it."

All the curious around the desk were still peering at the sketch. Mrs. Hilb said, "It'll take quite a while to make—"

"Not me," Dulcie assured her. "I sew fast. I'll have it finished in time to wear to the Heart Hop on Valentine's night."

Beany gasped. Dulcie going to the Heart Hop. That *was* fast work. Beany herself had, as yet, given little thought to it. Of course, there was Andy Kern for her to rely on—

If a bomb had been tossed in their midst, the sewing class couldn't have looked more jolted. The girls exchanged looks. Beany could feel the sudden antagonism of all those who were fearfully unsure of being asked to the big event of the year—the Heart Hop. And then to have a newcomer toss off in lordly fashion that she was going to it.

Mrs. Hilb was jolted for another reason. "Oh, no, my dear," she exclaimed. "The Heart Hop is less than three weeks off. Just those lace medallions bordering the hem—each one has to be whipped on by hand—and the skirt is miles around."

"I'll work extra on it," Dulcie insisted. "I'm to have a study hall—couldn't I get excused to come here? And I can work after school on the evenings I'm not carhopping at the Ragged Robin."

Mrs. Hilb laughed in rueful delight. Students who elected to use their study-hall period and stay after school in the sewing room were few and far between. "All right, Dulcie," she agreed. "And if you do finish it in time to wear to the Heart Hop, for heaven's sake, don't spill any punch on it. It'll be a knockout in our Easter Parade."

For the first time Dulcie looked around at the girls who would be her classmates. She must have felt their tacit banding together against her. For the first time her bouncy bravado failed her.

She turned to Beany and blurted out, "You're going to be in this class with me, aren't you?" Something like the child who clutches at the hand of the one he knows best, and says, "I'm scared—please stay with me."

"Yes," Beany said heavily, "this is my class."

All that day Beany knew sharp uneasiness about Dulcie's copying the dress which might already have been delivered from the Hollywood Shop to Jennifer Reed in Harmony Heights. She shared her uneasiness with Kay as they rode home from school.

"I just don't feel up to coming right out and asking Jennifer if she's bought it," Beany said worriedly. "Can you think of any excuse for us to go to the Hollywood and see if it's still there?"

"Couldn't you stop and sort of report to Dulcie's mother about how she got along at school?" Kay hazarded.

"I could if I wasn't so scared of that hoity-toity Madame Simone," Beany confessed.

They drove several blocks in silence before Kay said, "I could go in and buy a pair of nylons, even though she charges more than they do downtown."

They did just that. One swift look around the House of Hollywood and Beany drew a breath of relief. There was the Original on the model with the pleased simpering smile and a pair of long white gloves draped over her outstretched hand.

Praise be!

Mrs. Lungaarde, sewing in the back room, saw Beany. She came in and said in a low, hurried tone, "Oh, Beany, I'm so grateful to you for all you've done for Dulcie. Now we can settle down here. And you'll be the first person we ask when our house is finished and we have a housewarming party for Dulcie."

Madame Simone turned such a condemning look their way that Beany gravitated toward the front door, and Mrs. Lungaarde returned to the back room.

"Well," Kay sighed in relief, as they walked toward the Maffley car, "it was worth paying one ninety-five for a pair of one fifty-nine stockings to know that Jennifer decided against Simone's Original."

"Oh, yes. That snooty old buffalo."

They both giggled lightheartedly.

144

11

THAT first week at Harkness, with the new semester starting and the old one ending, was an unsettled one. The seniors who were "up" in their work were given days off. Jennifer Reed was one of those. Students who were not "up" scurried about, taking make-up tests, bringing notebooks to date, and finishing work in Shop for mid-year credits.

Beany scarcely saw Andy, who was putting final touches on a lamp in Woodwork for his mother, or Kay, who was working extra time so that her Heart Hop poster could be hung in the hall the next Monday morning.

And because of the confusion, the lack of routine, Dulcie Lungaarde managed to escape without too much notice.

But by the following Monday when classes were back on schedule, when Kay's colorful poster of the Heart

Hop hung in the main hall, two topics of conversation took over Harkness—the coming Heart Hop *and* Dulcie Lungaarde. Already she was referred to as The Passion Flower, Honey from Hodgepodge, or The Eye-fillin' Filly.

Tuesday, as Kay and Beany walked toward the lunchroom, they were halted by knots of students surrounding Kay's poster. A background of pink hearts and apple blossoms against which dancing figures were silhouetted. Kay, the artist, appealed to Beany, "The hair on that girl in the foreground doesn't look just right, does it, Beany?"

Before Beany could assure her that it did, one of the girls turned from her group to say spleenishly, "Why, no, Kay, you should have given her a pony tail and had her wearing a black lace and white tulle formal. Old pony tail is going to be right there in the foreground, as everyone in our sewing class has been told repeatedly."

As Kay and Beany moved on, Kay added ruefully, "So has everyone in Art. The Bitter One is having Dulcie do her dress in pastels on dark blue paper—oh, that black lace and white froth shows up lovely on it—and she's told everyone—"

"Did she say who—with whom she's going?" Beany asked.

Kay shook her head. "Only that she isn't going with any high-school *boy,* but with a college *man* who is a former Harknessite. If the little dope would just keep

146

still. The gals who haven't got dates hate her, and the gals who have dates with high-school boys hate her, because you know how, for the Heart Hop, it adds that extra something to go with an alum'. I keep wondering if she's going with Jag Wilson."

"I hope not," Beany said fervently, thinking of Jennifer and her moody reticence since she had returned Jag's pin. And then her heart gave an unsteady flip-flop. Norbett Rhodes was a college *man* and a former Harknessite. But it couldn't be Norbett. It must be one of those numerous college fellows who flocked to the Ragged Robin.

The thought of Norbett started the whole nagging train of thought. Where had Norbett gone? What was the mysterious something that had brought him out here? Did Norbett still think Beany Malone had a disposition like a wounded cougar? Had he said to Dulcie, "You're the only one I can depend on"?

Often, with these thoughts nagging at her, Beany was tempted to take off that jangly and reminding bracelet. But Norbett had asked her to wear it; he had said her wearing it would bring him luck.

She stopped now in the noisy hall and glanced down at the good-luck leprechaun. "Kay," she demanded, "when you look at this little fellow in his pointed cap and shoes"—she brought him into view by cupping him in her fingers— "does he sort of wink at you?"

"Um-hmm. Kind of a devilish wink though. Beany, you're all over being *wild* about Norbett, aren't you?"

"I—I think so," Beany said.

Kay returned to the subject of Dulcie. "I hardly think it's Jag Wilson. He's the type who would late-date her and string her along for kicks when he goes to the Robin. But he's also the type to take a 'prominent' girl like Jennifer Reed to a school prom. Did I tell you that our decorating committee thinks my idea of a wishing well in the middle of the floor is real great?"

Beany nodded absently. "And we throw in a penny to make a wish?"

"No, nothing so mercenary. A flower out of our corsages. You don't know where I could get hold of one of those old wooden washtubs, do you?"

Beany was just saying, "Gosh, no. They predated bustles, didn't they?" when the principal, Mr. Dexter, came toward her.

Like every student, her first reaction was, Now what have I done? But Mr. Dexter was wearing what Harkness called his warmed-over smile as he said, "Catherine,—I believe they call you Beady, don't they?"

Beany only nodded. She couldn't count the times she had corrected him with "Beany" instead of "Beady."

He said, "Jennifer tells me she's counting on you for the feature article in your next issue. I'm glad, for you do that type of inspirational writing very well—very well, indeed. But there's one idea I would like to have you

148

touch on. It's come up for frequent discussion in our faculty group—that is, the present-day familiarity between boys and girls on their dates." His smile was shaded with embarassment. "I believe you have a name for it—"

"More-thanning," Beany supplied.

He chuckled gently. "Yes, more-thanning. I think it would be timely if you mentioned that in your article."

He turned away in the direction of his office. Beany let out her breath in an exasperated heave. "Dad gives me an idea for my piece—the more freedom, the more responsibility—and I knock myself out, trying to write it. And now Mr. Dexter would have me tackle the more-thanning problem."

"But you could tie them together, couldn't you?" Kay suggested.

"I could if I had the brains of a goose," Beany admitted. "But I've written and torn up a dozen starts, because each one sounds like a sermon. Even Dad says so. He says I need a vehicle for it, so I can put it over more informally."

Kay said, as they dropped down at the lunch table where Andy and Dulcie were waiting, "We've got troubles, Beany and I . . . I'm in quest of a wooden washtub to put rocks and moss around for our wishing well for the Hop—"

"One of those old-fashioned jobs made out of staves, and all gray and warped?" Dulcie asked. "Seek no further. There's one on that place of ours. It's under a gutter to catch the leak. I'll make you a present of it."

Kay said, "Dulcie, you're a lifesaver. I'll drive you home after school and get it."

In front of Andy Kern was a stack of squarish white envelopes. He ran his eye down a page of names and addresses as he ate a sandwich. He asked, "What's your trouble, Beany?"

What's my trouble? Beany thought wryly. My biggest one wears her hair in a pony tail and is sitting next to me, and sometimes I hate her, and then again I want to fight for her.

Kay answered for her, "Beany's looking for a vehicle."

"But not the kind you ride in," Beany explained. "It's a method of carrying my article so it won't sound like a sermon."

"Tell us more," Andy urged. With a swift sleight-of-hand movement he reached over and took Kay's frosted cupcake and transferred it to his mouth. Kay laughed delightedly, and Beany said, "I brought an extra banana for you, Andy."

Dulcie added, "Do you like ribs, Andy? I can manage some for you from the Robin."

"Gnawed on by customers?" he asked.

"No, ungnawed. The cook's a friend of mine."

"All donations thankfully received," Andy said. "Let's hear about your problem, Beany."

150

"Well, I have to uplift Harkness, only Dad keeps warning me that if I make it sound preachy no one will read it. And now, to complicate life further, Mr. Dexter suggests that I touch on the problem of more-thanning."

Dulcie asked with pseudo-innocence, "Is Mr. Dexter in favor of more more-thanning?"

Beany's giggle was spontaneous. "Hardly."

"I know," Dulcie said with belittling scorn. "You're to write on the evils of. I can tell you just what to say—I know it all by heart. Because teachers are always backing me in a corner and dishing it out to me." She pursed her lips and imitated a reproving voice, "Boys don't respect a girl unless she has high standards. Oh, my dear, remember that a girl's reputation is like a precious jewel. Who steals my purse steals trash, but who steals my good name—" She dropped her prim mimicry to add, "Oh, my foot!"

Beany caught Kay's eye as Kay wadded up the waxed paper her sandwich had been wrapped in. They felt a little embarrassed somehow. It didn't seem right for Dulcie to be so frank, so flaunting. Beany stole a glance at Andy, who was peeling his banana.

Dulcie went on blithely, "Some of those little flat tires in sewing called me a more-thanner the other day. I guess they thought I'd sneak off in a corner and weep. I came right back at them. I told them I didn't have to sit home nights, listening to weather forecasts on TV." She laughed gaily. "All this talk about how a girl should be a model of virtue because a man must look up to her! Oh, well, they used to tell me if I ate crusts my hair would be curly—and I didn't eat crusts and my hair is still curly. They told me if I wasn't good, Santa Claus wouldn't bring me anything—and I was never good but I always did all right on Christmas—"

"So you know all the answers," Andy said, looking at her levelly over his half-peeled banana. "Did you ever figure out why restaurants stopped having sugar on the table in a free-for-all sugar bowl and used individually-wrapped jobs instead? The reason is that nobody likes to dip into the same sugar bowl everybody else dips in."

Beany saw the defiant color flare in Dulcie's cheeks, but before she could answer Kay put in, "Andy, how about us helping you address some of the invitations for the Heart Hop? The out-of-town ones ought to be on their way."

Beany, grateful for the interruption, added, "Yes, why don't we?" She made a small furor of pushing back lunch debris and getting out her ball-point pen, and explaining to Dulcie, "Andy's on the committee that sends the invitations to the old grads."

"I drew the ones who graduated in the last two years," Andy said. "And I've worked my way down to the L's."

Beany focused on addressing an envelope to a boy named Wilbur Lane.

Andy and Dulcie had never hit it off too well. After their first lunch period together, Andy had said to Beany on a low whistle, "The blond menace! I fear you've grabbed a bear by the tail, knucks. It's going to be hard to hang on, and yet you don't dare let go." And Dulcie had said to Beany, "I guess you haven't gone with very many boys, have you? If you'd gone with as many as I have, you wouldn't fall for old know-it-all Kern."

"Down to the M's," Andy was saying now. "Here Beany, you can deliver Mary Fred Malone's and John Esmond Malone's invite in person and save the committee postage. We don't have the latest address for Norbett Rhodes either. How about your sending that to him, too? By the way, did he ever answer about whether he wanted to sell his car or not? You asked him, didn't you?"

Beany couldn't look at him. Her heart started an uneven thumping. She kept on licking the flap of an envelope.

Dulcie spoke up. "You'd sure be a sap if you bought that car. It's a clunk, if I ever—" She stopped short.

Beany felt Andy's eyes leave her own flushed face and turn to Dulcie's. Dulcie tried to cover her slip by saying "This crazy pen of mine never writes unless I keep wetting it—and won't I look cute, going to math with green lips?"

Kay said innocently, "I think Norbett must have sold his car. It isn't in the Park Gate garage any more."

Beany got up hurriedly as the clang of the bell announced that first-hour lunch period was over. It had been an awful lunch hour.

It seemed a strange coincidence, when she reached home after school, that her father, too, should mention Norbett Rhodes and ask her to send him a message.

Martie Malone was typing in his study and he called to Beany as she passed his door.

"Beany, I had lunch with some of the newspaper people at the Park Gate today. And I happened to run into N. G. Rhodes, Norbett's uncle, in the lobby. It kind of shocked me to see him, for he looks bad—sick and worried. He's out of that political job of his now. You remember he was traffic manager up until about a year ago?"

"Yes, I remember." She remembered too that Martie Malone had written scathing columns, denouncing the traffic manager, so that Norbett's going with Beany Malone had something of the feuding family background of a Romeo and Juliet romance.

Her father was saying, "Rhodes has a printing business. And I imagine he had to neglect his business while he was in office. I stopped and visited with him for a while today."

"You did? I thought you two were enemies."

"Why, no, Beany. I lambasted him in my column because he was so lax about enforcing traffic rules. But there was never any personal enmity between us. He was

154

asking me today if you had heard from Norbett recently. He said his last letter to him in Ohio was returned. You have Norbett's latest address, haven't you? Write him right away, and tell him his uncle is very anxious to get in touch with him. Tell Norbett he looks sick and worried."

Beany couldn't very well say, Norbett doesn't want his Uncle Nate to know where he is. She couldn't even say, I don't know either, but a girl named Dulcie does.

She only fumbled out, "I'll tell him when I see—I mean, when I write—"

It seemed to her that her father, even as Andy Kern, gave her a probing look.

12

BEANY had such mixed feelings about Dulcie Lungaarde.

She blamed her bitterly for so many things. In the journalism room, Beany would glance up at the reminder on the blackboard: "Only five more days till deadline," then "Only four more days—" and she would think, I still don't know how to put Mr. Dexter's uplift piece together. I could think it through if I weren't so upset about Dulcie—Dulcie and Norbett."

Beany *had* been able to put her mind on the pencil drive for Korean children. At a meeting of their Scribblers' Club, she had enlisted their sponsoring of it.

"Soon as the stirring appeal comes out in *Hark Ye*," they promised her, "we'll all bring glass vases and set them up in the hall for pencils to be dropped into."

On Wednesday after school, Beany sat in the staff room, typing out the stirring appeal. Jennifer Reed had assigned Peggy Wood to write it, but Beany was doing it for her. For Peggy was even more heavily burdened at home these days. Her mother had taken a job in a downtown department store. Whenever Kay and Beany rode to school in the Maffley car, Kay stopped by for Peggy. "Oh, thanks, Kay," Peggy always said breathlessly, "I'd be late again if you didn't give me a lift."

On this Wednesday morning, Peggy had run out from her yard as Kay slowed to a stop. She was hanging up clothes, and her wet hands were purplish with cold. She wanted Beany to explain to Mrs. Brierly that she couldn't make it to journalism. She just had to wash school clothes for the younger kids—

"What about your write-up for the pencil drive?" Beany asked. And then as Peggy's round face turned more harassed, Beany added, "Look, I know all about it—why don't I just do it?"

"Oh, Beany, if you would," Peggy said gratefully.

"See what I mean?" Kay had said as she drove on. "You're always the pinch-hitter on that paper. Just give Jennifer time to simmer down, and she'll go ahead and ask you to take her place at the Springs Convention."

"She doesn't speak to me any more than she has to," Beany said.

This Wednesday after school, even as Beany typed, "A pencil means little to you or me," Jennifer Reed came into the room.

She asked, "Is that your uplift feature you're finishing?"

Beany's eyes lifted to Jennifer's dark ones which were neither friendly nor unfriendly. Behind Jennifer the sign on the blackboard read: "Only three more days till deadline." Tomorrow it would be two. Jennifer wanted all copy turned in by Monday morning so that she could arrange space on the dummy.

"No, I'm doing the write-up for pencils for Korea. For Peg. Things are pretty thick for her at home right now."

Jennifer didn't say as she had so often, "Beany, you're the old dependable stand-by for everyone." She only said curtly, "Keep it to one column. When will you have your feature in?"

"I don't know. I'm working on it, but I can't seem to get the right slant."

The old Jennifer would have said, "Let's put our heads together and see what we can come up with." But this new moody and reticent Jennifer only said, "Until it's turned in, I can't lay out the first page."

That was all Dulcie's fault too, Beany thought again. Jennifer Reed had never been so edgy before Dulcie came between her and Jag Wilson. And the extra-strained relationship between the editor of *Hark Ye* and the feature writer was because Dulcie was the protégée of the same feature writer.

A glance at Jennifer told Beany that Jag's fraternity pin was still missing from Jennifer's soft slip-on. Dark red, today, with the same white wings of collar framing her set face. Certainly this was no time for Beany Malone to bring up the Quill and Scroll Convention, and that still unfinished sentence of Jennifer's, "I have to fly out to my brother's wedding, so I thought—"

But it would mean so much to me to go, Beany thought heavily. It'd mean that just once I was out of the dependable old stand-by class. Every one of the Malones has been an OH at Harkness; every one but Beany. Every one of my friends here at Harkness is; and Beany's just the work horse.

It was all Dulcie's fault, she summed it up, as her fingers typed on, "Look through your lockers, your pockets, for those extra pencils."

Yet when any of the girls snubbed Dulcie, when any of the boys whistled after her in the hall or made coarse remarks about her, Beany felt a fierce championing of the girl with the burnt-sugar hair.

Dulcie was so blatant, so blundering. But so was she anxious to belong. In one school period Beany could veer from fury toward her to aching sympathy.

On Thursday morning in the sewing class, Beany sat across the table from Dulcie, who was deftly basting the black tulle border on her fluff of skirt. Mrs. Hilb was standing outside the door, talking to Melinda Page, the drama teacher.

Dulcie was wearing a flowered skirt and a white blouse, called a fiesta blouse. It had short puffs of sleeves, and its round and very low gathered neckline had occasioned considerable interest among the male contingent when Dulcie leaned over the drinking fountain in the hall. Beany was wondering if there were any way she could tactfully mention the blouse's too-low neck to Dulcie, when Dulcie leaned over the table to ask Beany in a near whisper, "Have you ever been to a Heart Hop?"

"Yes. I went last year with Norbett."

Beany's thoughts instantly dipped back to a year ago. . . . I was Norbett's girl then. No girl at the Hop was as far up in the clouds as I was. We practiced the samba and the Mexican polka at home for nights. And Norbett was in one of his cock-of-the-walk moods. He wouldn't even let me dance with Johnny or Carlton Buell. Oh, I'll never forget last year's Heart Hop. . . .

She burst out, "Dulcie, Norbett went off someplace with your father, didn't he?" She felt Dulcie stiffen, and she hastily tacked on, "My father wants me to give Norbett a message—he thinks it's important. When will they be back?"

Dulcie's face took on that closed look. "If we worried about my dad's getting home at any certain time, Mom and I would both be gray-headed by now." She shrugged. "Relax, kid. You've got Andy Kern to look after you. Why try to corner the market?"

160

She stood up, gathering her armful of shimmering yardage, and walked over to a sewing machine.

Beany tried to fit the notches on the waistband of her denim shorts to the notches on the front, and her fingers shook. She watched Dulcie running the sewing machine with blithe confidence, and she hated every inch of her, from her swirl of pony tail to her ballet pumps. What did she mean, "Relax, kid. You've got Andy Kern . . . "? Did she mean, "Relax, kid. I've got Norbett"?

Dulcie stopped her stitching to rethread the bobbin. Before she started again she glanced at the girl at the machine next to hers who was starting to stitch in a zipper. Dulcie said. "Hey, you've basted that in wrong. Give it here, and I'll pin it for you."

It was one of the very girls whom Dulcie had previously offended by bragging that she, Dulcie, never had to sit home and watch TV. With a ready smile, Dulcie reached for the girl's cotton skirt. The girl drew back and said nastily, "Oh, never mind. Go ahead on your formal that you *say* you're going to wear to the Heart Hop."

Dulcie looked slapped. She glanced around at the silent unfriendly girls. The low-cut blouse slid off a slumped shoulder, and Dulcie fumbled it into place before she turned back to her machine.

That was when Beany felt an ache of sympathy for her. And when another girl commented to Beany across the table, "Nothing would tickle me more than to see *somebody* and her formal left high and dry," she felt swift fury. She turned and faced the girl, ready with a defense for Dulcie.

Just then Mrs. Hilb and the drama teacher came into the room. Mrs. Hilb spoke to Dulcie, "Miss Page says she needs someone to let out seams in some of her Flora-dora dresses."

Melinda explained, "We've got a new Adeline to play in *Our Darling Daughter* at the Veterans' Hospital this afternoon, and our new Adeline has bulges until some of the waistbands won't meet."

"I told her you were the quickest sewer I knew, Dulcie, and that if you would be willing—"

"Sure thing," Dulcie broke in heartily before Mrs. Hilb's sentence was finished. "Let me at your waistbands."

She likes doing things for people, Beany thought. Dulcie, with childlike enthusiasm, scurried about to put away her own sewing. She gathered up scissors and needles and thread, and went out with Melinda.

The next day, Friday, Dulcie unwittingly gave Beany the "vehicle" she needed for her uplift article.

Beany hadn't seen her since she had left the sewing class Thursday, because Beany took Home Ec on Friday. She and Kay were at their locker when a bubbling-over Dulcie came hurrying up.

"Guess what. Melinda got me excused from classes yesterday afternoon, and I went out with the cast and

162

watched them put on *Our Darling Daughter* at the soldiers' hospital. The soldiers thought it was a riot—you should have heard the ripe remarks they yelled out."

"I know," Beany said. "Did they *tch-tch-tch* and say, 'Adeline, how could you?' "

"Yes, and 'What is the world coming to!' And no wonder. Imagine all that to-do in the last act over a girl holding hands. And with a meek little number in the choir. Imagine any girl, singing in a choir. I can't believe that parents and chaperones were such hard-shelled old fossils even sixty years ago."

"The way I hear it, they were," Kay said. "You ought to hear my grandmother tell about her courtin' days."

Dulcie snorted. "Thank Pete, I wasn't born then. I kept thinking of how shook that sheltered little Adeline would be if she landed at Harkness and talked to one of us for just half an hour."

Beany stared at her—and suddenly an idea took root. Not only took root, but started flowering. She breathed out, "Dulcie, that's it."

"What's it?"

"The vehicle. I can have Adeline coming back to life—like Rip Van Winkle—"

"But Rip only slept for *twenty* years," Kay reminded her. "And Adeline lived about *sixty* years ago."

"Oh, but everything is bigger and better today," Dulcie said. "Beany's Miss Van Winkle could sleep longer and harder."

"Dulcie, you saved my life," Beany said.

"I'd look pretty with a Purple Heart," Dulcie said with a pleased grin.

The bell rang, and they parted. Beany climbed the stairs to French, the idea yeasting inside her. It would all be in dialogue between the gay-nineties Adeline and a present-day Harknessite. What striking contrast it would make in costume, speech, morals.

She sat at her desk and answered students who said, "Hi, Beany," without hearing the exchange of greetings. She was hearing instead the discussion between Adeline and a Harknessite.

Andy took his seat, leaned across to ask, "What are you looking so far gone about?"

"I've got it—the vehicle I've been looking for."

"Surrey with a fringe on top, or a Ford convertible?"

"A little of both. It'll be like a play. It's even started writing itself."

"Look, Beany Shakespeare, don't be so carried away in your vehicle that you forget your date to go to the Pant tomorrow night. You and Kay and Johnny, courtesy of Andy Kern, head usher."

"Even if I'm carried away, I'll come back for that," she assured him.

So this was what it meant to be carried away by an idea! Beany sat at the dinner table with the Malones talking all about her, even *to* her, while all the time Adeline and a glib Harknessite talked back and forth in

164

her mind. Adeline was dressed in her lilac taffeta with its stayed collar, hampering sleeves, long and lined skirt, and narrow pinching shoes; the present-day girl in short-sleeved blouse, comfortably short skirt, and soft ballet slippers which were next to going barefoot.

Beany sat up late in her room, typing it on Johnny's typewriter, which had a rakish way of jumping an extra space or two. "Like a trotting horse breaking into a singlefoot," Johnny always excused it.

Her fingers flew.

ADELINE *(in unbelieving amazement):* You mean to say that when your escort takes you to the theater, he doesn't have to buy three tickets, so the chaperone can accompany you?

HARKNESSITE: Oh, groan! We wouldn't have an escort if we even mentioned chaperone.

ADELINE: But if you don't have a chaperone, who lays down the rules for you? Do your parents and teachers trust you to be—virtuous—and above reproach?

HARKNESSITE *(thoughtfully):* Well—yes. Parents and teachers trust us. But I guess a lot of us don't realize that it's a sort of solemn trust we should live up to.

ADELINE *(eagerly):* But supposing you don't? Isn't there any line drawn between 'nice' girls, and the girls we call 'fast'?

HARKNESSITE *(hedging a little):* We call them more-thanners here at school. We thought it was funny because the grown-ups in your time laid down rules about what a well-brought-up young lady could do and

then said, "—more than that no nice girl ever permits."
Nowadays the line has moved considerably—
ADELINE *(insistently):* But there is a line yet, isn't
there? *(Harknessite doesn't answer.)* You said yourself
that the girls were tagged "more-thanners" here. *(She
touches the arm of the Harknessite earnestly.)* I wish you'd
tell me whether it makes any difference or not.

Beany's fingers left the typewriter keys. She put her
elbow on the typewriter and cupped her chin in her
hand. She had a feeling that Adeline was real, and that
she was asking her an honest question, "What do you
think, Beany?" and that it called for pure honesty in
answering.

Always before Beany had skirted the question. She
had never had to face it with Norbett. Yet she would
have if Norbett hadn't stayed back in Ohio last fall. She
hadn't had to with Andy Kern, because Andy kept it
light.

For the first time she was asking herself what she,
Beany Malone, thought about more-thanning. She
thought of Mary Fred and her off and on times with
Sergeant Wally Thomas because he was the amorous
type. "Unless it's the real thing and you can start plans
for getting married, all this *amour-amour* seems a little on
the cheap side." And just last week Eve Baxter had said,
"Unless males have changed completely, I'll bet they still
divide girls into the nice ones and the easy marks." She
thought of Dulcie, who was defiantly proud of being a
more-thanner. Beany mentally saw the nudges between
the boys and heard their meaningful whistles, their

166

exclamations of, "Hot tamale!" as Dulcie Lungaarde walked through Harkness halls. . . .

No, I wouldn't want that, Beany realized.

She sat for a long time, staring into space. The house quieted about her. "Don't ever write anything you don't believe in," Eve Baxter always admonished. And Martie Malone said, "You have to put part of yourself in everything you write."

Very slowly she began to type—

HARKNESSITE: Yes, even though the line has been moved considerably from your day, there is still a line. A girl doesn't take a chaperone with her on dates today, but she has to take her conscience along . . .

The next morning when she went to Eve Baxter's for dictation she told her that the inspirational article which had been by way of an order from Mr. Dexter was now roughed out on paper.

"The idea came like an inspiration," Beany sighed. "But I had to work on it till way after midnight."

"Most writing," Eve Baxter said wryly, "is one-tenth inspiration, and nine-tenths perspiration. Let me run over it while you go down and put on the coffee."

"Make allowances for Johnny's typewriter hopping, skipping, and jumping," Beany apologized. "I'll rewrite it on one of the machines at the *Call* office."

Eve Baxter said thoughtfully when Beany returned with her coffee, "Nice job, Beany. Your own philosophy always comes through better when you put it on the lips of characters. You bring me a copy of your *Hark Ye* next Saturday with this printed in it."

She sorted through the stack of letters on her desk as she sipped her hot coffee.

"Are you going to answer the letters on whether to be loving or unpopular?" Beany asked.

"No, I've another idea to take care of those. Today we'll handle letters from boys in the army who have received Dear John letters."

A satisfying day for Beany. A satisfying evening.

Johnny took her and Kay to the Pantages—courtesy of Andy Kern, head usher. Kay sat beside Beany, and on the other side of Kay, Johnny. The seat next to Beany was on the aisle, and every now and then Andy dropped down in it, keeping a weather eye out for any customers who needed seating.

The story on the screen was a musical comedy about a theatrical family. Beany laughed heartily at the farcical situations; she hummed under her breath with the songs they sang. She thought suddenly, I'm happy. I'm so relieved that my uplift piece is shaping up. And I haven't thought of Norbett Rhodes since—well, not since Dulcie gave me the idea of putting my article in dialogue form.

Andy Kern slid in beside her and plopped three bags of popcorn on their respective laps. Beany had to lean across Kay to admonish, "Johnny, don't chomp so loud—and don't rattle your sack." For the story on the screen was reaching the emotional climax. The lost son, for whom the family had searched and grieved for years, was about to be found.

"Get out your handkerchiefs," Andy said. "The tear-jerker scene is coming up."

Tear-jerker scenes always brought tears from Beany. Andy leaned over and wiped away a tear, and patted her shoulder. "It's only a story, pie-face. The actors get paid for making you cry."

Riding home through the cold night in Johnny's drafty little car, they all sang together. As they walked up the front steps of the Malone house, Kay dropped behind to murmur to Beany, "Has Andy asked you to go to the Heart Hop yet?"

Beany shook her head.

"He'll ask you tonight, I suppose. Or maybe he just takes it for granted—with all our talk about it—that the four of us are going together."

Johnny had parked in front of the house because Adair's convertible sat in the driveway. He threw wide the front door. "Head for the kitchen, everybody. Just for the feed lot."

Martie Malone was sitting at the kitchen table, tinkering with an electric cord. In answer to Johnny's, "What're you doing, Pappy?" he answered, "I'm trying to get this electric heater working."

Beany's eyes widened as they roved over the table. Across from her father sat a glass half full of milk, and a plate holding a half-eaten sandwich. As though someone had left hurriedly. As though that someone had left so hurriedly he had not had time to pick up a still burning cigarette off the ashtray. Martie Malone smoked a pipe, not cigarettes.

Beany's heart began a harder thumping as she saw that mysterious something in its canvas case hanging over the kitchen chair where the someone had been sitting. Didn't any of her three companions notice it?

Johnny was saying, "Beany, you put together some hot chocolate while I build up some sandwiches."

Perhaps one of the other three did notice, for Andy Kern said, "Johnny, I'll have to skip the refreshments. Rosellen wanted me to pick her up a home permanent, and Downey's Drug will be closing."

Beany heard herself saying that it wouldn't take a minute to make cocoa, heard herself regretting that they had to hurry off, when, for the second time, every fiber in her was urging her guests, "Go, Go! Norbett has come back."

And somehow she said her good-bys to Kay and Andy as they went out the front door with Johnny, who was to drive them home.

13

AS BEANY hurried back to the kitchen, her father was calling down the basement steps, "They're gone, Norbett." And as Norbett's red head and plaid flannel shirt came into view, Martie Malone added disapprovingly, "There was no reason for you to duck like that."

"I heard Kay," Norbett said. "And you know how gabby her mother is with my aunt at the Park Gate. Hi there, Beany," he greeted her with a sheepish grin.

She said, "Hi, Norbett," faintly.

Norbett was back. His skin was burned to a red mahogany by sun and wind. His hair, so exactly the shade of their Irish setter, needed cutting. In his heavy flannel shirt and scuffed boots, he seemed a different Norbett from the one who liked to think of himself as a coming newspaper man. But he was as wire-trigger taut as of old.

Martie Malone said, "I think Norbett could eat another sandwich or two, Beany. And see if there's more milk in the icebox."

Cold milk wasn't good enough for the returned Norbett. Beany hastily mixed chocolate, sugar, and set the mixture on the stove for hot chocolate. She sliced more ham and cheese.

Her father said, "I was just telling Norbett about seeing his uncle a few days ago—and how anxious he is to get in touch with him."

Norbett set down his glass of milk. It had left a small rim on his lips—a mustache, as the small Malones used to call it—but he didn't bother to wipe it off. "Oh, sure, sure," he said mockingly, "he's very anxious to get in touch with me. Because he's very anxious to beat me out of what's coming to me."

"No, I don't believe N. G. Rhodes would beat anyone out of anything," Martie Malone said evenly.

Norbett flung out the same remark Beany had, "I didn't know you two were friends. I thought you were bitter enemies."

And Martie answered with the same easy laugh, "Why, no. Just because I nipped at his heels in my *Call* column when he was traffic manager doesn't mean that we're not friends outside of politics. . . . Why are you so mistrustful of him, Norbett?"

"I'll tell you why—"

He told it all in an angry outpouring. His Ohio uncle had owned some placer claims down in the uranium country, that part called Four Corners, where Utah, Arizona, Colorado and New Mexico touched corners. At his uncle's death the claims had been left equally to Norbett and his Uncle Nate here in Denver at the Park Gate.

172

About the first of the year, Norbett's Uncle Nate had written him, telling him he had a buyer for their claims, and that he thought it wise to sell the land when they had the chance. He had sent a release for Norbett to sign. His Denver uncle would then proceed with the deal and send Norbett his share, which would be a thousand dollars.

"Sounds like a good deal for you both," Martie said. "What makes you think your Uncle Nate is trying to gyp you?"

"Because I heard from a fellow named Ivor Lungaarde, who has done a lot of uranium prospecting down there, and he—"

Uranium! So Ivor Lungaarde had been bitten by the uranium bug, as Eve Baxter put it. That was why his wife worked as alterations woman at the House of Hollywood, and his daughter as carhop at the Ragged Robin.

"—he told me about all the rich strikes right around our land," Norbett went on. "Ivor told me not to sign it over to my uncle until we went down there and investigated. He said there were fortunes to be made in uranium down there."

So Norbett, too, had the get-rich-quick fever.

Beany's father was thoughtfully tamping tobacco into his pipe. He said, "I've heard my father tell about the old gold-mining days here. I remember his saying, 'For everyone that hits it big, a hundred go broke and die in the gutter.' Your Uncle Nate probably thought he was doing you a favor to sell your joint claims for two thousand, a thousand apiece for you."

"He didn't think anything of the kind," Norbett contradicted. "I know him better than you do. I know he's always pushed for money, because Aunt Mae has to go in for society—and entertaining. No sir, he thought he could have me sign a release because I was back there in Ohio, and he could go ahead and make the big money himself. Ivor Lungaarde said it looked that way to him."

Beany said, "Here, Norbett, here's a mug of hot chocolate." She put it before him, and he lifted it and drank it as though he didn't know or care what he was drinking. He flung out triumphantly, "Ivor and I went all over my ground down there." He indicated the instrument in its canvas case which hung over the back of his chair. "You ought've seen that old Geiger counter dance and jiggle all over the place."

So it was his Geiger counter, the detector of uranium, Norbett had been so mysterious about. So the lure of uranium wasn't as far removed from her life as she had thought when Eve Baxter talked about it.

"Did you really find uranium?" she asked.

"I brought home samples of ore," Norbett hedged. "Ivor says they look good to him. I drove back with them. Ivor wanted to stay down there—I guess his wife is always trying to talk him into staying home when he's here. I was just as glad, because he's the kind that always has to stop along the way and chin with every prospector—"

"What did you do with your ore samples?" Beany pursued.

"I left them at the assayer's. He's a friend of Ivor's, and he promised to run them through this evening. Ivor

174

says that when we get his report, we can lease the land for our own price, and be a lot better off than to sell it for peanuts the way Uncle Nate wanted to do."

Martie Malone got to his feet. "I'll leave you two to visit. The electric heater will warm up the garage room. I wish, Norbett, you'd go to see your uncle tomorrow and put all your cards on the table. A man is innocent until he's proven guilty. I've been rather haunted by him—he looked like a worried, sick man."

"I want to wait until I get the assayer's report," Norbett defended himself. "I want to know where I stand first."

In silence, Beany sat on one side of the kitchen table and Norbett on the other after Martie left. Silence, except for Norbett's nervous crunching of cookies. He muttered, "I haven't had anything to eat since morning. I drove all day so's to get the ore to the assayer. I was making a sneak for the garage room when your dad saw me."

"I wish you would talk everything over with your uncle. And then you wouldn't have to be dodging around like this."

Norbett didn't look at her. He was turning the green chocolate mug around and around.

"There's a reason why I can't, Beany. I was ashamed to tell your dad. But Uncle Nate sent me two hundred bucks when he asked me to sign the release. At first I thought I was going to fall in with him—and I needed the money, so I spent part of it. Then when I heard from Ivor, I began to think Uncle Nate was pulling a fast one. So I used the rest of the money for a bedroll and Geiger counter and plane fare. At that, I wouldn't have landed here broke, if I hadn't been charged so much for excess baggage."

He looked up, and Beany caught the impact of his unhappy dark eyes. "Beany, you're not still mad at me, are you?"

"No—no, I'm not mad at you."

Mad? Wild triumph clamored in her breast. Norbett had come straight to the Malones. He hadn't gone to see Dulcie. Hadn't she been a ninny to think he would? It was *her* hand Norbett was reaching for and kneading between his roughened and nervous ones. Hadn't she been a ninny to think, even for a minute, that he was the college man Dulcie was going to the Heart Hop with?

Norbett said uneasily, "I'd better make myself scarce before Johnny comes back. I heard your beau of the evening ask him to take him and Kay home." He stood up and picked up the electric heater and cord.

"Wait a minute," Beany said. "I've got something for you."

She hurried into the dining room and riffled through her Home Ec book for the squarish invitation to the Heart Hop. She came back, pulling the invitation out of the envelope.

Norbett didn't look at it right away. He said again, "I can't very well see Uncle Nate yet. I'd like to put through a big deal just to show him—I mean, he's always treated me as though I didn't know very much. Good grief, Beany, I want to get out of the poor-relation class, and this is my chance."

"I know," Beany murmured, and she felt the old longing to build him up. Norbett, who always wanted to feel important; who wanted to do favors, who hated to take them.

"What's that you've got?" he asked.

"An invitation for you. Andy—I mean the committee—asked me to see that you got it. The Heart Hop. It's a week from tonight. They want old grads to come to it. They've got committees all over the place to take care of the decorations and music and refreshments. Kay's even going to have a wishing well in the middle of the floor. Remember," she asked catchily, "last year when we went to the Heart Hop?"

"Sure, I remember." He bent over and read aloud, " 'For auld lang syne, my dear—' "

"For old time's sake," Beany translated, in case he didn't know.

"It sure would seem like old times for us to dance together. It seems like a thousand years. When did you say it is?"

He smiled excitedly into her eyes, and she felt her old pulsing excitement; she felt again the magic of last year's Heart Hop when she had gone with Norbett—cock-of-the-walk Norbett . . . .

"A week from tonight. You'll be back then, won't you?"

"I'll burn up the road getting back. I'll have my own car, so I won't have to dilly-dally around with Ivor. I'm leaving in the morning, as soon as I get the assay. Ivor knows men down at Four Corners with capital who are egging for good claims to lease—"

Beany, womanlike, was more interested in their going to the Heart Hop together. "When will you be back?"

"Can't say for sure, but I'll be back in time."

"And then you'll be through with all this hush-hush stuff and dodging around?"

He laughed exultantly. "Your durn tootin'! I'll be a uranium king. I'll be the conquering hero. Oh, Beany, I always feel on top of the world when I'm with you. I need you so. I want to feel that you're waiting for me. Beany, you're still my girl."

The arm that wasn't holding the portable heater grabbed at her and pulled her close.

Yes, she was still his girl. She could think she had forgotten him, and then he could reach out and pull her to him, and suddenly all the things that had filled her life—her dating Andy, her creative joy in doing her dialogue article—all of it was only dim background.

She said with a choked laugh, "I'll be counting the days. I'll start watching for you Thursday. Oh, Norbett, I wish I could tell everyone that you'll be back, and that I'm going with you—"

"Wait till I get back." He bent to kiss her—

But before their lips could touch, Red scrambled up from his place in the middle of the floor and streaked through the hall. The front door opened. It took Beany a startled moment to remember that other people were in the world beside Norbett and her.

"There's Johnny," Norbett said, and leaped for the back door. The cord of the electric heater dangled after him, and Beany grabbed it and threw it over his shoulder. She closed the door behind him.

178

She fell into a frenzy of picking up dishes off the table that might betray an extra presence to Johnny. But she need not have worried. Johnny came into the kitchen with a faraway look in his eyes—the look the Malones called, "the snows of yesteryear," which meant that his mind was on some old historical figure or event.

He had stopped in the hall to pick up a thick, shabby book. He said, sniffing, "Chocolate, huh. Pour me a mug, and I'll drink it while I read up about General Denver. Got to dig out all the salient facts of his life and turn them in to my history prof Monday morning."

Beany said, just to be saying something. "Oh, was he the one they named Denver after?"

"Why, no," Johnny said sarcastically. "They named Denver after General McGillicuddy. Go on to bed, stupe."

Beany went to bed.

It would be like old times, Norbett had said, to be dancing with Beany again. And so was it like old times for Beany to be tossing sleeplessly in bed and thinking of Norbett. Norbett had bent his head to kiss her, and she had lifted her lips to his— If only Johnny hadn't come in the front door at that moment.

Guilt assailed her. Fine thing for Beany Malone to write earnestly about nice girls and more-thanning, and then to be swept off her feet by Norbett's saying, "You're my girl."

Did every girl say to herself, "Oh, but this is different—we're in love"?

Sunday, Monday, Tuesday, Wednesday—four more days till she saw Norbett, if he came back on Thursday. Seven days before they went to the Heart Hop together.

She had given little thought to the Hop or what she would wear. Last year she had worn her pale green taffeta. But she had worn it, and Mary Fred had worn it, on so many, many occasions. She wished she had a glamorous new formal. She counted her money in her mind—the five dollars she had been paid by Eve Baxter today, plus about three sixty-five. No new dress. But if Mary Fred wasn't wearing her pink with the rows and rows of lace stitched on the skirt, she would wear that.

She thought of Andy. He had never once said, "Will you go to the Heart Hop with me, knucks?" Was he, as Kay said, taking it for granted that they would double-date with Johnny and Kay? She sat up in bed and pounded her pillow, dropped back again. Supposing Andy said to her, What color corsage do you want that I can buy for a buck and a half? What should she say?

Oh, dear, that buffeting wall of secrecy. She wouldn't be able to tell Kay or Johnny *or* Andy that she was going with Norbett Rhodes. Not until he returned, the uranium king, the conquering hero.

Yes, like old times. A long time of going to sleep for Beany Malone. A hard and heavy-eyed getting up in the morning.

Martie Malone was flying to Washington on a news assignment. There was all the scurry of his getting packed. Adair said, "I think you'd better take a bigger suitcase, Martie, so your shirts won't get so mussed. There's one in the room over the garage—"

"I'll get it," Beany offered swiftly. Norbett would have gone, but maybe he had left a message for her.

"Be careful of that second step," Adair cautioned.

Martie said teasingly, "Where's that carpenter of yours, Adair? The one who was going to have a brand new stairway for you in no time at all?"

"Just wait till I see him," Adair said with unwonted fire. "Just wait. I'm laying for that man."

Beany carefully avoided the treacherous second step, remembering her bruised and scraped shin which was only now completely healed. She opened the door, and looked around the cluttered room. Norbett *had* left her a message. It was pinned to Headless Hetty and read, "I'm counting on you and the good-luck leprechaun to bring your prospector luck."

Beany didn't wad up this note and throw it in a corner. She folded it carefully into a small square and stuck it in her skirt pocket. She turned the charm bracelet around, and looked into the blinking green eyes of the leprechaun. She wished he didn't have such a mischievous—even devilish—wink.

She stood there a long while before she remembered what she had come to the garage loft for.

Three suitcases were piled on top of each other behind the old baby bassinet. Beany took the medium-sized one. It was one of Adair's. It was a creamy tan and, as Beany straightened, she realized how light in weight it was, how good the handle felt in her fingers.

For a brief moment she swung it lightly, wishfully. This would be just the right size for a girl to take to the Press Convention in the Springs. If Jennifer gave her the

"Go" signal, she would drive up with Claude Metz, the senior co-editor who always read copy and took the paper to the printer. They would get there in time for the opening luncheon, and she would wear her shamrock blouse and the new green skirt.

If Norbett were here with me, she thought wryly, I couldn't even think about a Quill and Scroll Convention. It was only when Norbett was away that her heart had room for different yearnings.

14

MONDAY and Tuesday were days of pent-up ecstasy for Beany.

What a relief to have her stint done for *Hark Ye*. What a blessing that she had found the vehicle and worked on it Friday night and Saturday. She could never concentrate on it now. Not with Norbett's reappearing. Not with her mind and heart a-tingle with thought of their going to the Heart Hop together.

Jennifer Reed liked her uplift piece done in dialogue.

Beany saw her the first thing Monday morning before they even entered Harkness. Jennifer was getting out of her car, and Beany ran up to her and thrust her two typed pages into her hand.

Jennifer unfolded them, ran her eyes over the first page and gave a pleased chuckle. "This is a knockout. We'll be in solid with our Mr. Principal."

"I barely made the deadline," Beany said with a sigh.

"*You* barely made the deadline! Do you know I've torn up a half-dozen miserable efforts at doing my witty column? Whew, hasn't this Valentine issue been a headache? Mother has been nagging at me about shopping for clothes for my brother's wedding, but I told her I'd have to wait till we got the paper to bed."

Jennifer was acting and talking like the old pre-Dulcie Jennifer. As they started up the wide white steps, she shifted her books and her fur coat fell open. No wonder—no wonder! Beany caught a glimpse of a gold and jeweled pin on her dark sweater, and she said impulsively, "Oh, you and Jag have made up. Oh, I'm glad."

Jennifer's gay laugh was a little sheepish. "Yes—we're on again. You see, Jag asked me a long time ago to go to the Heart Hop with him. He stopped by yesterday to see if I'd still go with him—and he wants me to wear his pin again." They were pushing through the heavy door and into the maelstrom of Harkness' hall. Jennifer added with a shy smile, "Life is looking up for me."

Beany opened her mouth to say, "Life is looking up for me, too. I'm going to the Heart Hop with Norbett." She wanted to say it, to add, You remember Norbett Rhodes? She longed to take out her happiness and share it. It didn't seem right to keep it locked up inside her.

The bell for first-hour class was ringing. Jennifer hurried up the stairs on light feet.

And it didn't seem right not to share her gladness with Kay. That first day, Monday, Kay asked, "Has Andy asked you to the Heart Hop yet?"

Beany only shook her head and changed the subject.

Tuesday, Kay said, "Has Andy said whether he'll have the Kern car for Saturday night? Or will we go in Johnny's?"

184

Again Beany shook her head. Oh, this was bad—this riding under false colors; it gnawed at the edges of her happiness.

"Why don't I ask him about it at lunch?" Kay suggested, looking closely at Beany who was not looking at her.

"No," Beany burst out. "No. I mean—well, please don't."

"But I'm sure he's planning on taking you," Kay insisted.

And then Beany became not so sure. Andy was *different*. No one else seemed to notice it. Kay didn't, when at lunch period she prattled on happily about the wishing well for the Heart Hop and how they would put blue crêpe paper in the water to turn it a deep blue. Dulcie didn't, when she hurried into the lunchroom so late that she had to chomp down a sandwich hastily before the bell rang. Dulcie was finding that Mrs. Hilb had predicted truly about those lace medallions consuming hours of labor.

Outwardly, there was nothing different about Andy. He still called Beany "knucklehead" and "stupe." But she sensed some cool withdrawal in him. She thought uncomfortably of Mary Fred's saying, "Nobody ever fools Andy. He isn't the son of a police captain for nothing. That lad is smart and savvy and shrewd."

Andy, unlike Johnny, *was* the kind to notice a glass half full of milk, and a cigarette left burning on a kitchen table. Andy *was* the kind to read meaning into Norbett's car disappearing from the Park Gate garage.

185

Andy studiously avoided mention of the Heart Hop. He studiously avoided having a minute alone with Beany. And even while she was counting the days until Norbett would be back, she still wondered unhappily what Andy was thinking. Every time she glanced at the pretty and dependable watch on her wrist, she felt a small wincing of guilt. Even though Andy had said, "—and as the brush salesman says when he gives you a sample, 'No obligation whatever on your part, Madam.' "

But a girl was obligated to be honest and aboveboard with someone like Andy. That, too, gnawed at the edges of her ecstasy.

It was the same at home. Beany asked Mary Fred if she would be going dancing with Wally Saturday night, or if she, Beany, might wear the pink formal.

"Sure, hon, you can wear it. Because I won't be tripping the light fantastic with Sergeant Thomas. I've said my cold farewell to him."

It was after dinner in the Malone house. The dishes were done, and the two girls were in the dining room where Mary Fred was shaking out the table mats while Beany ran the carpet sweeper.

"Honest, Mary Fred, have you broken up with Wally? For good?"

Mary Fred leaned wearily against the sideboard. "For Mary Fred's good, if you know what I mean. Wally's a nice guy, only his idea of a date is—is not my idea of one. . . .Beany, about that pallid pink. You tell Andy to send you a sort of purplish corsage. Tell him it's sort of blah without something to set it off."

Beany rattled the carpet sweeper diligently. She made a great business of putting it away in the hall closet. Goodness, it was like steam inside her that she longed to let out. If only she could tell Mary Fred, "I'm not going with Andy. I'm going with Norbett. I went with him last year, and it was the most wonderful night in my life. I'm Norbett's girl again."

Beany's restless fingers reached for her heavy coat in the closet. She said, "Guess I'll run up to Downey's Drug and get some notebook paper. I've been borrowing from Kay for weeks."

Beany was just stepping up on the curb on the lighted corner by Downey's Drug when she heard her name called by someone in a parked car.

She recognized the Kern car and Andy's sister, Rosellen, who was in the front seat. Rosellen had been a polio victim years ago. Last year she had been in a wheel chair, but now she got about on crutches. Rosellen was fifteen and vivacious and pretty and folksy. Even crutches didn't hamper her from going places and being in things.

As Beany walked over to the car, Rosellen was rolling the window down and trying to keep her crutches from clattering to the floor. "Beany," she wanted to know, "did you ever have a home permanent?"

"No, I don't need one, not with braids. But Mary Fred has—I gave her one about a month ago."

"How did it come out? The girl next door told me that some of these home permanent jobs leave your hair smelling like burned rubber for a long time afterward—"

"Oh, no," Beany assured her. "Mary Fred's didn't."

"Look, Beany, you scoot in and get the kind Mary Fred used. Andy got me one, but it was the wrong kind—it was the kind to give a tight curl—and so I had him bring it back"—she giggled ruefully—"and he's not happy about it. He wouldn't let me go in for fear I'd slip on the icy walk. You go in and tell him the right kind— or gosh knows what he'll get."

Beany hurried in. Perhaps it was because Andy was irked at having to change the package of home permanent, for he said curtly to Beany, "All right, take over. If you can figure out what brand, what curl the gal wants, you're smarter than I am."

Beany got her notebook paper, too, and she and Andy walked out to the car together.

"Oh, swell!" Rosellen said happily when Beany handed her the box. "This is the kind it said on TV that you can put up yourself, just as easy as putting your hair up on pin curls."

"Oh, no," Beany said again. "You have to make curls all over your head no bigger than a dime, and sop every curl with one liquid, and then pour on the neutralizer. Couldn't your mother do it for you?"

Rosellen's face fell. "Not tonight—and not tomorrow night. She's going out tonight, and tomorrow night we're having company. And I washed my hair today to have it ready—I wanted it done tonight, so it wouldn't look like a brush heap for Saturday night."

"I'll do it for you," Beany offered. "I'm not doing a thing this evening."

"Would you, Beany? Oh, that'd be wonderful—"

"In case you're interested, you two," Andy put in with a man's disdain of beautifying methods, "I'm already five minutes late at the Pant, so let's settle all the hairdressing problems as quick as we can."

"It's settled," Beany said. "You drop Rosellen and me off at our house."

It was also settled, as he stopped in the Malone driveway and helped Rosellen out of the car and up the steps, that he would call back for her after his stint of ushering.

Because the stairs were hard for Rosellen to manage on crutches, Beany seated her in the kitchen. She gathered up all the bobby pins in the house, and fell to combing and twisting and pinning the mass of dark hair into dime-sized curls.

"It scared me when the girl next door said her home permanent smelled like burned rubber," Rosellen said, holding out bobby pins to Beany as she required them. "Because I want to look good and smell good for the big premiere Saturday night. Did Andy tell you about it?"

"Well—no—"

"He didn't? That's funny. They're having the opening for *Brief Interlude*—or is it *Happy Interlude?*—anyway, some kind of an interlude at the Pant; and the Hollywood leads, male and female, are making a personal appearance. Even though it was Andy's night to be off, he told the boss he could work, and he's going to take me. Oh, very deluxe, with Andy meeting the female star at the curb and escorting her in and presenting her with a corsage."

"Oh," Beany said. And again, "Oh." The first oh was of surprise, the second of relief—such great relief that her bobby pin gouged Rosellen and she breathed out, "Ouch!"

Beany murmured, "Sorry. Duck your head a little."

. . . Then Andy's plans for Saturday night did not include the Heart Hop in the Harkness gym or Beany Malone. She need feel no guilt in having another date. . .

"Didn't he ask you to the premiere?" Rosellen demanded.

"That's the night of the Heart Hop at Harkness," Beany hedged. She was twisting a wispy curl around her forefinger, but Rosellen jerked her head around to look at her, and the curl was pulled askew.

"Why, of course," Rosellen said. "I remember now. I remember Andy getting the Benny Boden orchestra for it. Benny's been saying no to all school dances, you know. But Andy got him because he knows Benny, on account of Benny's playing for special affairs at the Pant."

"The Benny Boden orchestra. Wonderful!"

It *was* wonderful. The sought-after Benny Boden orchestra would make the Heart Hop more of an event than ever. But even more wonderful was that—well, that Beany could continue to coast along, letting Kay and Johnny—even Dulcie Lungaarde—assume that she was going with Andy. Until Norbett came back. Then she could announce to the world, "I'm going to the Hop with Norbett."

Rosellen's head was tilted not down, but up, as she studied Beany's face. Like Andy, Rosellen, for all her gay chatter, was quick to grasp things. "So you've got another date for the Hop?"

"Well—yes," Beany stammered around the two bobby pins between her lips.

She knew what the next question would be—and it was. "Who are you going with? You got a new beau?"

She knew, too, that she would find herself evading. And oh, how sick Beany was of evasions, of saying, as she did now to Rosellen, "I—well, I can't tell you—not yet, because of a promise. . . . I'll scoot up and get some towels to wrap around your shoulders while I daub this gooey stuff over the curls."

Back in the kitchen, Beany emptied the bottle of milky, thick solution into a bowl; it did smell like burning inner tubes. Such a strong chemical might do something to her jewelry, so she slid Andy's watch off her left wrist, unclasped Norbett's tingly bracelet from her right.

She patted the dripping wad of cotton over each dark snail which clung tight to Rosellen's scalp. Beany had a question to ask, "Is Andy—mad at me—about Saturday night, Rosellen?"

Her answer came muffled through the towel Rosellen was holding over her forehead and eyes to catch the drip, "No—no, he isn't mad."

Beany daubed on. "There now. We have to wait fifteen minutes before proceeding with the next step, which is pouring on this goop that looks like water. . . . Does Andy ever get mad?"

Rosellen partly unsheathed her face, still patting at stray rivulets. "Does Andy ever get mad! Yeh—hoppin'.

But it's funny—he hardly ever gets mad over anything that happens to him. It's just when he thinks someone else isn't done right by."

An hour later when all beauty operations had been cleared away, when the new Mrs. Malone had joined them for cookies and tea, and Rosellen reached a hand to her head to say, "It's still wet, but I can tie a scarf around it," Andy called for her.

Beany answered the front door. Andy said as he stepped in, "Whew, what a fertilizer factory smell."

She stood, leaning in the doorway and plucked at his sleeve as he started through the hall toward the kitchen. "Andy, I guess—I guess you think I was pretty skunky not to let you know I was going to the Hop with—somebody else—"

His laugh was not pleasant. "You didn't have to let me know. I can figure out some things for myself. But you can keep on using old Andy and letting everyone think you're going with me, till such time as you're ready to spring the glad tidings that you're not. I'm always willing to oblige."

He started toward the kitchen, but again she detained him with a hand on his arm. "Andy, I'm sorry. It *was* skunky. I would have told you—and everybody—if I could have, only—"

"You're pretty crazy about this—someone else, aren't you?"

She only nodded, not trusting her shaky voice.

His eyes dropped to her bare wrists, and he asked, "Is this some more of the treatment, discarding the Andy Kern watch?"

192

"Oh, no! I took it off when I was sopping that smelly stuff on Rosellen's curls. But maybe—" she said hesitantly, "you'd rather I didn't wear it—maybe you'd like it back—"

"I'd like it where it belongs," he said brusquely, "which is on the left hand of Beany." He looked into her troubled face and said with a grave flick of smile, "I'm not the jealous possessive type—at least I work at not being that type. So you go on to the Hop, clobberhead. I feel better about it now that you've told me." And then he said a strange thing: "It wasn't your ditching me I minded so much—it was your being sneaky about the whole thing. That, from Beany, was hard to take."

The clatter of Rosellen's crutches in the hall interrupted.

15

BEANY went to school the next day feeling infinitely better. Now that Andy knew from her that she was dated for the Heart Hop, she could look him in the eye. Now she could count the days until Norbett's return without that one nibbling of guilt.

Ah, yes, as Jennifer said, life was looking up.

Beany sat at the sewing machine in third-hour sewing and stitched all around the edges of the pockets that were to be inserted in her denim shorts. Today, Wednesday, was just a day to get through. So was tomorrow. For Norbett would surely be back by tomorrow night.

He had left the Malone garage loft early last Sunday morning, to take back to Four Corners that important assayer's report. All he had to do was show it and lease the land. And Ivor Lungaarde said men were waiting and eager to grab it.

She had asked Johnny, "How long would it take—someone to drive back here from Four Corners?"

Johnny had thought a minute, computing miles and hours. "It'd be a good day's drive. But if you left down there bright and early in the morning, you ought to pull in here late in the evening."

Beany took her kidney-shaped pockets back to her sewing table. She was jittery with longing to see Norbett again. To pick up where they had left off when Johnny had so unceremoniously come in the front door, and so unceremoniously broken off their kiss before it started.

She sat on, daydreaming, as she turned and twisted a pocket and tried to figure out how to insert it in her shorts. Mrs. Hilb was out of the room.

Dulcie's formal was on a much slimmer version of Headless Hetty, and Dulcie was on one knee, pinning the lace medallions around the wide uneven border of black tulle on the skirt. Every scrap of time Dulcie could take from study hour, lunch period, and after school she had spent on that dress. She worked these days with a grim and weary resolution, paying no attention to what went on in the room about her.

Beany struggled on with her worrisome pocket. She was just planning to ask Dulcie how a slit pocket should be engineered into a pair of shorts when Jennifer Reed entered the room on light purposeful steps.

She came over to Beany's table and asked appealingly, "Do you suppose you could get excused a few minutes? I need help on being witty. Maybe if we put our heads together we could strike a spark—"

She broke off and her eyes went beyond Beany to the dress on the form. She froze in startled horror, as her eyes traveled over the lovely black lace bodice, the swirl of white skirt, the black medallions being pinned on it. Her eyes dropped to Dulcie, who was inching around it on her knees, with one hand under the transparent skirt, the other pinning on medallions.

Jennifer gasped out, "Whose—dress—is that?"

Dulcie got off her knees awkwardly, stood up and confronted the questioner. She took the pins out of her mouth to answer, "Whose do you suppose? Mine."

Jennifer's voice was harsh. "But I bought that dress— just yesterday afternoon. Mother went with me and we bought that very dress from Madame Simone—"

"Not this very dress, you didn't," Dulcie snapped. "I've been working like a slavey on it ever since I started sewing here."

Jennifer walked toward the dress and Dulcie. Her hands were clenched, and her voice shook in outrage. "You have no right to copy a dress that Simone insisted was one of a kind."

Dulcie gave her head and pony tail an insolent toss. "Who says I haven't?"

Every girl in the room had let fall her pinning and her basting. The three girls at machines stopped their stitching and turned in their chairs.

Beany stood up unhappily. "Jennifer, Dulcie didn't know you were going to buy that dress. She just decided to make one like it, because it was so—so unusual—and lovely—"

"To wear to the Heart Hop," one of the girls in the room put in with obvious malice toward Dulcie.

Jennifer and Dulcie were facing each other now, the dress in question between them. Jennifer rasped out, "You can't wear that to the Heart Hop. That's what I bought mine for—to wear to the dance first and then to the wedding reception when my brother is married. Do you think I'd wear my dress to the Hop, with you flouncing around in one exactly like it?"

Another girl spoke up, "She even cut a pattern off the bodice."

"Sure I did," Dulcie defied them all. "And I cut the pattern off this uneven piece of black that goes around the bottom. And I measured how far apart the black medallions were. And my dress isn't costing me any eighty-nine fifty, either. Only a sucker would pay that much. I don't care whether you wear yours to the Heart Hop or not. I'm wearing mine."

Again one of the girls interrupted, "Jennifer, why don't you tell Madame Simone that Dulcie copied one of her originals? I'll bet she'd make it hot for her."

Dulcie turned and looked about the room at all the girls who were sided with Jennifer against her. Beany couldn't help it—she felt again that defensive ache of sympathy for the blatant, blundering Dulcie. The one against the pack.

Jennifer Reed gritted out, "I'll take my dress back. I'll tell Simone about your copying it. I'll tell her I wouldn't have it if she gave it to me."

Perhaps it was the mention of Simone, and Dulcie's swift realization that her mother's job was at stake; or perhaps, like a cornered animal, she had to lash out in the only way she could think of. She hurled out at Jennifer, "You like to think of yourself as the one and only Jennifer in your one and only formal. Yes, and you even think you're the one and only with Jag Wilson. Well, just because you're wearing his pin doesn't mean that he isn't still hanging around the Robin to take me—"

"You scum!" Jennifer broke in, and stepped toward her, her open palm aimed at Dulcie's face—

Mrs. Hilb took that moment to walk into the room.

Jennifer's hand dropped shakily. All color was drained from her face. She looked around as though she, herself, was amazed at the lengths to which her fury had carried her. Without a word, she left the room.

Mrs. Hilb's cheery voice sounded strange in the tense atmosphere. "You girls don't look very busy," she scolded; and to Dulcie, "Have you got enough medallions to go around?"

Dulcie too lifted dazed eyes to the sewing teacher. "I don't know—yet," she finally muttered.

Beany asked if she could leave and go to the staff room for a few minutes.

At one side of the big room, Mrs. Brierly was holding her journalism class. On advertising, today. At the long work table, the staff photographer was trimming photographs, and the staff artist was cutting out some lettering on a linoleum block.

Jennifer's desk was in the back of the room. She was not working at it, but standing at the window. Beany walked up to her and stood for a minute beside her. Then she cleared her throat and said in a low voice, "Jennifer, I don't blame you for being mad about the dress. I wouldn't even blame you for taking it back to Simone and raising Cain—only—I wish you wouldn't. I mean, I wish you wouldn't tell Simone you're bringing it back because Dulcie's making one just like it—"

Jennifer's lips curled. "That's right. Dulcie's your protégée here, isn't she?"

Beany waited until a boy started reading a page on advertising rates. "It isn't that. But Dulcie's mother does alterations at the Hollywood. Simone—well, she's all honey-sweet to customers, but not to Mrs. Lungaarde. She'd be awfully nasty to her—she'd probably fire her."

Jennifer didn't answer, but stared out the window at the patches of snow on the flat roof of the gym. Beany floundered on, "You see, Dulcie's father is away from home a lot— What I mean is, Dulcie's mother needs her job. . ."

Jennifer said at last, in a low monotone, "No, there's no use making it tough for an innocent party. But I'd like to make it so tough for Dulcie that she'd never put foot in Harkness again. Dulcie! That's a joke. It means sweet and soft in Latin. She should have been named Brassy."

She turned away from the window and walked over to the dummy of the *Hark Ye* issue that would be proofread by Claude Metz and taken to the printer that afternoon. She began talking to the boy about the linoleum block.

Beany was dismissed.

Dulcie didn't join them in the lunchroom for the first-hour period. Beany ate a sandwich, scarcely knowing what filling was in it, and briefed Andy and Kay on the fracas in the sewing room. Andy only looked mystified; a male, Beany realized, couldn't appreciate the importance of an Original, or why one girl—especially a poised and self-contained girl like Jennifer Reed—should be ready to slap another girl for copying hers.

Andy only said, "I had a feeling all along, bright eyes, that you were courtin' trouble when you took up Dulcie."

Kay said, "Oh, Beany, I wish *you* weren't smack-dab in the middle of it. Do you suppose you could talk Dulcie into *not* wearing her black-and-white froth to the Hop?"

"That would solve everything," Beany mused.

She left the lunchroom and sought out Dulcie. She was sure she would find her in sewing, and she did. Dulcie was in the empty room, standing at her sewing table and cutting out more of those black medallions, which were inch-and-a-half-wide black roses. Dulcie looked drained and tired—and stubborn.

"Aren't you eating lunch?" Beany began. "I'll run down and get you a hamburger."

Dulcie only shook her head, and went on appraising odd-shaped scraps of lace, evidently leftovers from her bodice. "I haven't got time. Thanks, though. I have to work at the Robin this eve, so I can't stay after school. I miscounted those fool medallions, and now I have to figure out five more from these piddling scraps."

"Dulcie, why don't you take your time finishing your dress? You've got something else you could wear to the Hop, haven't you?" Dulcie's scissors went right on snipping out a slightly foreshortened lace rose. Beany pursued, "I talked to Jennifer and she said—well, she isn't going to raise a row at Simone's—"

"That's big of her," Dulcie commented.

"I think it was. I think you ought to wear something else."

For a few seconds Beany thought Dulcie was going to flare out in anger. Instead she said doggedly, "Ever since I heard of the Hop, I planned on wearing this dress so he'd see me in it—"

Beany's curiosity was too much for her. "Who, Dulcie?"

Dulcie looked at her, and her tired eyes grew rapt. "I'd tell you, Beany, because it's someone you know, only I thought it'd be fun to surprise you—all of you. But besides—oh, lordee—my having a date with him is so special, and he's so special—"

Her eyes lifted to the dress on the form and the space on the diaphanous skirt that called for five more black lace roses, and her lips gave a determined twitch. "So that's it, and your fine-feathered friend can go blow."

Classes were over at last. At their locker Beany and Kay tied scarves under chins, zipped up storm boots. Beany was just saying on a burdened sigh, "Let's call it a day," when they heard a shouted, "Hey, Beany, hold everything!"

It was Claude Metz, copyreader and deliverer of the *Hark Ye* to the printer. "I'm all snafu," he panted. "I just got word that the tryouts for the Forensic Contest are under way in the aud, and I've got to speak my piece or else. I guess you know what I'm leading up to, don't you?"

"I feel it coming on," Beany said. "You want me to take the dummy to the printer. But isn't there anyone else?"

"But I've got Mom's car," Kay put in. "We can drop it off."

"Wonderbar!" Claude said. "It has to be there by four-thirty, remember. And Beany, run your eagle eye over it for any mistakes I missed. I'll put out for a double coke for you two any day." He started off at a lope, turned back to add, "Hey, looks like you and I will be jaunting off together to the Convention at the Springs, huh?"

Beany's heart leaped up high and fluttery in her throat. "Why?" she asked around it. "Did Jennifer tell you I was to go?"

"No—no, I guess Jennifer hasn't been in any shape—what with down in the dumps, and up in the clouds—to make any formal announcement. But she's always calling you her man Friday and her stand-by. Oh, and my blessings for taking over for me."

As they walked down the hall, Kay said, "Beany, I don't think Jennifer will hold it against you—Dulcie's copying her dress, I mean. I just don't see how she couldn't *not* have you go with Claude to the Convention."

"She might," Beany said dubiously, remembering the chill in Jennifer's voice this morning when she said, "Dulcie's your protégée here, isn't she?"

The staff room was empty. On the long table, weighted down with a bottle of glue and the long scissors, lay the large-sized dummy of the paper. Beany sat down, pushed her scarf off her head, and pulled the paper to her. The rectangles and squares were filled with large X's which would be filled in with pictures. Beany

202

ran through them, checking to see that the number on the pictures coincided with the numbers in the squares. Here was the girl who had played Adeline in *Our Darling Daughter.* And the newly-elected basketball captain—

Never yet had Beany Malone's picture filled a square in *Hark Ye.* It seemed little enough to hope to see her picture for some accomplishment in the paper she drudged on.

She bent over the table, running her eyes over each write-up. She added a comma or two. Her own dialogue fantasy between an old-time Adeline and a Harknessite occupied two columns on the front page. Beany corrected her own misspelled "virtuous."

She opened the dummy wider to check the two inside pages. Under the masthead and the listing of the staff, was Jennifer Reed's column, "Between You and Me." How the school delighted in Jennifer's wisecracks and jibes. Beany's eyes skimmed over it, thinking idly as she did that it was less sparkling than usual. But then Jennifer had wanted help on it this morning, had admitted she was finding it hard to be witty.

This time her column was a glib punning on names and their fitness or unfitness to their owners . . . A Jack *Hornblower* had never been known to blow his horn . . . The coach hoped Al *Winfast* would live up to his name on the basketball team.

And then one name—Dulcie—seemed to leap out at Beany. Her pulses quickened as her eyes followed the next two lines— "And then we have Dulcie. Dulce in

Latin means sweet and soft. Hardly as fittin' for the girl with the pony tail as Brassy."

Beany breathed out, "Golly," and then "Oh, no!"

"What's the matter?" Kay asked.

"Look here."

Kay's blond head bent over Beany's, her eyes followed Beany's pointing finger. Kay, too, breathed out, "Golly—"

Beany sat, her finger on those two lines. By Friday noon the bundles of the Valentine edition of *Hark Ye* would be brought to this very room from the printer's. The *Hark Ye* salesmen (some of whom were girls) would have them distributed by two-thirty. The name Brassy would create a ripple of malicious amusement throughout the whole school. The name would stick, even as Jag Wilson's had. Beany could predict that from day after tomorrow, as of three-thirty, Dulcie Lungaarde would be Brassy Lungaarde.

It was too cruel, even though Dulcie had brought it on herself by her blundering, by her flaunting toss of pony tail. Jennifer had said, "I'd like to make it so tough for her, she'd never put foot in Harkness again." This could easily do it.

And suddenly Beany saw Dulcie's forlorn face that night at the Ragged Robin when the gusty snow had lashed at her. Beany remembered her thick voice when she choked out, "You're the first girl that ever offered to give me a hand." She remembered the warm-hearted, eager-to-please, wanting-to-give Dulcie in the Malone home that night.

204

Beany said in a thin voice, "I can't let that go to the printer's. I'm going to change it."

Kay repeated, as though her vocabulary were very limited, "Golly." And then, "Oh, Beany—you know how Jennifer is—she won't like it."

"I know."

She got up slowly and walked to the typewriter. Automatically she dropped her coat off her shoulders, slid in a piece of paper.

Kay only watched. They had been close friends for so long that she didn't need to put in words what lay behind her stricken eyes. She didn't need to say aloud, "You know, Beany, what it'll cost you if you change Jennifer's crack about Dulcie."

And Beany answered the unspoken words with a dry and tortured grunt, "At least I won't be in suspense any longer about going to the Quill and Scroll doings. I can go right ahead and wear that print blouse you gave me, and the new green skirt I was saving."

Her hands rested on the keys. Maybe if she were bright she could think of some other name to pun about. But she couldn't. A glance at the wrist watch Andy had given her showed that it was four-fifteen. There was no time to spare, trying to think up something. So she only copied the first line as per Jennifer's, "And then we have Dulcie. Dulce in Latin means sweet and soft." She changed the last line to read, "And so is the heart of the girl with the pony tail."

No, not bright at all, but it was the best Beany could manage. She reached for the scissors, cut out her typed words and glued them over Jennifer's.

She stood up and pulled on her coat and folded the dummy paper carefully; she fastened the photos and snapshots more firmly under their clips and walked to the door.

Kay followed silently.

But, at the door, Beany stood for a brief moment and looked back at the scuffed desks and tables. And at the blackboard, bare of any nudging reminder of deadline now. She was saying good-by. Not only good-by to all hope of jaunting to the Convention with Claude, but good-by to working on the *Hark Ye* staff under Jennifer Reed. Jennifer wouldn't make a scene—maybe she wouldn't even ask Beany Malone to resign as feature writer—but the gulf would be there.

"Let's go," Beany said, her stubborn jaw set and tight.

It was Kay who was blinking back the tears as she walked beside her down the hall.

16

THERE were times, Beany thought fondly, when Kay was very transparent. The next morning when she picked Beany up at the park entrance in the Maffley car and drove on toward school, Kay talked fast and with great enthusiasm about everything. As though, if she kept talking, she could divert Beany's mind from Jennifer's "Between You and Me" and the dire consequences of Beany's tampering with it.

"The red heart-shaped bids for the Hop will come from the printer's today. Our decorating committee decided to do the lettering on them ourselves so as to save money—"

Beany leaned over and turned on the radio to catch the eight-fifteen weather forecast. "Today and tomorrow will remain clear and sunny, slightly above freezing, little change in temperature. All roads are open and in good condition."

... Fine. Fine. No snow would prevent Norbett from burning up the road in getting back from Four Corners...

"I told Johnny any color corsage would go with my pale blue net. What kind is Andy getting you?"

Now it was Beany's turn to divert Kay's attention. Without answering that, she said hastily, "Johnny and Carlton Buell went to some campus meeting last night, and the darndest thing happened. Carlton came ambling into our house *alone* about ten-thirty—"

"Wasn't Johnny with him?"

"No. I heard a car stop, and it didn't sound like Johnny's. I went hurrying to the door because I thought—"

Beany stopped short. She couldn't tell Kay that she had gone running to the door with her heart thudding in her throat, thinking that Norbett had made it back sooner than he planned, sooner than Beany dared hope. She couldn't tell Kay how she had stared in disappointment at the blond boy next door and said, "Oh, it's you, Carl."

"How come Johnny wasn't with him?" Kay asked.

"That's what I asked Carl when he asked if Johnny was home. But it seems that Carlton had left the meeting early—he said he had something to do—"

"What?"

"He didn't say. He looked kind of sick, and I asked him if he was all right, and he said, 'Just a little punch-drunk.' "

"Is that all he said?"

208

"That's all he said for quite a while. He just sat there so sort of dazed, and I asked him if he wanted to practice the shag or samba for the Heart Hop—Johnny told us he was going—but Carl said no, he wasn't going to it. He said he had planned to, but something had changed his mind. It was the way he acted," Beany said slowly, "just sitting there, so jolted and shocked. And the way Red acted—you know how old Red always senses when anyone feels bad? He went over and put his head on Carlton's knee and whimpered so dolefully."

"Hmm," Kay mused. "What could have happened? Do you suppose it's more of his putting some girl on a pedestal, and her falling off?"

"Search me," Beany said puzzledly. "Carlton's not the talky kind . . . You going to stop by for Peggy Wood?"

Kay nodded. "She never gets off in time to make it on foot. I hear her father had to take some sort of a night-watchman job till he could land something better."

There was no sign of Peggy in front of the Wood's battered bungalow. Beany said, "I'll run in and get her."

Her knock was answered instantly by a boy of about twelve, who said in the sepulchral whisper used in a house where someone is sleeping, "Come on in. She's right there in the dining room."

Beany caught Peggy's eye and said in a whisper and with gestures, "Kay's outside."

Standing in the living room she could see, even feel, all the evidences of near poverty. The house wasn't as warm as a house should be on a cold February morning. Beany's practical homemaking eye saw the scuffed floors and the dingy curtains, so frayed they would never hold up through another washing. Shabby, faded wearing apparel was drying on a clotheshorse near a register.

From the dining table the girl younger than Peggy was gathering up cereal bowls. One of the smaller Woods was still eating. It was oatmeal, and he poured the last of the milk from a bottle over it, and asked, "Where's the sugar?" Beany heard his sister's whisper, "There isn't any. We won't have any till Mom gets paid Saturday."

Peggy herself was tumbling through the contents of a sideboard drawer. She turned her harried face to Beany to explain, "I'm hunting for mittens for Jackie. . . .Here, hon, you'll have to wear these, even if they aren't mates. I've got to hurry—"

She got her weathered green coat from the hall closet. She pulled out a wool scarf, hesitated, and then tossed it to the girl clearing the table. "Tessie, you wear this, so your ear won't ache again." And to Beany as they went out the door, "I won't need one in the car."

She was running a side comb through her limp disarray of hair as Beany opened the car door. No wonder poor Peggy always looked thrown together, a concerned Beany thought.

The three girls were threading their way through the crowded hall at Harkness when two boys of the *Hark Ye* staff pushed through to them to announce, "Hey, Beany and Peg, don't forget the coke and cookies in the staff room after classes tomorrow—the usual 'Thank God, the paper's out!' celebration."

Celebration? Beany felt a cold queasiness under her ribs. For Beany Malone, it would be not a celebration,

210

but the ax. She wondered with sick dread if Jennifer would wield the ax in private, or before all the staff.

One of the boys was saying, "We fellows will see to the cokes. I don't know which girl's turn it is to donate the cookies."

Peggy Wood said thinly, "It's mine."

"Well, bring a lot. You know that hungry horde."

As the boys moved on, Beany saw the blank dismay in Peggy's round face. Some twenty-one on the staff, not counting the sponsor, Mrs. Brierly. . . . "Where's the sugar?" the little Wood boy had asked. "We won't have any till Mom gets paid Saturday," his sister had answered.

The bell's ringing meant a hasty scattering. Beany caught Peggy's arm to say, "Look, Peggy, Johnny's been after me to make cookies, and I promised him I would tonight. I might just as well double the recipe."

Peggy lifted wretched eyes to Beany. "But it isn't your turn. You brought them for the last party. It's my turn."

"So what?" Beany discounted. "As long as I'm in the mess, a few extra doesn't matter. You've got more to do than I have—you forget it."

Peggy's grateful eyes said that she would not forget it.

The next afternoon Beany took out of her locker the shoe box of cookies. It isn't everyone, she thought grimly, who provides refreshments for her own execution. She slammed shut the locker door and started down the hall to the staff room.

She turned into its noisy hilarity. Some eighteen or nineteen of the staff were there. Sports reporters, society and club editors, circulation and business managers. Jennifer Reed, editor and writer of the column, "Between You and Me," was there. She was sitting in the back of the room, wearing her fur coat and with her stack of books on the desk in front of her.

Beany was greeted with noisy welcome. Someone extracted the cookies from under her arm. There was the clack of coke bottles, the little *pf-ff* as tops were pried off. Someone thrust a cold bottle in Beany's hand. Mrs. Brierly's admonition, "Don't leave any bottle caps on the floor," was scarcely heard.

Open copies of *Hark Ye* were much in evidence as staff members scanned them, chuckled over them. Peggy Wood was reading the plea for pencils for the Korean children, and she murmured, "Beany, you shouldn't have signed my name to it, when you had the work of writing it."

"It was easy enough. I just put on paper what I had said to the Scribblers'."

Beany stole a glance at Jennifer. She saw that Jennifer's issue of *Hark Ye* was folded between one of her books.

Beany made her way to the back of the room and stood beside her. "I don't know whether Claude told you or not, but I took the paper to the printer—"

Claude pushed up to them with a bottle of coke for Jennifer. "Yeh, our Beany saved me from a fate worse than death Wednesday." He tossed a cooky into his mouth, said as he chomped it, "Um-mm, and she can cook besides. Beany, let's elope."

212

Beany added distinctly so that Jennifer could hear her over the din, "And I proofread it for Claude, and made some—changes."

She braced herself for Jennifer's wrath. Jennifer didn't answer. She looked helplessly around the whole noisy room and said, "I promised Mother to be home early." She set down her bottle of coke, from which she had taken one sip, and hurried out the door.

Again Claude said in a low voice to Beany, "Make allowances for Jenny's not being herself. Same old heart trouble over the same guy because of the same third party."

Beany murmured, "I thought she and Jag had patched things up."

"The patch didn't hold. This is the way I heard the sad story. Jennifer phoned Jag at his fraternity house Wednesday night, and some undiplomatic drip told her Jag had gone to the Ragged Robin, which meant he would be very late getting in."

Beany had no comment. . . . Was there no end to Dulcie's trouble making?

She stayed only long enough to gulp down her drink, to somehow smile and answer the remarks aimed at her. Beany, the do-gooder, the uplifter of Harkness womanhood, they called her.

Kay was standing at their locker when Beany went for her wraps.

Kay, the unmechanical, who always had trouble twisting the dial to the combination of numbers known only to the two locker owners, bragged, "I worked and worked till I opened the door. I figured you'd be in no state to rassle with it. Well? What did she say?"

"Not a word."

"Not a *word?*" Kay echoed. She reached for Beany's coat and held it for her. "Maybe she hasn't read it yet."

"Maybe," Beany said in a lackluster voice. "Or maybe she's too much of a lady to make a scene in front of the others."

"She wasn't too much of a lady to reach out to slap Dulcie."

"She would have, too, if Mrs. Hilb hadn't walked in just then." Beany added between her teeth, "I wish she had clouted Dulcie a good one." She relayed to Kay what Claude had told her about the latest bust-up between Jennifer and Jag.

Kay shook her head, making clicking noises with her tongue all the way down the stairs.

Beany burst out, "I wish Jennifer had exploded. I even wish I had come right out and told her I changed what she said about Dulcie. At least, it would be over. Now, it'll be hanging over my head until Monday."

They pushed through the heavy door into the crisp outdoors.

"Don't think about it, Beany. Let's just go to the Heart Hop tomorrow night and have ourselves a fling—" Kay broke off to say exasperatedly, "Our committee is about to have the screaming meemies. Can you imagine it? The printer didn't get the programs for the Hop finished until today."

"You don't need them till tomorrow night." Beany climbed into the Maffley car. Somehow, programs for

214

the Heart Hop didn't seem worth a case of screaming meemies.

"Oh, but we've got all the finishing touches to put on them. It was my idea to frill paper lace around them to look like old-fashioned valentines, and we're doing the lettering ourselves to save expense. Adair offered to help me with it. So I thought of asking the committee over to your house tonight to work on them."

Beany didn't say instantly, Sure, all of you come over. . . . Norbett was sure to return this evening. She had looked for him all last evening while she baked that multitude of cookies. She had gone to the extra trouble of making filled cookies because he was partial to them. She had sat up until late—waiting. But tonight was Friday night. He *had* to come tonight. And she would like a little privacy—she didn't want the whole chattering decorating committee overrunning the house.

Kay, who took Malone hospitality for granted, didn't wait for Beany's invitation. She said, "Adair will have printing pens. Tell her I'll bring the white ink."

Beany spoke out of her own thoughts, "Kay, what's the cheapest thing we could buy at the Hollywood? I'd like to stop there—"

"To find out if Jennifer took her Original back?"

Beany nodded. Yet even though she was both anxious and curious to know what Jennifer had done about the moot formal, that still wasn't the real reason. Sometimes, when Madame Simone was busy with her best customers, Mrs. Lungaarde waited on the lesser trade. Beany was hoping that would be the case, and she could ask her very offhandedly, "Are you expecting your husband home over the weekend?" Or perhaps, "Have you heard from the folks at Four Corners?"

"A handkerchief," Kay said. "I noticed some there when I bought the stockings that time. Simone oughtn't to charge more than seventy-five for a fifty-cent handkerchief. You know, Beany, some day when we're feeling real pert and chipper, we just ought to go into the Hollywood and pretend we want a real snazzy formal—money no object—and try on everything she's got and—"

Beany carried on, "—and then with our noses in the air, tell old Simone, 'Sorry, these all seem so commonplace!' "

They knew they would never have the nerve to do it, but they planned on with gleeful malice, imagining themselves saying loftily, "We'll look in one of the French rooms downtown where there's more of a selection."

"But today," Beany said as they stopped on the Boulevard, "I'll buy a handkerchief."

The owner-manager of the House of Hollywood *was* busy. She was waiting on a slender, trimly-suited woman; and when Kay and Beany stopped in front of the handkerchief counter, Madame Simone called out, "Mrs. L, would you wait on these girls?" Her tone implied, they're scarcely worth my time.

She turned her lacquered smile and velvety voice back to her customer. "My dear, I'm happy to make the exchange. I really think this ice-blue brocade would be more appropriate for your daughter to wear to a wedding reception. It's less overwhelming—should we

216

say?—than the black lace and white tulle. You remember, Mrs. Reed, when your lovely daughter tried on the blue that day, we both said how it brought out her dark eyes and coloring?"

Kay nudged Beany, whispered, "Did you hear? Mrs. *Reed*. She's bringing the dress back for Jennifer."

The two girls were listening with such avid interest that when Mrs. Lungaarde approached them with a smile and asked what she could show them, Beany had to stammer blankly before she said, "Oh—oh, yes, a handkerchief."

Mrs. Christopher Reed was saying, "I really preferred the ice-blue on her myself, but Jennifer insisted. I don't know why she changed her mind so suddenly just day before yesterday."

. . . And she didn't know that the two girls at the handkerchief counter could have told her why. . . .

Madame Simone was telling her customer about a brocade bag which would be a perfect match for the ice-blue formal. They moved to the other side of the shop.

Mrs. Lungaarde said, "That dress is a little overwhelming, as Madame says. Of course, Dulcie can carry it off. She told me Jennifer was going to exchange it because she decided it wasn't her type."

. . . What a lot of things mothers don't know, Beany thought. But, at least, there had been no ugly scene, involving Mrs. Lungaarde in the exchange of dresses.

"These are all Madeira handkerchiefs from Portugal," Dulcie's mother was saying.

"I'll take this one."

And then when Mrs. Lungaarde was wrapping it, and Kay was edging toward the door, Beany asked, not at all offhandedly, "What about Mr. Lungaarde and Norbett? Do you know when they'll be back?"

"No, honey. I've learned to look for Mr. Lungaarde when I see him." She sighed. "I guess men get so wrapped up in business, they never think of sending word home."

The handkerchief cost a *dollar*, plus tax.

The big Malone dining table was a clutter of red heart-shaped dance programs, white tasseled cords, scissors, glue, and lacy paper doilies. A chattery assembly line, with some of the girls attaching the cords, some cutting the centers out of the paper doilies and frilling the edge around the programs; and lastly Kay and Adair lettering on the red construction paper in white ink, "Harkness High," and the date.

Beany wielded the glue brush, constantly glancing at her watch. Over the snip of scissors and talk of prom dresses, she listened for the chug of a car in the driveway or a step at the door.

Twice the leprechaun charm on her bracelet became entangled with the lacy paper ruffle she was gluing around a program and tore it. "Has that little man got it in for our Heart Hop?" one of the girls asked. "He does have an evil glint in his eye."

The telephone rang then, and Beany leaped to answer it. It could be Norbett, telling her that he was on his way back, and thus releasing her from her bond of secrecy. In the brief time it took her to traverse the distance between

218

dining room and the telephone in the hall, she visualized herself going back to the noisy room and announcing, "That was Norbett Rhodes. I'm going to the Heart Hop with him."

It was not Norbett. It was Sergeant Wally Thomas, asking for Mary Fred.

"She's not here, Wally. She and Lila—you know her friend Lila?—went out to the Student Union. There's to be a Valentine supper after the basketball game tomorrow, and they were to help set up tables for it."

"Has she got a date for it?"

"I—I think so," Beany imparted hesitantly. That seemed a little less harsh than to say, "She sure has. With the center on the basketball team."

Wally said dolefully, "You know she's mad at me, Beany."

Beany murmured an innocent, "Oh," as though she didn't know Mary Fred was—or why.

"Ask her to break her date and go with me," Wally pleaded. "Tell her it's my birthday, and I hate to spend a birthday all alone."

"I'll tell her," Beany promised.

She did tell her some ten minutes later when Mary Fred and Lila came in. Mary Fred threw back her head and laughed. "Wally's birthday, my eye! He had his birthday last June."

At last the Malone house was quiet. The committee had left with their two cartons of bids resembling old-fashioned valentines, all ready to present to each girl who walked through the door of the gym tomorrow night. All ready for the scribbling in of dance partners. All

219

ready for hanging on the wall afterward, or pasting in a scrapbook as memento of a happy evening.

A thought struck Beany. Norbett might have come. He might have been reluctant to come into a house full of company. He might have slipped off to the loft over the garage.

Beany went out the back door and climbed the rickety steps. The dead and stony chill of the room told her, even before she turned on the light, that no one was there. She stood, looking about the dismal clutter, and said aloud to Headless Hetty, "Oh, well, he'll be back late tonight sometime. He wouldn't miss going to the Hop with me."

And then, going down the steps, Beany forgot to step over the broken second step. Again her foot slid through it. The identical spot on her shin was scraped and bruised again. Just when it was completely healed. No best stockings were ruined this time, because she was wearing socks.

She thought, and then quickly banished the thought: The leprechaun with his green-eyed twinkle couldn't be an ill-omened charm, could he? He wasn't delighting in snarling up her life, was he?

220

17

IT WAS mid-afternoon the next day, which was Saturday and Valentine's Day, before Beany reached home. Her eyes scanned the driveway for a battered but rakish red car. There was none.

She had been so sure Norbett would be waiting. All during her taking of Eve Baxter's dictation, her driving to the *Call* office, and typing the copy, she had thought only of his coming.

And now no Norbett.

She entered the house and turned into the living room. Mary Fred, just returned from her riding classes, had pulled off her jodhpur boots to warm her cold feet. Johnny was sorting over mail. Adair came in, bearing pink roses in a pottery vase.

Beany asked, "Who are the roses from? Who for?"

Adair answered happily, "From my true love. And a telegram, saying he'll be home Monday—and happy Valentine's Day to us all."

Happy Valentine's Day!

Beany asked further, "Did I get a—any phone calls?"

"Not a one," Johnny said.

Beany said with thin humor, "Where is my public? Any mail?"

"Scads of mail," Mary Fred murmured.

There was. A sentimental valentine for each of them from Miss Opal in California. And from their sister Elizabeth and her small son, little Martie. Beany read in childish printing, "You are my valentine, Aunt Beany."

But not one scrawl from Norbett.

Mary Fred said, "Sit here on the couch on my feet, Beaver, and warm them—they're like petrified wood." She refolded the letter she was reading. "I ought to go up to my dude ranch." They all knew it was not *her* dude ranch, but rather the one where she had worked for two summers. "This is from the foreman, and he says the new owner is out for a brief visit. I ought to see about my job, before he hands it out to someone else."

Johnny, with his ever-ready enthusiasm, offered, "I can drive you up tomorrow. Let's the whole caboodle of us go, and make a day of it. It isn't far—"

"Eighty-seven miles," Mary Fred supplied.

"We're practically there," Johnny said.

222

Mary Fred reached over and picked up one of Beany's hands and scrutinized it. "I'll give you a manicure when I give myself one—provided you run up to the five and dime and get a bottle of polish remover. Let's see, you'll be wearing that washed-out pink creation to the Hop—a pinkish polish looks better with it than red."

Beany started to say, I'm not going to the Hop. But that would start all sorts of questions, and if there was anything she was weary of, it was questions and hedging answers. No, she would wait until the last minute and then—well, she didn't know what excuse she could reach for.

In the kitchen she ate a cheese sandwich which didn't seem to fill the hollow corners inside her. She started for the Boul.

She was just turning into the dime store when she heard her name called. It was Dulcie—her coat flying open, and her eyes shining. She clutched Beany's arm and said all in one breath, "Wait'll I show you what I got at Simone's—I wish you had your car, or I wish I'd see someone I knew to take me home, because I still have to press the miles of tulle in my dress—look!"

From a green sack and tissue wrapping, she rustled out a circlet of white flat flowers. "This is the bracelet." She clasped it around her wrist in demonstration, and drew still another, slightly larger, from the bag. "And this I'm going to wear around my pony tail to dress it up for evening."

Your hair doesn't need dressing up, Beany thought, but she said perfunctorily, "It's pretty," and felt suddenly desolate and left out.

"Simone's got these sets in a lot of different colors. You'd look good in one of these hair dodads on top of your braids. What color dress are you going to wear?"

Beany strove to keep her voice casual. "Oh, I'm not going."

"You're not going to the Heart Hop! Why?"

Why, indeed? Because she had fallen between two stools. Because Norbett, wanting to prove himself a smarter businessman than his uncle, had somehow been delayed at Four Corners. He might even have had an accident. . . . But none of this could Beany go into with the blithe and cocky Dulcie.

"Why, Andy has to be at the big premiere at the Pant tonight. Andy is the head usher, you know—and besides I hurt my ankle last night. Yes, Andy is to present the corsage to the star—"

She didn't lie. She didn't *say* she was going to the Pant with Andy. If Dulcie chose to think so. . .

But Dulcie was evidently thinking about catching a ride home. Carlton Buell had stopped his car in front of Downey's Drug. Dulcie only muttered, "Well, have fun," and ran toward it, the white flower bracelet still on her wrist, the circlet for her pony tail flapping in her hand.

On leaden feet, Beany turned into the store for polish remover. At least, she had saved face with Dulcie.

224

The rest of the day Beany managed to be evasive about her date for the Heart Hop. As Mary Fred applied the pink coating to her nails, she said, "You'd better try on that bargain formal of mine, in case it needs a stitch or two, or a few safety pins. I'm what you might call a little more developed in certain spots—"

"It'll be all right. Touch up this thumbnail again."

And then came the moment when Beany must tell the family, "I'm not going to the Hop." It came after dinner, when Mary Fred was looking on the mantel, the sink's drainboard, and the telephone stand in the hall and asking, "Has anyone seen my jangly copper earrings? I want to look glamorous for my All-American tonight."

The moment was precipitated by the front door opening on a swirl of cold wind and Kay Maffley, struggling with a huge suit box, an evening wrap, and silver sandals looped over her wrist, and saying, "Mother was going to a concert, so she dropped me off here because I thought it'd be fun for Beany and me to dress together."

Johnny was coming down the stairs. Mary Fred was at the closet, still searching for her earrings in coat pockets.

Beany announced, "I'm not going to the Hop."

She saw the *Why?* on every face. Kay spoke first, "You aren't! Didn't Andy ask you?"

"Andy had to be at the premiere—" She went into lengthy detail about that, remembering that Andy had said, "I'm always glad to oblige." She added lamely, "Besides, I hurt my ankle last night, and dancing might make it worse."

Mary Fred said peremptorily, "Let's see that ankle." She dropped to the floor, pushed aside Beany's sock, and examined it. "Tut, tut! Nothing a couple of Bandaids won't fix up," was Mary Fred's verdict. "Nothing to miss a hop for."

Johnny said, "Well, if you think we're all going off and leave you here to wither upon the vine—"

"I won't wither," she discounted, but she did feel not only withered, but discarded. "Come on, Kay, and I'll help you dress."

She was just zipping Kay's "stardust ballerina" of pale blue net when Carlton Buell yelled up the stairs, "Hey, Beany!"

Before she was halfway down the stairs, he had asked her, "How's about going to the hop with me tonight?"

As though she didn't know that Johnny had hastened through the dividing hedge between the Buells and the Malones and told him that Beany was stranded without a date. She started to say, "Now, Carl, you don't have to—" when he said, "You've pinch-hit for me so many times when I was stuck without a gal, that I thought maybe you would again."

Now that was a nice way to put it. Blessed old dependable Carlton. "You sure you want to go, Carl?"

226

"With you—yes. You go on and scrub behind your ears, and I'll tear home and do likewise."

Even if she hadn't wanted to go, she would have been pushed into it. Adair said, "I'll fix two of these pink roses and some greenery into a corsage for you." And Mary Fred thrust her dress at her, saying, "Here's my emaciated pink. Start climbing into it, while I hunt for the sandals."

With Adair and Mary Fred helping, with Beany and Kay in bouffant dresses, Beany's small room became too crowded. They all moved down to the dining room and the full-length mirror. The strapless bodice of Mary Fred's dress was plain; the skirt was almost solidly covered with rows of narrow white lace. The dress *was* a mite large for Beany. She tightened the self-covered belt.

Mary Fred said critically, "I might know there was some reason for getting a thirty-dollar dress for fourteen ninety-five. It's too blah. It does nothing for the wearer."

"Even the pink roses don't help," Adair worried. "It needs a note of contrast."

Carlton Buell appeared in his dark suit, a very white shirt, and black bow tie. He must have been teaching a class in swimming at his neighborhood house all afternoon, for his hair looked even more bleached. "Look at him," Johnny said. "All it takes is a black suit to make him look like a pallbearer or horse trader."

The attention of the female contingent was still on Beany in Mary Fred's pink formal. Their attention now turned to the bodice, which should cling a shade more snugly. Adair and Mary Fred agreed that a brooch on a chain would solve both the problem of holding the bodice snug and adding the note of contrast.

Adair brought down a piece of her own heavy gold jewelry. No, that wasn't right. She tried a cameo with a necklace of small pearls. No, not that.

Carlton said, "Hold everything," and ducked out the door.

He reappeared shortly with his mother, who carried an old and sizable jewelry box. "These were Carlton's grandmother's," she explained. She studied the pale dress, noted Beany's hand unconsciously tugging the bodice to a higher and tighter line in front. She sorted through the box and said, "Let's try this."

It was a brooch with a large amethyst set in antique gold, and surrounded by opals; the chain was of small amethysts. Brooch and chain held the bodice in place, and added just the right dark and purplish touch. It even dimmed the handful of freckles across Beany's nose.

Mary Fred beamed. "It gives you the demure Victorian look."

"It makes your eyes look lavender," Carlton contributed.

Bless families, Beany thought with a lump in her throat. Here was Adair, hurrying down the stairs with her own short blond fur cape and throwing it over Beany's shoulders. Here was Mrs. Buell saying,

"Carlton's father said for him to take our big car, so the girls' dresses wouldn't be mussed." Here was Mary Fred saying, "Yipes, my specimen of hardy manhood is almost due, and I'm not ready yet. But you look fabulous, pet."

"Fancy us, driving to the ball in state in the judge's car," Johnny said.

Beany couldn't let on to any of them that this last-minute going with Johnny's best friend—who was, after all, just the boy next door—was a far cry from the exciting, heart-filling evening she had looked forward to. . . . What could have held up Norbett? One read of dynamite explosions or cave-ins among uranium seekers. She wished she could confide her uneasiness to someone. Would she dare ask the secretive Dulcie if she had heard from her father—or Norbett?

Their foursome was late in arriving at the Harkness gym. The Hop was well under way. Kay and Beany were given the familiar, heart-shaped, beruffled bids at the door. They stood inside it, watching the milling dancers while Johnny and Carlton checked their armfuls of wraps in the physical ed office. The boys returned, pinning red carnations on their coat lapels.

"You'd never know the old gym," Johnny praised Kay, glancing at the false ceiling of red and white crepe paper. From it dangled satin ribbons with clusters of artificial flowers, courtesy of a downtown department store.

Kay commented anxiously, "I hope the wishing well looks like a real old-fashioned one."

"Let's dance," Johnny said. "We'll meet you at the well afterward."

Kay's parting remark to Beany was a murmured, "I'm just busting to see Dulcie—and see *what* college man is her date."

As Beany danced with Carlton, her eyes kept sifting through the dancers to see a girl in black lace bodice and a white, very diaphanous skirt. She kept watching, too, for Jennifer. Probably Jennifer would be wearing the ice-blue brocade—which was not *overwhelming*.

She didn't see Jennifer. Once she thought she caught a glimpse of a swirling black-touched skirt, but it was speedily lost from view among the other dancers.

The dance ended. Beany and Carlton gravitated toward the center of the floor. Beany explained, "The wishing well was Kay's idea. She was in despair over finding one of those old wooden tubs, when Dulcie came up with one. It does look real with all the rocks and moss around it, doesn't it? They blued the water with crepe paper. Oh, look, it's already full of flowers that girls have tossed in. Should we throw in a rose and make a wish?"

"The wish nearest your heart?" Carlton asked with his nice tilted grin. "What would yours be, Beany?"

"You're not supposed to tell," she evaded.

And I'm not supposed to be thinking about Norbett when I'm with you. But I'm worried about him. . . .

230

She was feeling for the pin under her pink roses when, glancing up, she saw the dress that had been the bone of contention between its maker and the editor of *Hark Ye*. She saw the burnt-sugar pony tail encircled with white flowers. Beany's curious eyes went beyond the girl to her escort.

In the pit of Beany's stomach, a clammy fish seemed to leap and flop over.

Dulcie's tall escort was a few steps behind her. He was half turned, dislodging from his shoulder one of the red streamers which had evidently caught and pulled loose from the ceiling. He turned, and his dark eyes met Beany's staring, startled, blue ones. She saw the jolted impact in his as he stood, stupidly holding that piece of red ribbon.

And she could only stare on, noting irrelevantly that his new haircut had left a line on forehead and cheek, lighter than the sunburned mahogany of his face. His black bow tie was slightly askew. But then a bow tie never rode straight on Norbett Rhodes.

She couldn't move. Only her fingers kept scrabbling for the pin under her pink roses. Some girl, backing away from the well, said, "If you want to make a lot of wishes, just pull off a petal at a time."

Johnny and Kay were converging upon them at the focal point of the well, even as Dulcie and Norbett were.

Johnny bellowed out, "Why, Norbett Rhodes! Then they did get hold of you? And you flew out? Kay was just telling me your aunt has been trying to phone you long distance—"

The three couples had stopped still. Norbett took his eyes off Beany and looked blankly at Johnny. "What for?" he asked.

Kay answered for him. "She wanted to tell you about your uncle. He was operated on this morning. Your aunt Mae told Mother this afternoon that he was pretty low. They were trying to get a transfusion for him, but he has that rare type of blood—"

The music struck up, drowning out her words. Johnny gave her a guiding shove toward Norbett. "Go ahead and dance with him, and tell him about it."

Norbett, with that same blank look, held out his arms to her, and he and Kay danced off.

And still Beany stood. The very rhythm of the Benny Boden orchestra seemed to pound out, *Norbett brought Dulcie.* She couldn't bear to look at the girl in the black and white formal, left with her and Johnny and Carlton. Beany kept her eyes on two girls who had taken off their corsages and were trying to decide which flower to toss into the blue, blue water.

Johnny said loudly and amiably, "We can't let that music go to waste. Let's dance."

Dulcie took a hesitant step toward Carlton and asked, "Will you dance with me?"

"I'd better stick to Beany," he said affably.

And the next thing Beany knew, Carlton was guiding her into the melee of dancers.

Norbett brought Dulcie. The sax seemed to be shouting it at her. Her mind was too numbed to think it through—only that: *Norbett brought Dulcie.*

"Is this a samba or a rhumba?" Carlton asked.

"I don't know," she said dully.

Beany had taught Carlton to dance. Whenever she danced with him, she found herself unconsciously guiding him, and pushing him this way or that while she counted under her breath. But as they danced this— either samba or rhumba—she had no heart to do anything but follow. And she realized in vague, uncaring surprise that Carlton had become a good leader.

He smiled down at her as the dance ended. "What's this about your having a bum ankle? Does it feel O.K.? Say the word, and we'll sit out."

"It's O.K." But she didn't know whether it was or not. She didn't care. She glanced at the wrist watch Andy Kern had given her. Ten after ten. Another hour and a half of this—of waving to friends, of hearing them say, "New dress, Beany?" "Where'd you get the ancestral jewels?"

She was thankful for Carlton, the dark-suited bulwark beside her. She was thankful for his talking about his Boys' Club, thankful for his silences. They danced the next dance and the next, without going back to the meeting point of the well. Norbett would be dancing with Dulcie now, after his brief dance with Kay.

The charm bracelet tinkled as she danced. Other times when she had been mad or hurt at Norbett, she had known only one impulse—to unclasp it and hurl it at him. Once she had done just that, bouncing it on his chest. She could even smile wryly to herself at such a childish venting of wrath. But this—this was something else again. She couldn't feel the hurt and fury a jilted girl should feel. She felt only numb and frozen.

Johnny sought her out for the next dance. He was having a wonderful time. He broke off his humming to the music to ask, "Wonder what's the matter with Dulcie?"

"Is something the matter?"

"Didn't you notice? Her eyes look red, like she'd been crying."

"She probably got some mascara in them," Beany said without feeling. "Johnny, let's go get some punch."

"Yeh, let's. Wait'll I signal Kay and Carl to come along."

Beany stood beside Kay, sipping the punch. Red, to match the color scheme. She pretended to be enjoying it and to be having a gay time with everyone around her. She tried not to look at the dancers sifting past. She didn't see any pony tail bobbing close to a lean sunburned face under red hair, the exact shade of their Irish setter.

234

Kay, as though reading her thoughts, said, "I don't see them. I'll bet Norbett decided to go to the hospital and see how his uncle is getting along."

"I doubt it," Beany said. "He was never one to be concerned about anyone else."

She felt Kay's puzzled and commiserating eyes upon her. "Beany, I just can't figure it—Norbett's bobbing up when we all thought he was back in Ohio. And with Dulcie. He didn't even know about his uncle's operation until I told him. It doesn't add up."

"It adds up," Beany said with a chill smile. "Remind me sometime, and I'll tell you how it adds up."

Norbett brought Dulcie. Maybe they were sitting up in the semiprivacy of the balcony, preferring that to being jostled about on the crowded floor.

Beany longed for the moment when she could open the door of her own little room at home and crawl into bed in the dark. But some hard stubbornness inside kept her from even mentioning going home. She wouldn't let herself be routed by one Norbett Rhodes and his date. Kay had worked long, drudging hours to make this dance a memorable event. And Carlton Buell had asked Beany Malone in order to keep her from withering on the vine at home.

The orchestra struck up a lively and clear-cut tempo. She turned to Carlton. "There's your Mexican polka that you like."

"It's no dance for anyone with a skinned shin," he demurred.

"Let's dance it," she urged.

They were dancing it, amid the reckless swinging of feet, when some boy's heel banged Beany right on the sore and vulnerable spot of shin. For a minute her left foot gave way under her. Carlton said, "Gosh, Beany, I was afraid of that."

Even then Beany clamped her stubborn jaw and said, "What's a friendly kick on the shin?" and went on dancing—and smiling.

They stayed until the dance broke up. They drove to the Ragged Robin and blinked lights for service; and a girl who wore glasses, whose waistline was a good two inches wider than Dulcie Lungaarde's slim one, served them barbecued ribs.

But when they arrived at the Malone house and Carlton helped her out of the car, she couldn't help limping. Carlton said, "Johnny, you take Kay on home in Dad's car. I'm going to dose up Beany's ankle."

He went into the house with her, helped her up the stairs, and ran water into the tub. Adair, hearing it, came out of her room in her taffeta housecoat. Carlton said, "You have Beany soak her foot in that hot water while I run over home and get some salve. I used it to heal a lot of scuffed shins and knees on my playground last summer."

He reappeared with the ointment and bandages. He and Adair helped Beany to her room. She sat on the edge of her bed while Carlton, as casually as though she were one of his kids on the playground, knelt beside her and dressed the ankle.

"That ought to do it," he said as he got to his feet. "It won't hurt to walk on it. Just take it easy."

"I'll be good as new in the morning. Thanks for taking me to the ball, Carl."

"The pleasure was all mine," he returned gallantly.

18

IT TROUBLED the big red setter the next morning when Beany made no response to his nudging. Beany lay in bed, a weary lump of lethargy, conscious of all the hubbub of the family's getting ready for nine-thirty Mass. She heard Adair say, "Sh-h, let Beany sleep and rest her ankle. She looked so done-in last night."

She lay there, hypocritically pretending to be asleep, when Johnny opened her door and tiptoed in and caught Red and pulled him out, scolding, "Don't be pestering our Beany, fella."

It wasn't her ankle. Under Carlton's bandage, it felt only slightly sore when she stretched or twisted her foot. She felt only sodden and numb, and quite inadequate to face the family. There would be bound to be questions and explaining—and evading—about Norbett's sudden appearance. With Dulcie.

Beany wanted none of it.

In the long stretch of silence while the family was at church, she half dozed. The house took on an accelerated commotion on their return. Mary Fred and Johnny pushed into her room, bearing a buttered and syruped waffle and a cup of coffee.

Beany sat up and said with false heartiness, "Oh, for Pete's sake, I'm no invalid. My ankle's right as rain this morning."

"We're taking off to Mary Fred's dude ranch," Johnny said. "Kay's going along, and Carlton. Do you feel up to coming along?"

"The sun shines bright," Mary Fred added. "And we'll coddle you."

Beany shook her head.

"That nice old Carlton is taking us in his car because his tires are better than Johnny's," Mary Fred said. "Can I wear your warm mittens?"

"Sure."

Adair called from the foot of the stairs, "Carlton's here and ready to go."

Mary Fred hesitated by her sister's bed. "Little Beaver, you've got more bruises than a bruised shin, haven't you?"

. . . No, not bruises. Just a numbness and an emptiness. . . .

"You'd better go on, Mary Fred," she said.

Mary Fred bent and kissed her. "Johnny told me Norbett was at the Hop. I want the whole gory story when I get back tonight."

In the quiet house, Beany got up and dressed and carried her breakfast tray downstairs. I've had enough of being babied by the family and myself, she told herself.

Adair was sitting at the telephone in the back hall. She looked up at Beany and imparted grimly as she dialed, "I'm going to get that carpenter out here today to figure on those garage stairs if I have to drag him in by the hair of his head. Wait, Beany, and I'll drive you to church."

"Oh, Adair, my ankle's fine. I can walk those few blocks."

Walking down Barberry Street, Beany buttoned her coat against the air that seemed suddenly as moist as a damp breath. A gray flannel cloud was sliding across the sun. Red walked in dignity beside her, matching his step to her slow, leaden ones.

At St. Mary's, she sat, and stood, and knelt automatically when those around her did. Her eyes followed the priest on the altar. You'd think the ice inside of her would melt, and, she'd start to *feel*.

The priest turned from the altar and said in Latin, "Go, the Mass is ended." The congregation filed out. Even then Beany sat on. A few others lingered, too. Beany had always wondered why some always stayed. Did they long, even as she, to stay on in this dim haven, dreading to go back into the world?

240

She couldn't analyze her feeling of loss. And of betrayal. It was more than being stood up by a boy for the Heart Hop; it went deeper than that. The very roots of her faith in human beings had been torn out. The very pattern of her life—that of believing in the goodness of others—had been broken.

All the while she had helped and defended Dulcie, blatant and blundering though she was, Beany had believed in her loyalty. All the while she had kept Norbett's secret and defended him in her heart, she had believed in him. Deceitful, snide, the two of them. She wished she could be furious or hurt. That would be better than this state of shock she had been in ever since she looked up and saw Dulcie and Norbett together.

Unseeingly, she watched the altar boy snuff out the candles. She heard low voices in the choir, and the organist running her fingers over the keys. The tenor began to sing "Ave Maria." They must be practicing it for a wedding. Or maybe a funeral.

The familiar chords of the organ and the sweet untroubled tones of the tenor poured about her. The music, infinitely tender and compassionate, probed through her numbness. The hurt started—such unbearable hurt, that she thought huntedly, What'll I do? Oh, what'll I do?

Someone touched her shoulder, and a voice, thick with Irish brogue, said, "Sure and it's a foine thing for a girl to be dancin' the night through and then draggin' to the last Mass, and fair fallin' to sleep."

Her startled eyes lifted to Andy Kern's teasing ones. He looked closer at her wan, joyless face, and dropped down beside her. He caught up one of her limp hands and said in swift concern, "What's the matter, hon?"

She said, "Norbett took Dulcie to the Heart Hop," and then, totally without warning, began to sob.

He slid closer to her and waited until the singer took a high note and held it, before he said, "Tell your Uncle Dud about it."

He bent his head and listened while she gulped it out. Norbett's calling her from the airport, his vowing her to secrecy, his returning from Four Corners—

"And ducking out of the kitchen when we came home from the Pant that night," Andy filled in. "I sort of figured it that way, though I didn't know where he had dropped from."

The organ music and the song had broken off; there was more low-voiced discussion in the choir loft overhead. Beany went on, "I gave him the invitation to the Hop. He said—it'd be—like old times—to dance with me—again—" She fumbled in her pocket for a handkerchief. "I thought—he wanted—to go with—me—"

"I thought you wanted to go with him," Andy said. "That's why I put business before pleasure for a change and backed off the scene." The organ music rose; the singer started the song again. "Hey, let's get out of here," Andy said, "before I think I'm at my own wedding—or funeral."

He helped her from the pew, and they walked on out into the vestibule. The music made only a soft background here. "Who *did* you go to the Hop with?" he asked.

"Carlton—next door. Johnny went out and dragged him in, so I wouldn't have to stay home. And then—I saw them"—her voice broke again—"Norbett, and Dulcie, in her new dress—"

Andy gave a low whistle. "I'd call her what she ought to be called if I weren't in church."

Beany gave a dismal pretense of a laugh. "Jennifer said the name Brassy was more fitting than Dulcie. I changed it because I knew how it'd stick. I wish," she added with vicious weariness, "I'd left it alone."

"You mean you changed Jennifer's 'Between You and Me'? You do stick your head in the lion's mouth. What did she say about your bit of editing?"

"Nothing—yet. She will tomorrow. I've given up all hope of going to the Press Convention at the Springs," she added thinly.

"Beany, you're the stuff heroes are made out of," he commented. "I knew from the first that that gal Dulcie was a menace."

"I don't know why we're blaming her," Beany said, still under the impression that she could laugh. "After all,

Norbett *took* her. I'm even through*er* with Norbett than I am Dulcie."

The last lingerers were sifting out of the big room. Each opening let in a chilling white breath. And still Beany and Andy stood in a corner of the dim vestibule. The stout lady organist and the balding tenor came down the stairs. There was the delaying flutter of his adjusting ear muffs, and of her stooping over to rezip an overshoe. She smiled at Beany and Andy. "Oh, I do hope it's nice for the wedding tomorrow."

So that's what the "Ave Maria" was for.

Andy said, "No, Beany, don't be through with Norbett. Only I wish you were through letting him hurt you. You bruise too easily. Norbett needs someone like you for a ballast. I know him—remember, I used to be a bus boy at the Park Gate? I liked the guy—I felt sorry for him. His uncle's a well-meaning fellow, but his aunt's a cold old ewe, if I ever saw one—"

Beany put in, "Mary Fred always calls Norbett 'old show-off Norbett,' and 'cape-and-sword Norbett.'"

"Yeh, he's a show-off, but it's because he never felt wanted. He has to act cocky, because he isn't sure of himself. He's always been made to feel like a poor relation."

Beany didn't want to remember back to Norbett's lashing out at her, telling her she didn't know what it was like to be a poor relation. But Norbett's outbursts were so unpredictable—

244

She broke out wistfully, "Andy, if you wanted me to— I mean, we could go steady. We always have fun—*you* never hurt me. *You* always keep everything light."

Why, I'm throwing myself at Andy, she thought. But she wasn't ashamed. For suddenly she longed only for the unruffling, the warm and gay intimacy that would be hers as Andy's girl.

He stood, cradling her shaky hands that were wet with her tears. "Yeh, I play it light, because I don't want any going steady and getting involved. You'd be my pick if I did. But not now. Because I'm enlisting in the Marines soon as school is out."

"Andy, not really?"

"Yep. It's been gnawing at me. I don't know whether it's the call of duty, or whether I want to get those years behind me. Beany," he said soberly, "I don't think going steady is the way to work things out—not for kids in high school. Not for someone like you or me. Not for anyone, until they can start thinking about who's going to sing 'Ave Maria' at their wedding. See what I mean, turnip?"

"Yes," she murmured. He was saying it differently, but he meant what Mary Fred did when she said, "It ought to be love—the real thing. . ."

"None of us know," Andy was saying, "how we're going to grow and change—used to be I could eat a dozen candy bars a day, and now I hate the fool things.

245

What I mean is, we're still fumbling along, sort of getting measuring sticks. Listen to old Andy, the philosopher! But everything we do, everyone we come in contact with, changes us. Take you, knucks. Before I knew you I always fell for the dolls, the pulse-beats. I never will again. I suppose I'll always be looking for something of Beany in any girl."

And that, too, was saying what Mary Fred said, Beany realized vaguely: That you become a series of different you's, as you go through life.

Andy was suddenly the blithe, keep-it-light Andy. "I'll walk you home, if you'll ask me in for a cup of coffee. I was just starting out when I saw Red holding down the step, and I checked to see which Malone was going to get locked in church."

He shoved open one of the heavy double doors. Beany noted in surprise that a fine, tinsely sleet had coated Red's dark fur and the church steps. She explained her limp as they went down the steps, "My sore ankle got whacked at the dance last night."

His grip tightened on her arm. "In other words, last night just wasn't your night. Lean on me, grandmaw."

They turned in the Malone gateway, and Mike greeted them with his usual tempestuous onslaught. Andy fended him away from Beany's ankle. As they walked toward the porch, Beany saw that Adair was again standing at the foot of the garage steps with the ruddy-faced man.

"Who's the gentleman caller?" Andy asked.

"That's Adair's now-you-see-him, now-you-don't carpenter," Beany answered with little interest. "Dad teases her about trying to pin him down. She'd like nothing better than to have those garage steps in before Dad gets home tomorrow."

It did look as though Adair might be coming closer to getting her way, for the carpenter was measuring the width of the steps with his slide rule.

Beany and Andy went in the front door. The quiet emptiness of the house struck her, before she remembered that Mary Fred and Johnny had gone with Carlton and Kay to the dude ranch. Andy pulled out a chair for Beany in the Malone dining room. "You sit here in state, m'love, and I'll rustle you a cup of tea, coffee, or milk—or what would Miss Malone prefer?"

"There'll be coffee," Beany said gratefully. "Johnny always makes enough for a threshing crew."

She shivered as she slid off her coat, turned so she couldn't see the image of her eyes in the mirror. What a drab day—what a drab world. She heard voices in the kitchen, and when Andy appeared with two cups of coffee, he imparted, "Adair's got her carpenter at the kitchen table, figuring how many two-by-scantlings he'll need for the job."

Andy made conversation. He told Beany that Rosellen had enjoined him to tell her that Charles of the

Ritz couldn't have done better for her hair than had Beany Malone.

"It didn't smell like burned rubber?" Beany asked.

"It smelled like violets in spring. You were nice to give the kid a hand—two of them."

"It was fun," Beany said.

She held her coffee cup poised at the sound of the front door's opening. Someone called, "Beany, are you home?" and she answered, "Yes, here in the dining room."

The someone came through the living room and stopped in the doorway of the dining room in awkward unsureness. The two at the table looked up in amazement at Dulcie Lungaarde.

19

FINE sleet frosted Dulcie's burnt-sugar hair as she stood irresolutely in the doorway between the rooms. As usual, her coat was flying open when it should have been buttoned. She looked wetly bedraggled—and chastened and fearful.

Andy swiftly got to his feet, more in belligerence than in courtesy. "What do you want?" he demanded.

"I want to talk to Beany," she said, breathless and driven. "I walked in from our house because I had to—"

"Because you had to gloat over her, I suppose. And when you get through here, you might walk on to Jennifer Reed's and do some more gloating. That's your dish," he said with savage sarcasm.

. . . Rosellen had said, "Yes, Andy gets hoppin' mad, but hardly ever for anything that happens to *him.*"

Beany said, "Come on in." She had to remind herself, Now don't start feeling sorry for her.

Dulcie didn't move. She seemed to wince as Andy's lashing voice went on, "In case you think Beany's stock increased at Harkness by sponsoring you, think again. You've done nothing but keep her in hot water ever since you started. She's lost out with Jennifer Reed—"

Beany kicked him under the table. No use going into that Dulcie-Brassy routine, she thought drearily.

Andy did swerve from that topic, but went on, "And then as a nice big 'thank you' to Beany, you take her date for the Heart Hop. Heart Hop," he sneered. "A lot you cared about turning it into a heartbroken hop for anyone else. Just so you got to go to it and show off your dress. Do you know where Jennifer Reed was last night? She came to the Pant alone and sat in one of the back seats and cried. Because you did such a good job of messing things up with her and Jag. And now you have the nerve to come here for a nice little talk with Beany. About what a lovely time you had with Norbett, no doubt?"

"No," Dulcie cried out thickly. "I didn't come for that. I had to tell Beany what—what really happened—"

"Sh-h-h," Beany cautioned, squirming uncomfortably. She wanted to say, Don't yell so, you two. For she was remembering that Adair and the carpenter were in the kitchen—out of sight, but not out of hearing. Andy, in his anger, had forgotten. And Dulcie, coming in the front door and through the living room, had no way of knowing anyone else was within earshot.

250

Beany's hushing went unnoticed. Dulcie went on desperately, "Norbett and Dad were forever getting back from Four Corners, but then Dad always is. They didn't come till Saturday afternoon, and I was crying because my date for the Hop fell through. And—well, I asked Norbett to take me."

The tight clamp around Beany's heart miraculously loosened. This was different. Then she hadn't been *exactly* betrayed by the two people she trusted. Life wasn't *completely* a broken pattern. . . .

Andy's voice was cold and distinct. "I could have told you that. I could have told you that Jag Wilson doesn't take his late dates to school proms."

"I didn't expect Jag to take me," Dulcie flung back. "It was someone else. And I wouldn't have wanted to go to the darned old Hop either, except that I told everybody I was going to it in the dress I made. And I thought if I just went for a little while—"

"Oh, sure, sure," Andy mocked. "What was a little thing like Beany's being left high and dry compared to your showing off?"

"She said she wasn't going," Dulcie defended herself.

Beany laid a restraining hand on Andy. "I did tell her that. I let her think I was going to the premiere at the Pant with you. I did it to save face."

Andy grumbled, "You'd have been welcome to come."

But his anger was not abated. He had more to say to Dulcie. "All right, all right, but let me tell you something. You're not going to get very far with all your snuggling up to every fellow that stops at the Robin. This won't be the first time some one of your numerous dates wriggles out of taking you to a school dance. And what do you think these fellows toss around about the cozy blond they're late-dating?"

Unexpectedly, Adair appeared in the doorway between the dining room and kitchen. She said reprovingly in a clear carrying voice, "Andy, hush. You're not being fair to Dulcie. She hasn't had it as easy or as normal as other girls. She's never lived long enough in one place to build up friendships, nor had the kind of a home she could invite a boy to. She told me that the first night she came here. Imagine living in seventeen different places in seventeen years! I can't imagine what her father is thinking of—"

"That's all right, Adair," Dulcie defended. "He keeps thinking he's going to hit it big—and then we can have a swell house, and I can have a car—"

Adair's eyes flashed. "It would mean more to you to have a home *now* where you could put down roots. I could cry whenever I think of your mother, wanting to stay in one place long enough to have ivy growing over the front of the house." And to Andy, "What else can Dulcie have but late dates, as you call them, when she has to work till ten or eleven at the Robin? How else could she get home?"

Andy muttered sheepishly, "Yeh, I guess you got something there." He reached for the leather coat he had thrown over the back of a chair. "Guess I shouldn't have blown my stack. I better be ankling on, so's to get to the Pant for the Sunday matinee. Be seeing you at school tomorrow, Beany."

Adair stood on in the doorway as the front door closed behind Andy. Almost simultaneously, the back door opened and closed, which meant that Adair's carpenter had left. What must the poor man think of this tearful tongue-lashing scene he couldn't help overhearing?

Adair brought in two cups of coffee. "Here, Dulcie, sit down and drink this." Dulcie sat at the table wordlessly. Adair added, "I need one, too." Beany noticed that her stepmother's hands were unsteady as she pushed the creamer toward Dulcie.

An awkward silence fell. Beany glanced at the windows, half-coated with wind-driven sleet. "This came up all of a sudden while I was in church."

Adair put down her cup. "I wonder about our young folks. I'll turn on TV, and see what they say about road conditions."

She left the two girls at the dining table.

A dejected Dulcie turned her coffee cup around and around in her saucer. She said at last in a frayed voice, "It was a heartbroken hop for me, all right. Seeing another girl there with the boy I wanted to be with."

"What girl?" Beany asked wonderingly.

"You."

"Me?" Beany gasped. "But I was with Carlton." No answer from Dulcie. Beany breathed out, "Gosh, was it Carlton you planned to go to the Hop with?"

But even as she asked it, stray bits of evidence fell into place. From that first afternoon when Beany had driven Carlton's car to the Robin, and Dulcie had come hurrying up with a beaming smile on her face. . . Dulcie's telling her mother, "Don't worry about Jag Wilson. There's someone else my heart goes pitty-pat over." . . . A college man, and a Harkness graduate. And Carlton himself? He had told Beany she would pay through the nose for the use of his car by teaching him the shag. "Oh, have you got yourself a girl?" she had asked. Carlton's flush had answered for him.

Dulcie said with a flare of pride, "He liked me. At first he always came to the Robin with Johnny. And then he started coming by himself. You know how bashful he is—but one day when I was waiting on him, we got to talking about the Heart Hop, and he said he wasn't a good dancer, and I said I didn't care about that. And there were a lot of people around, yelling at me for extras on their orders, and he said, 'We'll have to get together on all the details.'"

"Didn't he?" Beany asked. "Why? Because Carlton isn't the kind ever to stand a girl up."

Dulcie stared down at the dark liquid in her cup. She said dismally, without looking at Beany, "He came out Wednesday night to fix up the details. And he saw me more-thanning with Jag Wilson."

"Oh, no!"

Dulcie went on in that same hopeless voice, "It was the night after Jennifer and I had that fight in sewing, and I was so furious at her—she called me 'scum.' Jag came to the Robin that night, and I asked him to take me home. We parked in front of our house. Maybe you don't know it, Beany, but girls more-than-it for other reasons besides being crazy about a fellow. I had some sort of idea that I was getting even with Jennifer when I led him on that night. A girl can always lead a fellow on. And while we were in a clinch, a car went by. I just thought it was someone I didn't know—"

"It was Carlton," Beany filled in. "When he came in Wednesday night, he said he left the campus meeting early because he had some place to go. I'll bet he stopped at the Robin to take you home. And when you were already gone, he drove out to your house to talk about your date for the Hop."

"I've gone with so many boys," Dulcie mused sickly. "I've even thought I was wild about a few—and then I met Carlton. No boy ever treated me the way he did. When he'd take me home, he'd walk me to the door and just squeeze my hand, like I was something precious. Oh, I know it sounds corny, but whenever I'd hear that, 'Some day my prince will come,' it seemed like it was written about me—and him—" The aftermath of a sob, like a huge hiccup, shook her.

Beany patted her shoulder, thinking, My goodness, I never thought of Carlton being anybody's prince. Shy, clumsy, crew-cut Carlton. She said aloud, "He's such an idealist."

"He never made late dates with me," Dulcie's thin voice went on. "So he never saw me in anything but that sappy uniform. I wanted him to see me in my black lace and white tulle formal. All the time I was sewing those pestery black medallions on, I didn't care how tired I got, because I was thinking of how I'd look—"

"When you saw him on the Boul yesterday," Beany asked, remembering Dulcie's sudden leave-taking of her when Carlton's car stopped at Downey's Drug, "what did he say?"

"I asked him what time he was coming for me that night, and he just looked at me and told me he had seen me in the car with Jag, so he thought I was going with him. That's the first I knew it was Carlton that passed us."

"Did he say he wouldn't take you?"

"No. I was the one that told him I had someone else to go with. How could I go with him when he treated me as—as though everything was over? He wasn't mad or mean—he took me home. And then—then he didn't even want to dance with me—"

Beany remembered. Carlton had answered Dulcie's, "Will you dance with me?" with a good-natured, "I'd better stick to Beany."

Another unhappy silence before Dulcie asked, "Beany, do you think he'll ever—even notice me again?"

She asked it in such driven honesty that Beany had to answer it honestly. "No—being Carlton—I'm afraid not." She told Dulcie about Carlton and the little brunette behind the fountain at Downey's. "He had the same jolted look on his face Wednesday night. Somehow, he has to put a girl on a pedestal."

Dulcie gave an acrid laugh. "It serves me right. I always thought I was getting away with something, piling up dates the cheap and easy way. It kind of hurt me because Mom never guessed I . . . . She always trusted me."

A pause while the TV blared loudly, and was then lowered. Adair was trying to catch a weather forecast.

"It served me right, too," Dulcie muttered, "that I had a lousy time at the dance. Norbett said he had a date with you—he wanted to take you. He wasn't even very polite to me. We only stayed for one more dance after he saw you and after he danced with Kay. He said I'd shown off my dress enough, he wanted to leave. He wanted to go to the hospital and see how his uncle was.

Anybody that wants Norbett, the old grump, can have him."

I don't know whether I want him or not, Beany thought. Not after his putting me through the jumps this last time. And then she remembered bleakly: I've thought that before; and then he comes on the scene, and there's old Beany Malone eating out of his hand again.

She asked on a sigh, "What about the big uranium deal? Did they lease the land for a lot of money?"

"I don't know. I'm so used to Dad's big talk of making a quarter of a million, and then Mom or me having to dig up for groceries." She got uncertainly to her feet. "That reminds me, I have to stop at that little creamery that stays open on Sunday—"

Adair interrupted by coming into the room. "I missed the weather forecast. Can't you stay, Dulcie?"

"No. Mom will be worried if I don't appear with the groceries. She has enough to worry her, putting up with that old phony of a Simone. I wish she didn't have to."

"Maybe she won't have to much longer," Adair said.

Beany said, "I'll see you at school tomorrow, Dulcie."

"Not me," Dulcie answered shortly. "I'm not going back. I'm no treat for anyone there, and it's no treat for me with Jennifer Reed hating my guts—not that I blame her."

"You go back to school," Adair said firmly. "Everybody makes mistakes, and you can't keep running away from them."

"Did you see the nice little squib about you in Jennifer's 'Between You and Me'? Didn't you read the Valentine issue of *Hark Ye?*" Beany asked.

"I was too busy sewing on my dress. I wouldn't have read it anyway, because it's Jennifer's paper."

"Here's mine," Beany said, getting it from the sideboard. "Here's where she mentioned you." Heaven knows, Beany thought, Dulcie might as well profit by that tampered-with allusion to her. The tamperer would be paying dear for it by this time tomorrow.

Dulcie read Jennifer's two lines about Dulcie and *dulce* without comment. Adair said, "Read Beany's on the front page."

"You gave me the idea for it, you know," Beany reminded her.

Dulcie read it through. She commented with a self-belittling chuckle, "Too bad Dulcie didn't give herself some of those ideas on how far a nice young lady should go."

Adair interrupted again as Dulcie turned to leave. "Wait just a minute. I'll take you home. But I want to show you a length of tweed a friend of mine sent me from England. Wait, till I get it."

She ran upstairs, and returned with the folded yardage of heavy tweed with green and gray flecks in it. Adair said, "Beany, I ran some water into the tub and shook some Epsom salts in it. You'd better soak your foot again. See, Dulcie, I wanted to ask you about this. You're so good at sewing and designing." She was shaking the folds out of the material.

Dulcie's dressmaking instinct lighted her eyes. "Oh, it's beautiful! Gee, there's a lot—"

Beany left them. She was sitting on the edge of the bathtub when she heard them go out the door.

What a changeable day it was! As Beany dried her foot and thought, Why, I have to look twice to see whether the ankle is swollen or not, the *snick* of sleet on the window ceased. A half-hearted sun tried to slant through the rivulets on the window and catch the crystal stopper on Adair's perfume bottle.

Beany had to run down the stairs with one shoe off and one on to answer the ringing telephone. It was Mrs. Buell, Carlton's mother.

The Buells had caught the newscast on TV that told of dangerous sleet-covered roads in the mountains and the large number of accidents. Carlton's alarmed parents had been trying for the past hour to get a call through to the Willow Creek dude ranch to see if their young folks had arrived safely. They had just succeeded.

"The Judge talked to Carlton, and he admitted they'd had a bad time getting there," Mrs. Buell said. "So we told them all not to think of coming back this evening, but to stay overnight."

260

"Yes, that'll be better," Beany agreed.

"I knew you folks were just frantic with worry, too," Mrs. Buell ended. "I knew you'd be so relieved to get the news."

Beany was replacing the receiver when Adair came in the front door, saying, "Oh, Beany, the streets are like glass. Let's call Mary Fred's dude ranch and find out if—"

"They're all right," Beany told her. "The Judge telephoned them. He told them to stay over and come back tomorrow."

Adair leaned weakly against the newel post. "Thank Heaven. I've been imagining the most horrible things ever since it started to sleet. I always seem to worry harder about you kids when Martie isn't home."

Beany thought guiltily, Everyone else was worried sick about the four in Carlton's car—everyone but me. I was so wrapped up in my own woes that I never gave them a thought.

It's always like this when I'm upset about Norbett Rhodes. I don't seem to have room in my heart for anything or anyone else.

261

20

BEANY was always to remember that next day, Monday, as a day of surprises.

One of them awakened her. It was the sound of old lumber being hammered and pried from its moorings. She heard the protesting screech of nails and the thump of boards as they fell to the frozen ground. Glancing out her window, she saw Adair's carpenter and a helper busily demolishing the old garage steps. A strong February sun was already routing the thin crust of ice on ground and roof tops. Already steam, like a chiffon veil, was lifting from the garage roof and their cement driveway.

"Well, well," Beany greeted her stepmother. "You certainly must have put the fear of God in your carpenter."

"I hope so," Adair said fervently. "In more ways than one, I hope so."

At school that morning, Beany stood at her locker and wished Kay were here with her instead of temporarily sleet-bound at the Willow Springs dude ranch. It might ease the queasiness under her ribs to say to Kay, Should I hunt up Jennifer and get the ax, and have it over with? Or wait till I see her sixth hour in journalism?

She didn't have to wait. Coming out of Assembly second hour, she saw Jennifer in the hall ahead of her, and she thought suddenly, Anything would be better than this waiting. She hurried after the slim girl in her dark sweater and tailored skirt. She even called to her, "Jennifer—wait!" just as Jennifer was turning into the library.

Jennifer greeted her with her usual serene smile. "Hello, Beany. I've been wishing I'd have a chance to talk to you."

Oh-oh! Here came the ax.

They sat down at one of the tables inside the library. Beany sat tensely on the edge of her chair. Jennifer said as she dropped her weighty books, "Goodness, I don't know why I'm always carting around a ton of books. Look how the left sleeve of my sweater always wears thin."

Preliminary small talk, Beany thought.

"Do you have to hurry on to your next class?" Jennifer asked.

"No—sewing. And Hilb is always nice about the ones of us on the *Hark Ye* staff if we don't show up."

There's the opening, Jennifer. Go ahead and tell me I won't be on the staff, as of now.

"Yes, Hilb is swell," Beany's editor murmured.

There was the low babel of voices around the circular counter as pupils returned books and checked them out.

One of the student librarians, a Japanese girl, brought over to their table a book on newswriting Jennifer had said she wanted. Jennifer thanked her; she began talking to Beany about the book.

A sudden gust of rage swept through Beany. Why didn't Jennifer speak her piece, instead of being so contained and chit-chatty?

Beany burst out, "I knew you'd be mad about my changing your column, but I had to. I was mad at her, too—I mean, I blamed her for a lot of things, but I didn't want everyone here at Harkness calling her Brassy—"

Jennifer's puzzled eyes rested on Beany's flushed face, "What are you talking about, Beany?"

"My gosh, didn't you read your column? Didn't you know I took out that Brassy part about Dulcie?"

Jennifer said slowly, "No, I didn't know—because I didn't read it. I couldn't bear to—I was ashamed of it. I was so furious at her, I couldn't help taking a vicious crack. And then—the paper no sooner went to the printer's than I realized how petty, how mean I'd been—"

"I thought you knew," Beany said in equal amazement.

"And you took out the Brassy part?" Jennifer began to laugh shakily. "I wish I'd known before—I've put in such miserable days." She dropped her elbows to the table and bent her head a little so that the fingers of her two hands loosely cupped her face. She spoke through her spread fingers, "Oh, Beany, I'm glad—so—glad—you changed it. I had no right to use my column to feed personal grudges. I always thought unhappiness made you a bigger person. It didn't me—it made me small and hateful."

Beany listened in limp relief. Jennifer wasn't mad. Beany Malone was not to be ousted from the *Hark Ye* staff.

"Then Saturday night," Jennifer went on, "when—well, when Jag and I patched things up once more, I was more ashamed of it than ever—"

"Saturday night? But I heard you went to the premiere at the Pant—alone."

Jennifer's hands dropped from her face. Her laugh was still shaky. "I didn't go *home* alone. I don't know how Jag knew I was there—he wouldn't tell me—but he came to the show and sat beside me, and took me home."

Beany stole a look at the navy-blue sweater. The off-again, on-again pin was anchored there.

"And so all is forgotten and forgiven," Jennifer said throatily. "I'm not too sure his roving eyes and that flashy Jaguar won't make trouble between us again; but I can't help liking him, and he—well, he always comes back."

This thought flashed through Beany's mind: yes, and even if Jennifer had seen Jag and Dulcie more-thanning when they were parked there on South Wyman she could still forgive Jag. It wasn't only because Carlton was an idealist that he couldn't forgive it in Dulcie. . . . Eve Baxter was right when she said, "Customs change, but human beings don't. Men always feel the need to look up to a woman. It's always been up to the girl to set the pace."

She roused to hear Jennifer saying, "Mrs. Brierly and I were talking about the Quill and Scroll Convention in the Springs that I won't be able to get to. Beany, would you like to go in my place?"

Beany opened her mouth to say, Oh, yes, I'd love to.

Surprisingly enough, the words didn't come. Surprisingly enough, now that it was put to her, her heart didn't leap with delight. She didn't know why. For a month now, she had ached to hear Jennifer say just those words, "Would you like to go in my place?"

Instead she found herself asking, "What about Peggy Wood? Wouldn't she like to go?"

"Yes. And Brierly thinks maybe she should, because she's a senior. But Brierly will leave it to me. And I think

266

you deserve it. You're the one who's always helping everyone out in a pinch—you ought to get some reward."

But I like doing it, Beany thought wonderingly. I must be goofy, but nothing makes me so happy as when someone turns to me for a favor. I got a kick out of writing that piece on Korean pencils for Peggy. It was fun, giving Rosellen a permanent that night. If you enjoy doing things, that's reward enough.

"Oh, Jennifer, let's have Peggy go. She's been having it so rough at home." Beany had an instant's picture of Peggy, hanging freezing clothes on a line; of Peggy's harried face as she tumbled through a drawer's contents to find two mittens for her small brother. "It'd give her a big lift."

"Well—" Jennifer hesitated.

"Only, Jennifer, do you suppose we could somehow give her a hand with clothes and things? You know how it is—her father was out of work so long, and there are so many kids—?"

She had been wrong to think Jennifer wouldn't understand about out-of-work fathers and hardships. Jennifer hitched her chair closer. Her eyes lighted. "Why couldn't the staff give her one of those cardigan and slip-on sets? It wouldn't be much, divided by eighteen or nineteen, and it'd be perfect for the daytime sessions—"

And I could have her come over some evening and give her a home permanent—"

Their eager plotting was interrupted by a girl who, in utter disregard of "Quiet!" signs all about her, was calling out, "Oh, there you are, Beany. I wanted to ask you if you'd rather have green—"

Dulcie Lungaarde was coming their way. She was wearing a chartreuse blouse and a skirt with flowers, big as cabbages, of the same shade. Beany thought with swift understanding, She'll never dress like all the other girls. It's part of Dulcie to like gaudy colors—overwhelming, as Madame Simone would say.

Dulcie stopped short and cast a frightened look at Beany's table mate. And then, as though girding herself for something she had made up her mind to do, she walked straight to Jennifer and said, "I'm sorry I copied your formal."

Beany held her breath as Jennifer looked up at the speaker. With wondrous relief, Beany saw Jennifer's faltering smile, heard her say, "I guess I needn't have—have got in such a tizzy over the whole thing."

Dulcie had one more remark—it, too, was evidently rehearsed. "I appreciated what you said about me in your column." And then the wooden Dulcie turned back to the real one. "That was sure swell of you after my being so skunky."

A slight wince passed over Jennifer's face. She opened her lips to answer, but Beany forestalled it by saying quickly, "We were just sitting here, talking about Peggy

Wood, and her going to the Quill and Scroll doings this coming week end. You know her, don't you, Dulcie?"

"Yes, she's in Design with me." She added bluntly, "What's Peggy going to wear? Cripes, I never saw anyone with such tacky clothes."

"We were talking about it," Beany said. "Don't tell anyone, but the staff is going to give her a sweater set as a sort of going-away present."

Dulcie's eyes sparkled with warm interest. "What else'll she need? Won't she need a formal?"

"Yes," Jennifer said, "For the big wind-up banquet, she will."

Dulcie offered instantly, "Why couldn't she take that one I made? I'll bet it'd be classier—"

She stopped in embarassment with a look of little-girl fright at Jennifer. Jennifer only laughed. "The fightin' formal? But Peggy's bigger than you, Dulcie."

"Shucks, I could let it out. It's got wide seams, and you know how stretchable lace is. She wouldn't even need to press it," Dulcie went on with growing enthusiasm, "if she folded it carefully and then hung it in the bathroom and let hot water run—"

"We've got just the right size suitcase for carrying clothes without a lot of folding," Beany put in.

They were three girls, united in the common bond of clothes for another girl. Dulcie said, "Only, Beany, you get it over to Peggy that I want her to wear it, and that she can't possibly hurt it. You're the one that can do

269

favors for people so they hardly know you're doing it. You tell Peggy," she added, a forlorn note in her voice, "I'd like to think of someone wearing it—and having fun in it."

The bell for first-hour lunch rang. Beany and Jennifer stood up. "What did you start to ask me, Dulcie?" Beany wanted to know as they all moved toward the door.

"Oh, yes, about lining. First, Adair and I thought we would keep it for a surprise, but then we decided—"

"Keep what for a surprise? I've had enough surprises."

"I'm making two jackets out of that tweed of Adair's—one for you, one for me. I'm getting excused to go down and get the lining. And I wanted to ask you if you'd like green or gray."

"Green. But won't it take you forever to make two jackets, Dulcie?"

"Not me," Dulcie said, and grinned blithely over her shoulder as she went hurrying on. "I'll bet I'll have yours made by Easter."

Jennifer watched after the bobbing pony tail. She said simply, "Beany, thanks—thanks again."

Andy Kern was waiting for Beany outside the lunchroom. "What's happened to my harem?" he asked as he shoved open the door.

"I'm all of it today. Kay's absent." Beany explained about the trip to the dude ranch, and the sleety roads detaining them overnight.

"And where's our misunderstood menace?"

Beany chuckled. "She won't be here either. And don't call her a menace. Adair gave her a great big chunk of tweed, and Dulcie's hurrying downtown to get lining for *two* jackets. One for herself, one for Beany."

"Don't tell me there'll be another free-for-all in the sewing room over two somethings just alike."

Beany laughed again. "Hardly. I'm not Original-minded. . . . I've been talking to Jennifer. I'm so relieved. She didn't chew me out about the column—"

"I hoped she'd be all sweetness and light," Andy said, pulling out a chair for her. "There's nothing like a reconciliation with the one you love—"

Beany didn't sit down, but stood beside the chair, staring in wonderment at him. "Andy Kern! So you were the one who called Jag Wilson Saturday night and told him Jennifer was at the Pant. Yessir, and then you even seated him next to her."

His grin was a little sheepish. "Cupid Kern, I was known as in them days."

"How *do* you get your shirt on over your wings?"

"Sit down, sit down, and don't be standing there with your mouth like a capital O," Andy scolded. "I have a question for you. Do you know what a g-n-u is?"

"Um-hmm. It's a three-letter word you can use in Scrabble. It's in the dictionary—it's an African antelope."

"I do like an educated girl. Do you know what Mama Gnu said to Papa Gnu when he came home one evening?"

"No."

"She said, 'I have gnus for you.'" He didn't give her time to say, "How corny can you get?" but went on with something of triumph. "I have news for you, chowderhead. Did you know that Adair's carpenter is Ivor Lungaarde, Dulcie's father?"

"No!"

"Don't contradict your elders."

"What makes you think so?"

"I know so," Andy said. "When I left your house yesterday, he was just leaving and he offered me a lift. Yeh-boy, he was sitting out there in the kitchen and heard the whole stormy scene—my telling Dulcie off, and then Adair's telling me off, and making that stirring speech about poor Dulcie not having roots because her father is too much of a rover—"

Beany's fingers slowed in their unwrapping of a sandwich. "Oh, my gosh," she breathed.

"The old fellow was pretty shook. The two of us had quite a heart-to-heart talk. Maybe he's fed up with chasing uranium anyway, but he sounded like he was about to change his ways—"

272

"He must be. He was hard at our garage steps this morning."

"I gather that he's such a good carpenter that he can get work without even asking. He told me he was going right ahead with the addition on their house. I told him it wouldn't hurt Dulcie any to have a home she wasn't ashamed of. I even intimated that a gal behaved better in a house than she did in a car."

"Poor old Dulcie," Beany murmured, hearing again Dulcie's drained voice as she confessed that Carlton Buell was the prince she had dreamed about.

"I have no tears to shed for Dulcie," Andy said.

"She's all right," Beany defended. "She needs a new coat worse than I do, but she'll work like a gopher to get mine done for Easter. Be nice to her, Andy."

" 'Be nice to her,' she says. Let's not carry this too far. I don't go around slapping gals down, unless they need slapping down. . . . Haven't you got anything better than cheese sandwiches?"

"I'll do better by you tomorrow. So the carpenter is Dulcie's father. I can't wait to tell Adair. Will she be surprised!"

Andy stood up. "Well, as long as Kay isn't here to sponge off of, I'm going to break down and buy me a hot dog. I'll even buy you one, knucks."

Beany looked up at him. "Oh, Andy, it'll be awful next year when you're in the Marines. I'll miss you."

He flashed his crinkly grin at her. "It'd be awful*er* if you didn't. Mustard?"

"Lots," Beany said.

21

SHE couldn't wait to tell Adair. She hurried home from school. Yet, anxious as she was to impart her news, she stood inside the Malone gate, looking over the wide driveway for the sight of Norbett's car.

No red car.

Maybe Norbett was bobbing out of her life and back to Ohio as unceremoniously as he had bobbed into it. Maybe it was better, she tried to tell herself. In the month since he had come, she had seen him only three times. The first time they had quarreled heatedly; the second time they had picked up the old rapture; and the third time they had stood by Kay's wishing well at the Hop and stared in startled shock at each other. They hadn't even said hello.

Yes, maybe it would be better if she never saw him again. Maybe in time she'd get over this unfinished feeling that was both longing and desolation.

She walked on slow feet to the porch. She opened the door and called out, "Adair, where are you?"

Her stepmother appeared at the head of the stairs, holding a slip off a plant. "Big night at the Malones," she said, as Beany climbed the stairs. "Martie will be in on the six twenty-five plane. Johnny telephoned to say they were on their way home. I thought I couldn't go wrong if I put half a ham in the oven. Maybe you could add to the festive occasion by making cookies."

Beany nodded. She asked, "Do you know what the Mama G-n-u, gnu, said to Papa Gnu when he came home one evening?"

Adair carried along, asking like the interlocutor in a minstrel show, "No. What did Mama Gnu say to Papa Gnu when he came home one evening?"

" 'I have *gnus* for you.' And I have for you. Your now-you-see-him, now-you-don't carpenter is Dulcie's father."

Adair, instead of being astounded, laughed in delight. "I have *gnus* for you, honey. I've known he was, since that first evening Dulcie came here."

"You knew?" It took almost a full minute for that to thoroughly soak in. "You mean you said what you said yesterday about Dulcie not having a chance, or roots, or home to entertain in *on purpose?* I wondered why you stood there in the kitchen doorway, instead of coming into the dining room. You *wanted* him to hear you."

"I certainly did. The first night when Dulcie told me her father was always dashing off on some get-rich scheme, I figured it was probably uranium. I agree with Eve Baxter—gambling is all right if it doesn't work a hardship on the ones a man is responsible for. I was just waiting to give Ivor Lungaarde a piece of my mind, and the chance came yesterday. But I was scared. That's why I didn't tell you. I was scared my meddling might make things worse."

"But it didn't, did it?"

"No, he worked like a buckskin mule to finish the garage steps. He wanted to get paid so he could buy material to work on their own house. He's a top builder. He told me yesterday he was offered the contract for the carpentry work on the new wing of the sanitarium out near South Wyman. But he didn't know whether he would take it or not—it might tie him down too long." Adair smiled meaningfully. "Today he told me he was taking it."

"What are you doing with that slip off a plant?" Beany asked.

"For Mrs. Lungaarde. She came down from the Hollywood Shop and had lunch with her husband and me. It was more fun, planning with her about draperies and braided rugs. She wants one of these long planters. I promised her slips off all Miss Opal's plants."

She held out the wisp of shiny-leafed plant. "I don't even know what this is."

"It's philodendron," Beany said. "Don't you remember Johnny asking Miss Opal if Philo Dendron was the husband of Rhoda Dendron?"

"Does this Philo look to you like he'd grow and multiply?"

"I think so," Beany said dubiously. "You snip it off at the joint, and then plant it and keep it soaked till it starts."

"In coffee cans?"

"Flowerpots are better, because they have a hole in the bottom. There's some up in the room over the garage."

Adair said, "There are? Up in the garage loft?" And then, with more urgency than the occasion seemed to call for, "Beany, will you go up and get some?"

"I'd better make the cookies."

"Please, Beany, go on up in the loft and get the flowerpots," Adair urged. "You won't have to worry about falling through the new steps."

Beany went up the steps of new and solid unpainted pine. She opened the door into that cluttered and dingy room.

A day of surprises. And this was the most heart-thudding surprise of the whole day.

She noticed first that the electric heater was giving out rosy warmth. She noticed next—and that's when her heart began its uneven thump—the tall, lean frame on the lawn glider, which until today had been piled with lawn chairs and the croquet set. A lavender blanket covered the sleeping figure. A tousled red head was burrowed into a pillow.

She could only stand and gape, taking it all in. A dark suit coat was hanging from one of Headless Hetty's shoulders. Shoes were tumbled in front of the makeshift bed. A carton of books had been pulled close to the glider to act as a bedside table. On it sat an empty soup dish and a glass.

Adair had fixed Norbett a bed here. And brought him food. And then, pretending an urgent need of flowerpots, had sent Beany for them.

The sleeper was the picture of heavy exhaustion. Even the opening and closing of the door hadn't made him stir. One arm, in a crumpled shirt sleeve, hung as limp as the arm of a sawdust doll, the lax fingers touching the floor. She couldn't bear to break such a sound and weary sleep.

She could tiptoe past him and get a couple of flowerpots for Adair, and close the door stealthily behind her.

But the flowerpots were piled behind a bobsled that leaned against the wall. As she leaned over to disengage a few of the top ones, the sled fell over with a resounding crash and Beany, leaping to one side, stumbled against the glider.

Norbett jerked up, blinking stupidly through the winter dusk of the room. He looked around, taking a few dazed seconds to orient himself. Even under his sunburn, his face looked haggard and slack with sleep.

Beany said inanely, "I'm sorry, Norbett. I was getting some flowerpots. For Adair. Why did you come out here? There's that extra bed in Johnny's room. You aren't hiding now, are you?"

"No," he mumbled. "I just thought it'd be quiet out here—and I guess I feel at home up here."

A moment's silence, and then he blurted out, "I'd have been back last Thursday only my fool car went to pieces. It's done for at last. So I had to wait around and come back with Ivor. He can find more reasons to stop and kill time. And then we walked in on Dulcie, bawling her eyes out because she was out on a limb—"

"Yes, I know."

"And besides, she told me you had another date with your friend, Andy, and wouldn't be at the dance—"

"Yes—I didn't want her to know *I* was out on a limb." She stood the sled back against the wall. She asked curiously, "Where have you been since you left the dance?"

"At the hospital with Uncle Nate."

"How is he?"

"He's better now. But all Saturday night and all day yesterday, we didn't think he'd pull through. He's got that negative O blood. I was the only one whose blood matched, so I gave him a transfusion. The doctor said it was what pulled him through."

280

"You ought to sleep some more."

He didn't answer that. He said with weary vehemence, "By darn, I wish I'd listened to your dad that night he told me to go to Uncle Nate and put all my cards on the table. But no, I thought I was so smart; I thought I could put over a big deal that would make that two-thousand offer of his look like peanuts."

"Didn't you, Norbett?"

"Naw. The assay wasn't good enough. From the way Ivor talked, I thought we'd be millionaires. He's a good fellow, but he sure shoots a long bow. No, we had to take up the two-thousand offer Uncle Nate told me about in the first place." He added, "But it was my old red blood that pulled Uncle Nate through."

"Oh, Norbett, I'm glad." Funny old cocky Norbett. So happy to be on the giving—not the taking—end. Even if the giving was a pint of his blood.

He went on, "Uncle Nate wants me to help him get his printing business on its feet, too. I'd like it—it isn't so different from writing copy for a paper. So I'm staying on. You should have heard Aunt Mae! This scare about Uncle Nate kind of thawed her, I guess. She's begging me to stay with them now."

"So you won't go back to Ohio?"

"I'm staying right here. I'll take a light load at the university and work with Uncle Nate. . . . Sit down by me, Beany."

He hunched up, making room for her on the glider. In this very glider Norbett and Beany had spent so many hours last summer. It squeaked softly under her weight, and Norbett said on a laugh, "Our little birdie, remember?"

He reached out and caught her right hand and the charm bracelet jingled. "I was afraid you'd take it off."

"No, I didn't take it off."

"But you're still wearing the wrist watch that policeman's son gave you—"

"Andy Kern," she corrected.

"You can take it off," he said belligerently. "If you want a watch, I'll buy one for you." His arms reached out and pulled her close; he kissed her full on the lips. "There! That's the one Johnny did us out of. I'm back—and you're my girl, Beany."

The long-delayed kiss. She waited for her heart to give its old mad fifteen-year-old leap. She waited for the enchantment, the sweet and reckless glory. She waited for the feeling of, I'm Norbett's girl—nothing else matters.

And that was the biggest surprise of the day. She felt none of it. The glider squeaked again as she drew almost gently away from him. She seemed to hear Mary Fred's saying, "I'll bet if Norbett came back you'd get over all that starry-eyed worship. . . . You're a different you from the fifteen-year-old Beany."

No—no unreasonable, unreasoning ecstasy filled her heart, but in its place was something even more exciting. A lightness, and easiness—and exultance. She was free at last of having Norbett toss her heart hither and thither.

"There'll never be anyone like you," Norbett said. "I'll always need you."

"I'll always be here when you need me."

"Don't sound so lofty and stand-offish. We'll be going steady."

She shook her head. Queer, she not only felt older than that other Beany, but even a little older than Norbett with his restless, unpredictable moods. "No. No, I don't want to go steady—not with anyone. Not yet."

"We won't argue about that now," he said. "Not when I'm short on sleep—and blood."

She said musingly as she sat beside him, "Norbett, remember that first night when I met you at the airport and we came up here? And you thought nothing mattered except putting through a big uranium deal. You wanted this little leprechaun on the bracelet to bring you luck on it, so you wouldn't feel like a poor relation—"

"I don't feel like a poor relation now," he broke in. "Last night when I was sitting up with Uncle Nate, he said it was like having a son looking after him."

"That's what I mean. You got what you wanted, only it wasn't what you thought you wanted. And that night, I thought that if I didn't get to go to the Quill and Scroll affair in the Springs and have my picture in *Hark Ye,* my world would go to pot. But when I had the chance to go, and to get my picture in *Hark Ye,* it didn't mean anything to me. I guess," she added honestly, "we both wanted to show off how important we were."

Norbett didn't answer. The glider swayed gently, with the "birdie" chirping almost drowsily. She mused on in a low voice, "And yet we're both happier than if we had got what we wanted." Another drawn-out silence.

"Funny, isn't it? I guess maybe that was our good luck. Maybe that's why the little man on the bracelet had such a devilish twinkle."

No sound came from Norbett, except heavy breathing. She turned her head to look at him. In his hunched-up, uncomfortable position, he was sound asleep. And no wonder. A blood donor yesterday morning. Sitting up two nights with his uncle.

She stood up very softly and, even more softly, adjusted the pillow under his head. Even as she stood in the heater's roseate glow looking down at him, her thoughts began to wander. . . . If Peggy Wood took Dulcie's formal, maybe she should take that larger suitcase. . . . She tried to picture Andy in his Marine uniform. It would be fun, sending him cookies when he was away. . . .

Goodness, she musn't stand here daydreaming when she should be making cookies for a hungry crowd.

She tiptoed over and picked up three flowerpots, tucked them under her arm, and opened the door. It would be time enough to call Norbett when dinner was ready.

On the platform outside, her hand let the knob slide silently into place. She drew a deep breath. It was good to have room in her heart for everything, everybody, in her life. Each day suddenly seemed as full of promise as a bright package to be opened.

As she shifted the flowerpots the charm bracelet clinked against the side of one. She righted it on her wrist, her fingers straightening out the leprechaun in his pointed hat and pointed shoes. The lowering sun caught momentarily on the emerald eyes.

Beany chuckled softly. It wasn't a devilish twinkle after all. It was only a wise and knowing one.

About the Author

Lenora Mattingly Weber was born in L Missouri. When she was twelve, her adventurous far set out to homestead on the plains of Colorado. He she raised motherless lambs on baby bottles, gentle broncos, and chopped railroad ties into firewood. At the age of sixteen she rode in rodeos and Wild West shows. Her well-loved stories for girls reflect her experiences with her own family. As the mother of six children and as a grandmother, she was well qualified to write of family life. Her love of the outdoors, her interest in community affairs, and her deep understanding of family relationships helped to make her characters as credible as they are memorable.

Mrs. Weber enjoyed horseback riding and swimming. She loved to cook, but her first love was writing.